mm    JN

BK

Dear Reader,

Home, family, community and love. These are the
values we cherish most in our lives—the ideals that
ground us, comfort us, move us. They certainly
provide the perfect inspiration around which to build a
romance collection that will touch the heart.

And so we are thrilled to offer you the Harlequin
Heartwarming series. Each of these special stories
is a wholesome, heartfelt romance imbued with the
traditional values so important to you. They are books
you can share proudly with friends and family. And the
authors featured in this collection are some of the most
talented storytellers writing today, including favorites
such as Tara Taylor Quinn, Janice Kay Johnson,
Jillian Hart and Shelley Galloway. We've selected these
stories especially for you based on their overriding
qualities of emotion and tenderness, and they center
around your favorite themes—children, weddings,
second chances, the reunion of families, the quest to
find a true home and, of course, sweet romance.

So curl up in your favorite chair, relax and prepare
for a heartwarming reading experience!

Sincerely,

The Editors

**CYNTHIA THOMASON**

writes contemporary and historical romances and dabbles in mysteries. She has won a National Readers' Choice Award and she won the 2008 Golden Quill. When she's not writing, she works as a licensed auctioneer for the auction company she and her husband own. As an estate buyer for the auction, she has come across unusual items, many of which have found their way into her books. She has one son, who is an entertainment reporter. Cynthia dreams of perching on a mountaintop in North Carolina every autumn to watch the leaves turn.

You can read more about her at her website, www.cynthiathomason.com.

HARLEQUIN HEARTWARMING

# Cynthia Thomason

## *Dilemma at Bayberry Cove*

HARLEQUIN®
entertain, enrich, inspire™

Recycling programs
for this product may
not exist in your area.

ISBN-13: 978-0-373-36574-6

DILEMMA AT BAYBERRY COVE

Copyright © 2012 by Cynthia Thomason

Originally published as THE WOMEN OF BAYBERRY COVE
Copyright © 2004 by Cynthia Thomason

www.Harlequin.com

**Printed in U.S.A.**

# Dilemma at Bayberry Cove

This book is dedicated to the memory of Amanda Sue Brackett. Dear sister, sweet angel, your flame still burns brightly in my heart.

And a special thank-you to Florida attorney Adam Chotiner, writer Zelda Benjamin's son-in-law, whose expertise in the field of labor law kept me on the right track. Any mistakes are entirely mine and not his.

# CHAPTER ONE

LOUISE DUNCAN, who regularly apologized to friends and business associates for being late, was fifteen minutes early this morning.

The Fort Lauderdale legal firm of Oppenheimer Straus and Baker didn't officially open until nine, but when Roger Oppenheimer had called her at home the previous evening and told her to be in his office at eight, Louise knew she'd be on time. She'd been waiting ten years for this call.

She exited the elevator on the top floor of the Moroccan-style building that had graced Las Olas Boulevard since the 1940s. Continuing down a wide hallway flanked with offices, Louise stopped outside Mr. Oppenheimer's door. She knocked lightly and responding to Roger's request, stepped inside.

He turned from the bank of windows and smiled at her. "Right on time, I see, Louise." He gestured for her to take a seat in a deep-tufted green leather chair, and he sat in a similar one on the other side of a mahogany coffee table. He lifted a chrome serving pitcher from a silver tray. "Coffee?"

Louise smiled back at him, growing even more confident in the cordial atmosphere. "I don't know. Did you make it yourself?"

Roger chuckled and poured a cup for himself and one for Louise. "Yes, I did." Then he set his mug on a coaster and molded his thick fingers over the edges of the chair arms.

Louise peered at him over the rim of her mug. It wasn't her imagination. The good humor of the last moments was fading from his features. His eyes had narrowed, the lines around his mouth deepened. The time for small talk was over. That was fine with Louise. She was ready to hear the good news.

"Perhaps you know why I called you to the office so early, Louise," he said.

She set down her mug. "I think I have a pretty good idea."

"I wanted to speak to you in private, without the interruptions of normal business hours."

*And so the others who have been considered for the promotion wouldn't be around when you tell me I'm the one who got it.* Louise allowed herself a bit of mental gloating. "I think that was a good idea, Roger."

He moved his hands to his knees and leaned

slightly forward. "As you know, since Harker Penwright left, the firm has been considering moving someone from inside the organization to his position of junior partner."

She nodded. Oh, yes, she knew. The promotion had been the subject of whispered comments at the water cooler and murmured predictions during happy hours. Two days ago, Louise had gotten wind of what she believed was the true inside scoop from her administrative assistant, who'd heard from Oppenheimer's own assistant. The promotion was going to Louise.

"We all knew that a decision was forthcoming," she said.

Roger cleared his throat. "Right. And that decision was reached last night. It probably comes as no surprise to you that you, Ed Bennett and Arthur Blackstone were the principal candidates for the promotion."

Louise folded her hands in her lap and connected her gaze with Roger's in that direct way she was famous for in the courtroom. "I had assumed as much, yes." *Oh, this was going to be so sweet.*

Roger looked away from her penetrating stare and seemed to find something fascinating in the weave of the green-and-tan carpet. The first hint of unease prickled along Louise's spine.

After a moment, he looked up. "There's no easy way to say this, Louise. Especially since I am fond of you on a personal level. And of course I admire you on a professional one."

Louise turned cold to the tips of her fingers. She held her breath.

"We've decided to give the position to Ed," Roger stated with agonizing blandness.

Louise shook her head, replayed the stunning announcement in her mind several times to be sure she'd got it right. She leaned forward and stared at Roger's face, at the capillaries expanding and reddening in his plump cheeks. "You what?"

"I'm sorry, Louise, but in the end, all three of us agreed that this decision was best for the firm."

Uncharacteristically, words failed her. She blew out a long breath, blinked several times and finally uttered, "Roger, I have seniority over Ed by more than a year."

"I know, and we took that into consideration. Unfortunately, there were other factors that weighed more heavily in our decision."

"Other factors? May I ask what they were?"

"Louise, I don't want to go into this…"

"Roger, you owe me an explanation. You know you do."

He sighed heavily. "All right. Basically we feel that Ed projects a more appropriate image for the firm. He's wonderful with the clients. They like his give-and-take attitude with regard to decision making. He oozes confidence, Louise...."

"And I don't?" Great, if there was one trait that clearly defined Louise Duncan, it was confidence, not pretended or fleeting, but real, no-nonsense confidence that Ed Bennett could only dream about.

Roger remained calm, his tone of voice even. "You do, of course, and for the most part your work in the courtroom is exemplary, but..." He rolled one shoulder, resettled his bulk in the chair. "Frankly, Louise, we've had complaints. You come across as somewhat intimidating, forceful."

"I'm an attorney, Roger. It's my job to be forceful."

"To an extent, yes. But you shouldn't necessarily act that way toward our own clients. Ed is dignified, solid, almost courtly. He's stable and reliable, the picture of old-company trust. In the field of corporate law, Louise, his demeanor is most impressive."

"You're saying I'm not stable?"

He had the nerve to smile. "I'm certainly not suggesting you need psychiatric help, but to a client who's contemplating putting the future of his empire in our hands, you come on a little strong." He threaded his fingers together, resting his hands in his lap. "Let me put it this way. Ed Bennett bonds with the clients. He's both compassionate and capable. And while there's no doubt that you're a top-notch litigator, Louise, you do have a tendency to bully everyone around you."

Louise couldn't believe what she was hearing. Ed Bennett was a complete toady in his perfectly tailored black suits, and shirts starched to such gleaming stiffness that he crackled when he swung his arms. And he was getting this promotion over *her*. Her pride was wounded beyond repair. Her dreams were shattering like old crystal. And so she heard herself utter words of self-betrayal and corporate capitulation. "I can change," she said. "I can listen to stories about backyard barbecues, and kids' educations, and family vacations to Aspen. That's what Ed does. I can do that, too. I can be nice."

"Of course you can, Louise, but not by nine o'clock this morning." He stood, effectively dismissing her. "I hate to cut this short, but

Arthur Blackstone is due at eight-thirty, and I have to do this one more time. It's not something I enjoy, I assure you."

She stood up. "If you expect me to sympathize with you, Roger, you're going to be disappointed."

He chuckled a little. "I don't expect that at all. But please consider some advice. Take a break from the firm, a vacation. A couple of months. You've earned a mountain of personal days over the years. Sanders and Martin can take over your workload for a while."

"You're suggesting I run off to some Caribbean island and sun myself for weeks?" The thought was ludicrous.

Apparently oblivious to the absurdity of his idea, Roger said, "Yes, that's a great plan. We want you on board, Louise. But take some time for yourself. Come back refreshed, renewed."

*And more in tune with Oppenheimer Straus and Baker, Stepford attorneys.* "Fine," she said, opening the door to the hallway. "I'll see you in a few weeks, Roger."

She passed Arthur Blackstone midway down the hall. He stopped her with a light touch to her elbow. "Did you just come from Oppenheimer's office?" he asked.

"I did." A worried frown tugged at his lips. "Don't worry, Art," she said, empathizing with his soon-to-be-victim status. "It's not me."

He exhaled. "Sorry, Louise, but if not you, then who…"

"Just one word of warning. If Roger offers you coffee, you might want to lace it with a shot of bourbon."

AT NINE O'CLOCK that night Louise polished off a pint of Ben and Jerry's ice cream, licked the carton lid and tossed the empty container across the room into the wastebasket. Then she leaned forward on her sofa and reached for a cardboard box on her coffee table. Roger Oppenheimer had made it clear that her job wasn't in jeopardy, but she'd thought it advisable to clear her desktop of personal effects, since she might be gone for a couple of months.

She felt around in the box until her fingers grasped a chrome picture frame. Pulling it from the box, she stared at the portrait of her parents, both of them dressed in the white coats of their medical profession. Linda and Fritz Duncan had wanted their daughter to study medicine and join their successful OB/ GYN practice. Louise had staunchly refused, and followed her heart into law. Her parents had supported her decision and had always remained proud of her accomplishments.

"You should see me now, folks," Louise said to the glossy image. "I deserved that promotion. I worked hard for it."

Still holding the photo, she stood up, crossed the imported-tile floor of her fourteenth-story condominium and went out on the balcony. A breeze from the ocean, less than a half mile away, washed over her. Revived, she looked across the rooftops of nearby buildings and settled her gaze on the silvery black sea, rippling to shore from the distant horizon. "What am I supposed to do for two months? Where am I supposed to go? I already live in paradise.

"Where do people go when they are told to mellow out and become one of the good guys?" A bark of bitter laughter came from her throat at the inanity of Roger Oppenheimer's advice. Louise was a powerhouse in the courtroom. Aggressive, unyielding. Wasn't that what a lawyer was supposed to be?

If not, maybe she'd chosen the wrong profession. But she loved the law. She couldn't give it up now. So where did a person go to learn to be a nice, people-person kind of lawyer?

And suddenly she had the answer. She'd

go to that little town in North Carolina where
her best friend lived. What was the name?
She struggled to remember it through a haze
of muddled thinking. Bayberry Cove. That
was it. A homey little burg on the edge of
Currituck Sound near the Outer Banks. Vicki
had moved there six months ago and now,
deliriously in love and pregnant, she hated to
leave the town, even to check on her antiques
store in Fort Lauderdale. Endlessly praising
the quiet virtues of the place, Vicki had
repeatedly invited Louise to come for a visit,
but Louise never had time.

   She turned away from her grossly
mortgaged view and went into the apartment
to call Vicki. *You've got plenty of time now,
honey,* she told herself. *And if Bayberry Cove
can't turn you from a lioness into a pussycat,
I don't know of any place that can.*

TWO DAYS LATER, on a spectacular May
afternoon, Louise drove her black BMW down
Main Street, Bayberry Cove, North Carolina.
To her right was a row of two-story buildings
with granite cornerstones proclaiming each of
them to be over a hundred years old. To her
left, a typical town square with ancient trees
dripping shade over brick sidewalks and cast-
iron benches. A perfect place for people to

stop and enjoy the simple pleasure of a picnic lunch or lazy afternoon chat.

The only problem was that while Louise could admire the pastoral solitude of a leafy town green, she wasn't a picnicker, and she wasn't much for small talk. She was a woman to whom every minute was precious and not meant to be squandered. She pulled into a parking space and approached an elderly man seated on the nearest bench.

As she came closer, he shielded his eyes from the sun and grinned with obvious interest. Accustomed to such blatantly admiring looks, Louise settled her ball cap low on her forehead and flipped her long black ponytail through the opening at the back.

"Hi there," she said, flashing the man a sincere smile. "Can you tell me where I might find Pintail Point, the home of Jamie Malone?"

He looked her up and down, murmured directions and gestured into the distance with a gnarled finger.

Louise thanked him and headed out of town to a two-lane road he'd identified as Sandy Ridge. She turned right and in three miles spotted the causeway that would lead her to where Vicki lived with her husband.

The tires crunched on loose gravel as she drove across the narrow spit of land. Dust settled on the wax on her car. When she parked at the end of the point, she got out and walked toward a neat little houseboat with geraniums in the window boxes. She heard a welcoming squeal before she actually saw her best friend.

"Oh, you actually came!" Vicki crossed the wooden bridge from the boat and ran toward Louise.

"It's me," Louise stated unnecessarily. "Now slow down or you'll pop that baby out four months ahead of schedule."

Vicki threw herself into Louise's arms. "Don't worry about him. He—or she—is as protected as the gold in Fort Knox, and not going anywhere." Keeping her hands on Louise's shoulders, Vicki stepped back and fired questions. "How was your trip? How long can you stay?" She darted a glance over her shoulder where her husband, the totally gorgeous and charmingly Irish Jamie Malone, was approaching at a leisurely pace with his odd-looking dog beside him.

"Cover your ears, Beasley," Jamie said to the dog. "All this squealin' and squawkin' is typical womenfolk jabber."

He placed his hands on his hips and grinned

at Louise. "Well, well, Miz Lady Attorney. Fancy seeing you on Pintail Point."

She sent him a smug look. They'd had their disagreements in the past, especially about the divorce Vicki had claimed she wanted from the virtual stranger she'd married thirteen years before when he'd needed a green card and she'd needed money. Thinking she was doing her friend a favor, Louise had had the mysterious Mr. Malone investigated and subtly intimidated—until Vicki had fallen head over heels in love with him and shredded the divorce papers once and for all.

Louise took a step toward him. "Come on, Jamie. I know you're glad to see me." She angled her cheek toward his face. "Give us a wee kiss now."

He laughed and obliged her.

"So this is the love nest?" she said, walking to the boat. "The famous *Bucket O' Luck* I've heard so much about."

"This is it," Vicki said, keeping pace with her. She stopped and pointed across Currituck Sound to a hill rising next to Sandy Ridge Road. "And that's going to take her place in a few months when it's finished."

A partially completed house crested the hill, its bare timbers rising toward the afternoon sun. "Very nice."

"It will be. But for now, it's the *Bucket* or nothing." She opened the door and waited for Louise to precede her inside. "So talk, Lulu. What's the real reason you're here? You were very vague on the phone. I never thought you'd come."

Like the true friend she was, Vicki listened to Louise's tale and sighed at the injustice of it. "What are you going to do now?" she asked when Louise finished her story.

"Well, this looks like a nice place," Louise said. "I'll probably stay here for a while. Maybe Oppenheimer is right. Maybe I do need some downtime."

Vicki shot a glance in Jamie's direction. He hunched his shoulder in male confusion. Louise laughed. "I don't mean *here* here," she said. "I'm not moving in with you. I meant here in Bayberry Cove."

Relief washed over both faces. "Oh, well…" Vicki said. "If our house was ready, there'd be no problem, but we only have one bedroom on the *Bucket* and…"

Louise waved her hand to dismiss her friend's concern. "Enough, Vic. I don't want to stay with you two any more than you want me to. Just direct me to a motel. Anything in town will do."

Vicki shook her head. "That's a problem."

"Why?"

"There are no places to stay in Bayberry Cove."

"What? Nothing?"

"Nope." Vicki looked to Jamie for a suggestion.

He thought a moment and finally said, "There's always Buttercup Cottage. I could ask Haywood if he'd rent it."

"There you go," Louise said. "Of course, I've never churned butter or made my own candles...."

Vicki laughed. "It's not like that. It has indoor plumbing and electricity."

"Good. Show me the dotted line I sign on."

"You'll have to talk to Haywood Fletcher," Jamie said. "His family owns the place. I think you probably recognize his name."

Louise winced. "How could I forget the attorney who claimed he'd found flaws in that perfectly executed divorce decree I wrote for Vicki?"

Jamie laughed. "Don't blame Haywood for that. It was a stall tactic I used to buy time until Vicki admitted she loved me. Haywood will treat you fairly, but there might be one problem."

"What now?"

"My mother used to work for Haywood. She

told me that his son is coming home sometime soon. He's a semi-retired commander from the navy, and there's a chance he might want to move into the cottage."

Vicki groaned. "Oh, no. That place would be perfect for you, Lulu. When is Wesley due to arrive?" she asked Jamie.

"Ma didn't say. Probably not for a while. And anyway, he'll most likely stay at the mansion in town with his father."

"So, where is this cottage?" Louise asked. "I'm going to check it out so I know it's worth grappling with the town's only attorney over a lease agreement."

"That's the best part," Vicki said. "It's right next to us, just a mile farther down Sandy Ridge. You can't miss it. It's stained a delightful color, like—"

"Don't tell me," Louise said. "Buttercups."

TEN MINUTES LATER, Louise drove onto the pebble driveway of Buttercup Cottage. Besides the identifying color, a wooden placard above the front door confirmed that she was at the right place.

She stopped in front of the entrance and got out of her car. "This looks fine," she said, imagining the hypnotic effect of raindrops on the sloping tin roof, lightning bugs twinkling outside the double casement windows. The sound of waves lapping the shoreline behind the house reminded her that she was only steps away from the protected bay.

Louise walked around the side of the house. "I suppose I could look through the windows. No one's living here now."

She peered into a bedroom. A double bed covered by a bright quilt looked cozy. The ceiling fan, dormant now, would stir up a nice breeze on warm evenings.

The next window provided a view of a compact bathroom with a porcelain vanity under a small medicine cabinet. "Adequate," she said, and proceeded to the back of the house.

Pleased to see that the rear door had a window in the upper half, she walked up to get a look at what was no doubt the kitchen. She was just leaning into the glass when a man appeared in her view, and the door swung open. Louise jumped back a step, but not far enough. Without warning, she was doused from chest to ankles with the grimy contents of a large pan.

She hollered, and shook her hands free of water mixed with unidentified substances. Then she watched in horror as rivers of rust permeated her new white capris. She

stared at the open door where a man in a cap
emblazoned with a gold insignia stood with
the now-empty pan dangling from his hands.
She glared into bright aqua eyes and snapped,
"Look what you've done."

## CHAPTER TWO

HE STOOD THERE gawking at her as if she'd descended out of the sky. "Wow, look at you," he finally said. "I'm sorry about that. I didn't see you out here."

She glanced down at her pants again. "That's comforting. It's nice to know you weren't lying in wait...."

He disappeared into the house. Gone.

She leaned across the open doorway. "Hey!"

He came back with a roll of slightly soggy paper towels. "Here. Dry yourself."

She unwound about a dozen squares and began patting her clothes. When she swiped along her arms, she jerked her face away. "This stuff stinks. What is it?"

"I don't know. It's been in the pipes for something like five, six years. I can't remember when somebody last stayed here." He ran a sympathetic look down her legs. "I'd say it contains a good bit of rust, though."

She scowled at him. "Obviously you're a chemistry wiz."

He almost smiled. "Hardly. Unfortunately, I'm not much of a plumber, either. The pipes under the kitchen sink are winning this battle."

"Look, while you're joking about skirmishes with copper pipes, I'm fighting real germ warfare. Do you think I could come in and use the universal antidote to all this grime?"

"What's that?"

"Soap, Mr. Chemist. Plain old bacteria-eating soap. There is soap in this place, right?"

He moved aside. "Oh, sure. Plenty of soap."

She stepped through the door while digging her car keys out of her pocket. Her first look at the interior of the small kitchen confirmed the plumber's story. Sections of old pipe and numerous tools stood in puddles of murky water on the floor in front of an open cabinet, along with various lengths of shiny new PVC tubes waiting to replace their worn-out predecessors.

Louise picked her way across the disaster area and turned around. "Can you do me a favor? My car's out front. Would you bring in the smaller of the two suitcases from the trunk?"

"Bring in a suitcase?"

She almost laughed at the expression on his face. "Don't panic. I won't disturb your work. I'm not moving in this minute. I haven't even signed a lease yet. But I do need to change clothes." She tossed the keys, and he snatched them in midair. "Good reflexes, chemist. I'll be in the bathroom."

WESLEY FLETCHER DIDN'T like chaos in his life. He'd spent years eliminating as much of it as possible from his daily routines. He started every day with the same rituals. He ate his meals at the same times. He hardly ever watched a new show on television, preferring a select number of tried and true ones.

That's why he was determined to fix the pipes in Buttercup Cottage before it was time to prepare dinner. He glanced at his watch as he walked around the side of the house. He had only two hours left to accomplish the task, or after eating his thick, juicy T-bone, he'd be cleaning the broiler in the bathroom sink. This day would have gone so much better if the one plumber in Bayberry Cove hadn't told him it would be forty-eight hours before he could make a house call.

And now Wesley was carting a suitcase weighing at least twenty pounds back to his home, where a half-crazy lady was occupying his bathroom and making claims about moving in. That was chaos of a sort that could turn his already cockeyed day upside down.

It wasn't that he didn't owe her a favor. He did. Nearly drowning her in liquid muck was a pretty nasty thing to do to a woman. A woman whose clothes and demeanor indicated she was not from around here. And that was the biggest mystery of all. Who was she and where had she come from?

He entered the house and set the suitcase by the bathroom door. Tapping lightly to get her attention, he realized he didn't even know her name. "Ma'am?"

She opened the door about ten inches and, now hatless, presented him a view of a face that could rival any movie star's. "Call me ma'am one more time, chemist, and I may have to slug you. The name's Louise. So what's yours?" she asked him.

"My what?"

"Name," she coaxed. "I should at least know who to send the bill for my new pants."

Maybe she wasn't kidding. He couldn't tell. Maybe he should buy her new pants. He didn't know the protocol for this circumstance. But he did know his name, and he told her. "Wesley Fletcher."

"Okay, then, Wesley. Move away from the door so I can open it and get my case inside."

He went back to the kitchen and scowled at the sink. His first day back in Bayberry Cove was certainly not going according to plan.

LOUISE TWISTED THE TAILS of her floral print blouse into a knot at her waist and zipped up her shorts. She brushed her hair, gathered it at her crown and whipped the mass through a thick elastic band. In her mind she listed all the details she should consider before contacting Haywood Fletcher about renting the cottage. "Obviously some repairs are needed," she mumbled to herself, and then froze with her hand on the doorknob.

"Haywood Fletcher!" she said aloud. "The guy just said his name was Wesley Fletcher. He's no clumsy, blue-eyed plumber. He's Haywood's son, the navy man who Jamie said might have his sights set on my cottage."

She left the bathroom prepared to negotiate for Buttercup Cottage. Finding her adversary flat on his back under the sink, she tapped the sole of his sneaker with her big toe. He pushed himself out and sat up, leaving his cap behind collecting drops of water from the faucet above.

Draping well-muscled arms over bent

knees, he looked at her for a second and then ran tapered fingers over close-cropped, wheat-colored hair.

"Oh, no." He groped under the sink and retrieved his cap. The gold insignia had taken on the same rusty hue as Louise's capris, and he frowned at the ruined embroidery.

"Looks pretty bad," Louise said, allowing herself a little smile. "I know how you feel."

"I have others."

"Navy officer issue, right?"

He nodded and stood up. "You look better."

"I think I washed off anything that might enter my bloodstream and communicate a fatal disease."

He smiled. "I apologize again. I really didn't see you. The back door was just the easiest way to dump the corroded water, and I never expected anyone to be outside."

"Isn't this the type of town where folks just pop up on their neighbors' doorsteps for a piece of apple pie?"

He smiled again, revealing even, straight teeth. "In town I suppose that's true, but out here on the sound, visitors are pretty rare. Besides, nobody knows I'm here. This place has been vacant for so long there's not a soul who would have a reason to stop."

"Except for me, you mean."

"I guess except for you, and I'm a little curious about why you're here." He went to an old wooden kitchen table and lifted the lid on a red cooler. He pulled a can of Coke from a pool of melting ice and held it out to her.

She sat on one of the four spindle-back chairs—the one with all its spindles—and popped the top. "I wouldn't have snuck up on you except I didn't see a car when I drove up."

He opened a can for himself, sat across from her and nodded toward the backyard. "My Jeep's in the shed. I put it there because the salt in the air can be rough on the paint."

They each took a few sips of soda before Wesley spoke again. "So…why *are* you here? And even more important, I suppose, who are you?"

She set her Coke down and folded her hands. "My name's Louise Duncan. I'm a friend of Vicki Soren—" She stopped when she realized she was about to give Vicki's maiden name, the one she'd used until six months ago. "Make that Vicki Malone."

"Malone?" He nodded in recognition. "Jamie's wife? The one who married him so he could get a green card all those years ago?"

"That's the one."

"My dad told me those two found each other after something like thirteen years. He said he had a hand in keeping them together after all that time."

Louise scoffed. "I guess you could say that. I was Vicki's lawyer, and I drafted the faultless divorce settlement she presented to Jamie. And then your daddy took it upon himself to concoct a number of loopholes. No offense to your father, but he's a crafty old buzzard."

Wesley chuckled. "None taken. In the Fletcher family, that's a compliment." He eyed her over the top of his can as he took a long swallow. "So you're a lawyer?"

"That's right." She looked directly at him. "And I've heard every shark and bottom-feeding joke you can think of, so you can keep them to yourself."

He affected an innocent shrug. "Believe me, I wasn't going to make any cracks."

She relaxed. "Okay then. Now as for why I'm here in Bayberry Cove, I'm on vacation, sort of." Seeing no reason to delay the inevitable, she announced, "And I've come to Buttercup Cottage because I want to rent it for a couple of months."

He set the can down with a metallic thump. "Sorry. It's not available."

"Why not?"

"Because I'm living in it."

"But you could live anywhere."

"So could you."

She took a deep breath. Engaging in a war of words with Wesley Fletcher was not likely to get her anywhere, especially since the cottage she now obsessively wanted to rent was in his family's name. "Look, I might consider renting something else, but my friend told me there is nothing available in Bayberry Cove—no motels, no seasonal places even."

"That's true, but you could point that BMW down Sandy Ridge Road, and in ten or fifteen miles you'll hit some quaint little towns with enough gingerbread bed-and-breakfasts to make your mouth water." He picked up his can and pointed it in a direction roughly behind him. "Or head to Morgan City and get a room at the Comfort Inn. They have a free continental breakfast."

"That's almost twenty miles away." His answering shrug was impassive, and Louise had to struggle to control her temper. She drummed her fingers on the tabletop and watched for any sign of capitulation. Nothing.

"I think we can reach an agreement here," she finally said. "I'm only in your town for one reason. My friend lives a mile from this cottage and I want to spend time with her."

"That makes sense."

"And I know that your father lives in a big house in town. Jamie Malone told me. Couldn't you stay there for a couple of months? Then when I leave, you could move back to this place."

He shook his head. "I'd rather not. It's really not convenient."

Logic wasn't working, and now Louise wanted to rent Buttercup Cottage with a craving that was almost scary. She changed tactics. "I'll pay you, of course. And I know this time of year demands higher rates. Would you say a thousand dollars a month is a fair price?"

He barked with amusement. "For this little waterfront gem?" He leaned toward her across the table. "Here's what I think is a fair price. Assuming I can get the pipes fixed…" he glanced around the small kitchen "…and assuming these old appliances are in working order, which I haven't tested yet since you stopped by and interrupted me. And assuming that when I get up on the roof and walk around I won't find any leaks…then I'd say a fair price might be about four hundred a month."

Now they were getting somewhere. In fact, Wesley was turning out to be a decent guy. "You'd do all these repairs and only charge me four hundred a month?"

"No. I said that would be a fair price. Actually, I'm not going to charge you anything because I'm not renting you this house."

She stood up, sending her chair scooting along the worn linoleum floor. "I see what's happening here," she said.

"You do?"

"Absolutely. Don't move. I'll be right back."

He looked at his wristwatch. "Can I at least move back to the sink? I'm behind schedule already."

She glared at him, then picked up her keys from where he'd left them on the counter, and stomped through the kitchen to a parlor, where a few old pieces of furniture were haphazardly arranged. She picked her way through a clutter of old magazines and knick-knacks and stepped out the front door to her car. Opening the passenger door of the BMW, she snatched her purse from the front seat. When she went back to the kitchen, Wesley was under the sink again.

"Excuse me," she said.

He scooted out and stood up.

Louise moved to within inches of him and waved her checkbook in front of his eyes. "How much? Name your price."

He stared at her and slowly shook his head. "Are you crazy?"

"I want to rent this place, Wesley Fletcher. And I mean to have it. I've played games with your father in the past, but I'd rather not play games with you. Can't we just settle this here and now?"

His blue eyes turned flint-gray, and Louise took a step back. *Be nice, Lulu,* she said to herself. *Be compassionate and caring like Roger says. Don't intimidate.* She took a deep breath. "Please, Wesley. I'll pay whatever you say."

He crossed his arms over his chest and regarded her with serious intent. After a moment he turned his hands palms up. Louise experienced a gratifying rush of victory at the obvious gesture of surrender.

And then he said, "The place isn't for rent. That's final."

His was as resolute a face as she'd ever seen in her life. It was a granite and steel countenance that would be perfect at a peacemaking summit between world powers. Or above the green felt of a high-stakes poker table. And it was a face that wasn't going to change.

Louise marched into the bathroom, stuffed her soiled clothes into her suitcase and her feet into her ruined sandals and wheeled the bag back to the kitchen. Wesley was under the sink again, but his shadowed gaze snapped from the gaping pipes and remained fixed on her face.

"I suggest you let the local postman know you're living here, Wesley," she said. "The bill for my clothes will arrive in the mail. Since I don't have an address, you may send your check in care of the Malones."

The corner of his mouth lifted in an odd little grin that might have been endearing on a young boy, but was simply maddening on Wesley. "Aye, aye, Counselor," he said.

She stepped to the sink, carefully avoiding contact with his bent knee, and gave the old enamel spigot one quick flick of her wrist. The rewarding squeal and shimmy of old copper tubing filled her with satisfaction. Water spurted through the pipes, hitting Wesley Fletcher square in the middle of his smug face. Louise smiled down at him, grabbed the handle of her suitcase and exited Buttercup Cottage.

## CHAPTER THREE

WESLEY DROVE HIS Jeep Wrangler onto the gravel road leading to Pintail Point, the home of his long-time friend and Bayberry Cove's resident artist, Jamie Malone. Wes had been home less than twenty-four hours and there were plenty of people he needed to see, but on this picture-perfect morning with the sun shimmering off the blue water of the sound, it was Jamie he wanted to talk to.

After he determined that Louise Duncan's black BMW wasn't anywhere in sight, Wes parked under a couple of tall, sweeping sea pines. He walked toward the houseboat, scanning the yard until he was convinced Louise wasn't there. Then he fixed his gaze on the picnic table where Jamie's dog, Beasley, was napping. The long-legged beast opened his golden eyes, crawled out from under the table and emitted a low-pitched bark of welcome. Then he plopped down at Wesley's feet.

Wesley scratched behind one of the animal's

floppy ears. "Hey, Beas, how are you? Energetic as ever, I see."

Jamie burst out the door of the *Bucket O' Luck* and strode toward them. "Wes Fletcher, I heard you were home." He held out his hand. "Good to see you."

"Same here." Wes resumed a reconnaissance of the property while answering Jamie's questions about his retirement.

After a few minutes of conversation, Jamie snapped his fingers to get Wes's attention. "She's not here, buddy."

Wes was forced to focus on Jamie's face. "Who? I don't know what you're talking about."

"Sure you don't. I'm talking about Louise Duncan, who stopped by here yesterday after you doused her with what she described as some sort of sewage."

Wes scrunched up his face. "It wasn't sewage. It was rusty water from the kitchen pipes. And did she mention that she gave as good as she got?"

Jamie smiled. "Oh, yeah. That was the part of the story she enjoyed telling most."

Wes shook his head. "She's one strange woman. Bossy, pushy, demanding…"

"Don't forget drop-dead gorgeous," Jamie added.

Wes laughed. "I guess that's true, too. And determined. She wouldn't take no for an answer when it came to renting the cottage."

"We heard. Frankly, my wife, whom you haven't met, but who is the sweetest woman on this green earth, is a little ticked at you. She was hoping you'd move in with your dad."

Wes shrugged. "I've been given a grant from the National Oceanic and Atmospheric Administration to fund a project on marine ecology. I need to be on the water."

"Why didn't you tell Louise that? She might have understood why living at the cottage was so important to you."

"She didn't seem interested in anyone's motives but her own. And have you ever tried to get a word in with her?"

Jamie chuckled. "A few times. Your point's well taken."

"So where are the women now?"

"You just missed Vicki. She drove into Bayberry Cove to meet Louise at the Kettle. She stayed at a motel in Morgan City last night, but she's determined to find a place in town to rent for a couple of months so she can just sort of kick back."

Wes pictured the Bayberry Cove Kettle at eight-thirty on a Saturday morning. The restaurant would be packed, and he had no doubt who in the crowd would be the center of attention.

LOUISE TURNED ONTO Main Street and looked at the digital clock on her dashboard. Already ten minutes late, she reluctantly slowed to a frustrating, but law-abiding, thirty-five miles an hour and scanned the street for available parking. She settled for a spot two blocks away from the Bayberry Cove Kettle, got out of her car and walked briskly to the entrance.

She threaded her way through the crowded restaurant to where her friend was seated. "Sorry I'm late," she said, hanging her purse over the back of the chair and sitting down.

"Don't apologize. I only got here five minutes ago. I took my time, since I remembered it was you I was meeting."

"Funny." A pleasant-looking waitress came to the table. "What's good here?" Louise asked Vicki.

"Everything's great, isn't that right, Bobbi Lee?" Vicki said.

Louise gave Vicki a knowing look. So this well-rounded waitress in the red-checkered dress was the notorious Bobbi Lee Blanchard she'd heard so much about, the woman who'd chased after Jamie Malone for years.

"Not a bad choice on the whole menu," Bobbi confirmed.

"In that case," Louise said, "I'll have two eggs over light, hash browns, wheat toast and a side of bacon. And, of course, coffee—large."

Vicki ordered scrambled eggs and an English muffin and waited until Bobbi Lee had gone to place the order before she said, "What happened to yogurt and fresh fruit?"

Louise shrugged. "I'm in the country now. Fresh air makes me hungry." She pointed to Vicki's bulging belly. "It could be worse. Look what it did to you."

They chatted about Vicki's store in Fort Lauderdale, her new house, the wood carvings Jamie was sending to a Boston gallery for a summer showing. "Enough about my life," Vicki said when they'd finished their meal and were sipping coffee. "Be honest, Lulu. How are you going to stay in Bayberry Cove for two months? You're going to die of boredom."

"No, I won't. I like this town. It's cute and cozy. With the exception of Wesley Fletcher, the people seem nice. I'll find things to do. Maybe I'll help you shop for baby stuff."

Vicki's eyes sparkled with amusement. "You? Baby shopping? One trip to Infants

'R' Us in Morgan City and you'll be begging for mercy."

Louise nodded. "Maybe. But I'd like to give the town a try—if I can find a place to stay. I'm not driving nearly twenty miles each way to the motel."

Vicki set her mug on the table. "Sorry things didn't work out for Buttercup Cottage. And even sorrier that Wes gave you such a hard time. I've never met him, but Jamie's always told me what a super guy he is."

Louise arched one perfectly shaped eyebrow. "Believe me, Vic, there are things about him that definitely fall into the super category."

"Ah…so what Bobbi Lee just told me is true. Commander Fletcher is a hunk."

Louise smiled. "Close enough. He's way too clean-cut for my taste, but with a little roughing up, he could be the mountain man of my dreams."

"Somehow I can't see a career navy guy turning into Grizzly Adams."

Louise was about to respond when Bobbi Lee returned. "Can I get you anything else, ladies?"

Louise grabbed the check just as a customer approached the table demanding Bobbi's attention.

"Hi, Earnest," she said. "You want the usual?"

"That'll be fine, Bobbi Lee. Just wrap it up and I'll take it back upstairs to my apartment. I've got a whole day's worth of bookkeeping ahead of me."

Louise stared at the man's balding pate as he walked behind Bobbi Lee toward the counter. "Vicki, did you hear what that man said?"

Vicki tucked a strand of honey-blond hair behind her ear. "Something about a take-out order."

"Right. An order he can take up to his apartment." She pointed to the ceiling. "His apartment upstairs."

Vicki was clearly baffled. "So?"

"This street is lined with two-story buildings. There must be living quarters on the second floor of most of them. All I have to do is find one that's empty."

"What are you going to do?" Vicki asked. "Check every building on the street?"

"If I have to."

"Would you like me to help? I promised Jamie I'd work with him on his exhibit today, but he'll understand."

"No. Go on home to that gorgeous husband of yours. I'll wait and pay the check." As Vicki stood to leave, Louise looked out the window to the park across the street and grinned. "I won't need your help anyway, Vic. I know just who to ask."

WES WAS LUCKY. He pulled into a parking place right in front of the Bayberry Cove Kettle just after a customer backed out. Glancing around at the spots nearest him, he confirmed the absence of a black BMW and couldn't decide if he felt relief or disappointment.

He opened the door to the restaurant, and Louise breezed through it wearing a midthigh sundress splashed with sunflowers and held up with inch-wide shoulder straps. A flurry of gastric activity began in Wes's stomach that made him forget his earlier cravings for pancakes and bacon.

She stopped in front of him and locked her mesmerizing pale lavender eyes with his. A shock of recognition—no doubt as profound as Wes's own—shimmered in her gaze for mere seconds before mutating to an amused familiarity. Nothing seemed to faze this woman for long.

"Well, well, Commander." She placed a fist on her hip and gave him a self-assured grin. "You clean up pretty well."

His fingers twitched at his side. He resisted

the ridiculous urge to salute. He literally *was* a commander, but he didn't feel in charge of this encounter. "Good morning, Louise," he said, reassured by the commanding tone of his voice, at least.

"You look refreshed, Wesley," she said. "I assume you slept well in your seaside retreat."

"Very well, thank you." That was a lie. The window air conditioner in the master bedroom had cranked and hissed in competition with the twenty-year-old compressor in the refrigerator. But outdated appliances weren't all that had kept him awake most of the night. He was staring at the main reason for his restlessness. "And you?"

"Like a top," she said. "The motel you so generously recommended had all the amenities of, well...a motel." She flipped a shimmering column of black hair over her shoulder. "But you'll be glad to know that I may have solved the problem of my living quarters."

"Oh?"

She raised her eyes to scan the tops of the buildings on Main Street. "I can't imagine that there isn't a room to let above one of these Bayberry Cove establishments. I can be quite comfortable here in the middle of everything that goes on in your little town."

"That is an interesting solution, Louise. I'm sure you'll find the nightlife in town quite stimulating. Have you checked with any of the shopkeepers yet about vacancies?"

"I don't need to go door-to-door," she answered smartly. "I've already made one friend in Bayberry Cove who will be helpful." She pointed to the park across the street, where an old man sat on a bench.

Wes smiled when he recognized the familiar figure who had occupied that particular bench for most of the last five years.

"He was kind enough to give me directions to Pintail Point yesterday," Louise continued. "I'm sure he'll help me find a vacancy. I'll bet he sees everything from that vantage point. And I'll bet he knows everyone in town."

"That's probably a good bet," Wes said.

Louise inclined her head toward the restaurant door. "You enjoy your breakfast, Commander. By the time you've finished, I'll have signed a two-month lease, and we'll practically be neighbors."

"I don't doubt it." Wes glanced at the old-timer in the park. Mason was a tough cookie in most of his dealings, but if anyone could talk him into the lease deal of the century, it was Louise. "Why don't we meet back here in, say, forty-five minutes, and you can let me know how you made out," Wes suggested. "I'll even spring for coffee and promise not to pour any on you."

Amazingly, she seemed to like the idea. "Forty-five minutes it is." She gave him a grin and left.

"Hi. Do you remember me?" Louise said to the old man sitting under the sprawling oak tree.

He looked at her with surprisingly clear blue eyes that were still apparently capable of appreciating her obvious attributes. Sliding over to give her room on the bench, he motioned for her to sit. "I may be old," he said, "but my memory's as fresh as last night's dew for things that catch my fancy. Did you find your way to Pintail Point yesterday?"

She sat, then angled toward him with her elbow on the back of the bench. "I did. Your directions were perfect. I'm counting on you knowing every little thing about this town. That's why I've come back for your help today."

He layered his hands over a thick wooden walking stick and appraised her with an intensity that suddenly seemed strangely familiar. "What is it you need, young lady?"

Louise squirmed on the bench seat just a little, suppressing the feeling that she knew this man as more than just a passing acquaintance from the previous day. It was more than his eyes. Though his skin was creased with wrinkles and slack on his face, she detected a once-square jawline, punctuated by a strong chin that thrust forward with authority.

She told him about her search for living quarters and that she was hoping an apartment might be available in town. He nodded, asked her a few questions about her intended length of stay and her reason for being in Bayberry Cove.

She answered truthfully, and when she'd finished, he thought a moment and then replied. "There's a small house out on the sound about four miles from here," he said. "Has a sign above the door that says Buttercup Cottage. I think you'd like it there."

Louise laughed. "I would indeed, but it seems someone beat me to it. A man is already living there...."

His scraggly white eyebrows lifted in surprise. "Do you know his name?"

"Wesley Fletcher," she said.

The beginning of a smile curled the man's thin lips. "So, the boy's come home," he said. "I wondered when I caught a glimpse of him going into the Kettle."

"He has. I tried to bargain with him—"

"Oh, you can't bargain with Wesley. He's as stubborn as his father."

Louise nodded. "So I've experienced."

The old man chuckled. "You'd best leave the cottage to him." He pointed across the street. "Now, then, see that furniture store? McCorkle's New and Used?"

Louise nodded again.

"You try that place. I know the upstairs is vacant, and I think it's in pretty good shape. 'Course, all these buildings are showing signs of age. But I expect that one will do."

"And who should I see about renting it?" Louise asked.

"Ask for Suzie or Evan McCorkle. They run the place. You tell them that Mason told you to inquire." He winked at her. "You'll get the apartment. I guarantee it. Just have Suzie draw up a simple agreement saying you'll pay three hundred a month for the next two months. Tell her to give you a copy and that'll be that."

"Really? It's that easy?"

"You run along and get your suitcase. It'll be that easy," he assured her.

And it almost was. Evan McCorkle, gray-haired, well-fed and a living, breathing folk-art archetype of middle-class virtues, was at first reluctant to rent to Louise. She determined from what she deciphered from snatches of his whispered debate with his wife that Evan thought Louise might play loud music or entertain guests at odd hours.

But Suzie McCorkle argued that she had a good feeling about Miss Duncan, and couldn't she always trust her feelings? In the end, it was Suzie's intuition and the mention of Mason's name that clinched the deal. By the time Louise entered the Bayberry Cove Kettle to meet Wesley Fletcher for coffee, she had a signed lease in her hand. "The place is a bit dusty," she explained to Wes, "but I can fix it up. And I bought a few pieces of furniture from the McCorkles. I'll be very comfortable there."

Truthfully, it would take her a good two days to even make the place livable. The furniture needed sprucing up. The cobwebs alone would fill up a trash can, and the grime on the windows all but obliterated the view of Main Street. But Louise wasn't about to admit to Wes that any of those details were more than a passing inconvenience.

"Sounds like everything worked out for you even without Buttercup Cottage," he said, while filling her coffee mug.

"Absolutely." She stirred her coffee and

let a smug grin convey her feeling of self-satisfaction. "And the best part is I got a great deal, and don't have to write any rent checks to the Fletchers."

He smiled down into his own cup before leveling a serious gaze on her face. "That's not necessarily so, Louise. If you look at that document carefully, you'll see that your rent payments should be made out to Mason D. Fletcher Enterprises."

Louise darted a glance out the window at the old man in the park. "His name is Mason *Fletcher?*"

"'Fraid so," Wes acknowledged. "Your landlord is my grandfather." When he noticed the puzzled look on her face, he added, "Mason Delroy Fletcher owns these entire three blocks of Bayberry Cove, Louise. So no matter what second-story apartment you chose, you would be supporting the Fletchers."

He took a long sip of coffee. "And we certainly do appreciate your patronage."

# CHAPTER FOUR

VICKI MALONE CAREFULLY removed a china dinner plate from the packing box. She stacked it on top of others on an old wrought-iron and glass table in the kitchen section of Louise's apartment. "These dishes are really pretty, Lulu," she said. "I love the cherry blossom design."

"The best the Morgan City Wal-Mart had to offer," Louise responded. "And within the limits of the dollar amount I set to furnish this place."

Vicki swiped her finger through a layer of dust on the single kitchen counter. "Are you really going to sleep here tonight?"

Louise snapped plastic gloves onto her hands and dipped a cleaning rag into a solution of vinegar and water. "Absolutely. Two nights in a motel is enough for me. I'm looking forward to all the..." she paused, glanced around the room at the work that still needed to be done, and gave Vicki a rueful smile "...comforts of home. Have I mentioned how grateful I am to you two for your help?"

Jamie Malone, intent on turning an old oak bureau into a utilitarian work of art, shrugged off the comment. "Forget about it. What are friends for?"

"Besides, you've mentioned it about a hundred times," Vicki said. "With the three of us working, we actually might have this place in order by this afternoon. It's going to be lovely," she added. "The curtains and linens and pillows you bought are adorable and will add a lot of charm to this room."

Louise stared at her dearest friend. Vicki loved pottery and flowers and chintz, so Louise allowed her to use words like *adorable* and *charm*. Louise's viewpoint was that a person needed towels. So what if they had a little lacy trim on the hem? So what if a plate had a cluster of cherries painted in the center? It would still hold a microwave dinner. "That's the look I'm going for," she said with a grin.

When she finished unpacking dishes, Vicki picked up a candle that had been sitting on the table, and examined it closely. "I didn't know you were into these things. Did you buy this at the Bayberry Cove Candle Company?"

"Hardly, since I've never heard of the place.

The truth is, I didn't buy it at all. It was outside my door this morning when I got here."

"It's a beautiful shade of blue," Vicki said. "Did you read the tag taped to the side?"

"Tag? No. I didn't know there was a tag."

"It says, 'Look to the sky and look to sea for this tranquil shade of blue. Light it tonight and it will bring comfort to your home and you.'"

Louise walked over to the table and took the candle from Vicki. "Very touching," she said, "if not exactly poet laureate material."

"If you didn't buy it," Vicki said, "I wonder where it came from."

Jamie turned off the power to his electric sander and set the tool on top of the bureau. "I'd guess that Suzie McCorkle left it," he said. "She's interested in that kind of stuff. Candles, crystals, things like that. It's probably her way of wishing you domestic harmony."

Louise pictured the mousy woman with the shoulder-length gray hair neatly pinned back from her forehead with two barrettes. A New Age lady? Well, why not? Louise looked at the mattress and box springs and the "nearly new" plaid sofa she had bought from Suzie's shop the day before, and another explanation came to mind. "Maybe she's just thanking me for buying a few things."

Jamie ran his hand over the surface of the dresser and picked up the sander again. "Maybe. She would do something like that—quietly leave a candle without expecting recognition. She's a nice woman."

The origin of the candle solved, Louise returned to her struggle with the first of three windows that looked over Main Street. After scrubbing for ten minutes with the vinegar solution and following up with industrial strength glass cleaner, she was finally able to see the sun dappling the sidewalks in the square across the street. She yanked another batch of paper towels from a roll and feverishly wiped the stubborn glass with a circular motion. "Just have to eliminate a few more streaks," she huffed, "and then a bird with a bad case of cataracts might actually knock himself silly trying to fly into this place."

"For the love of Saint Pat, Louise," Jamie said above the steady whirr of his sander, "you'd better quit now before you rub a hole in the glass."

"Jamie's right, Lulu. You're taking out your frustration on the window."

Louise laid her forehead against the nearly clean pane and sighed. "You're right. I still can't believe I didn't notice the name *Fletcher* on that lease. Four days ago, if I'd had a client who'd done something as stupid as sign a document without reading it carefully, I'd have seriously considered not representing him."

Jamie looked at Vicki and was unsuccessful at hiding a grin. "And what difference does it really make now? You have a place to stay at a reasonable rent—the *only* place available, as I see it. Why do you care who owns the building?"

"But they're so smug," she said. "Wesley practically crowed when he told me that his family owns this building."

"They own Buttercup Cottage, too," Vicki pointed out. "And that didn't bother you when you thought you could rent it."

"That was yesterday, before I knew them." She gestured out the window, where people in the square were now visible through the sparkling glass. "And that old guy over there…Mason Fletcher. Now that I think about it, he was smug, too. And I can just imagine Haywood. He's probably more smug than the rest of them."

Jamie hunched a shoulder in a sign of agreement. "Smug, clever…there's a fine line between the two if you ask me. You have to be clever first in order to justify being smug.

And as for your signing the lease, my advice is to forget about it. You're on vacation from lawyering, so you might as well relax and enjoy yourself." He walked to the middle window and with his fist cleared a three-inch circle through the grime so he could see the street below. "Bayberry Cove is a really nice little town."

Louise let out a long breath and followed his gaze. It was Sunday morning, and families had gathered on the square. Fathers pushed children on swings and women chatted on benches.

"Yes, it is," she admitted. "And you're right. I'm going to relax just as soon as I get this place clean. And right after you tell me how old man Fletcher got all his money."

Jamie went back to the bureau, picked up a piece of sandpaper and began smoothing the edges by hand. "That's an interesting story," he said, his words a soothing accompaniment to the rasp of the paper. "Mason was in his early twenties when he took a small inheritance his father left him and traveled from Bayberry Cove to Arizona. He invested in a silver mine out there with some other fellas, and as luck would have it, they uncovered a rich vein that gave them each a good stake for their futures."

Louise dipped her rag again and attacked

the middle window. "So he came back to North Carolina and bought Bayberry Cove?"

Jamie chuckled. "Not all at once. He made his real fortune in patents. Sold one to Henry Ford that revolutionized the assembly line process. And then, bit by bit, he started buying up property around here and dabbling in various ventures. He built Buttercup Cottage for the love of his life, the woman he married."

Louise stared down at the old man under the oak tree. She wasn't surprised to learn a romantic soul lurked behind his knowing blue eyes. Smugness aside, Mason Fletcher had a soft spot. "Who was she?"

"An Arizona gal. He married her out there and took her away from all that soaring rock and desert and brought her to the sea. They say she loved being on Currituck Sound, and Buttercup Cottage was his gift to her on their second anniversary." He stopped sanding and looked first at Louise and then at Vicki. "He called her Buttercup. He was a man very much in love, apparently. Still is, twenty-some years after her death."

"Haywood was their only child?" Louise asked.

"The only one who survived the polio

epidemic," Jamie answered. "Haywood had two sisters, twins. They both died."

Louise watched as Mason Fletcher rolled a colorful plastic ball toward a group of children in the square. "That's sad."

"And Haywood only had one child—Wesley." Jamie blew a film of sawdust from the top of the bureau. "Can't say he didn't try for more, though. He's been married four times—which is why he shies away from wedded bliss today," Jamie added with a hint of bitterness in his voice.

Louise resumed scrubbing. "So Haywood is quite the ladies' man as well as a renowned legal mind. I can't wait to meet this paragon of Bayberry Cove society."

"You will meet him," Vicki said. "The only woman in his life now is Jamie's mother, Kate."

"But didn't you tell me that Jamie's mother works for Haywood?" Louise asked.

"We said 'used to,' as in she used to be his housekeeper. Now she's a bit more to him than that."

"Yeah, but not his wife," Jamie said with that same edge of rancor in his tone.

Louise spritzed a generous amount of cleaner on the window and began rubbing it dry. As the solution evaporated, a group of men standing on the sidewalk in front of the Bayberry Cove Kettle came into her view. There was no mistaking the tall, lean figure waving goodbye to the others and heading across the street. She quickly cleaned a larger section and watched Wesley Fletcher walk toward his grandfather. "Speaking of the Fletchers, the youngest one just appeared on the square."

Vicki levered her pregnant body off the chair. She stood beside Louise at the window. "Is that him? Is that Wesley?"

"In the flesh." Louise admired the stretch of a snug T-shirt over his chest and his muscled thighs extending from a pair of gray jersey shorts. "Or the next best thing to it, anyway."

"Ohh…" Vicki's one syllable rolled into several seconds of blatant admiration.

"Don't stare at the poor man, ladies," Jamie said from the middle of the room. "You couldn't be more obvious."

Vicki laughed. "You're just jealous because there's someone in Bayberry Cove who is *nearly* as good-looking as you are."

"Maybe a little," he admitted. "But Wes is a good friend. And he's the town's favorite son. He was born and raised here and all the locals followed his exploits through the naval academy and beyond. I'm content to stand in his shadow as the adopted son."

Louise drummed her nails against the pane. "I wonder why he's not married."

"He was, once," Jamie said. "To a girl he met while he was at Annapolis. She was a journalist in Washington, a couple of years older than him."

"What happened?"

"She went her way, covering stories around the world, and he went his, to wherever the navy sent him. Tough to make a marriage work under those circumstances. They divorced after a few years."

Louise drew her friend's attention back to the window. "Look, he's a runner."

Both women watched as Wesley stretched his legs and arms. He jogged in place a moment before taking off around the perimeter of the square.

"He runs a few times a week when he's in town," Jamie said, adding that he started the regimen at precisely the same time each day. "Now get away from the window and give the man his privacy."

"No way," Louise scoffed. "He doesn't want privacy. He's running in the middle of the town square!" Determined to raise the window, which probably hadn't been opened in a decade at least, she struggled until old paint finally cracked and the glass slid upward with a stubborn hiss. She waited for Wesley to sprint around to the street side again and then leaned out the window. "Ahoy, Commander," she yelled. "Good morning."

He looked up, shielded his eyes. "Good morning to you, Louise," he called. "How are the new digs?"

"Couldn't be better," she said, propping the window up with a yardstick.

He tossed her an offhand wave and jogged around the corner. Louise continued to watch. His legs churned with nearly effortless grace. His arms pumped rhythmically at his sides. He was all fluid, powerful motion, an image of focused elegance. She nudged her friend. "So, what do you think?"

"Oh, you're right, Lulu. I've never seen a man more outrageously…" Vicki fumbled for the right word and glanced over her shoulder at her husband "…sinfully *smug* in my life!"

Louise hooted with laughter. "See? I told you. But on him it does look good."

LOUISE'S APPROACH TO LIFE in Bayberry Cove was characterized by good intentions. First, she intended to take Jamie's advice. Once the apartment was in good shape, she'd kick back, relax, read a few good books. She'd definitely brightened the day of the owner of Books by the Bay when she'd walked out of the shop Monday morning with ten novels.

Second, she intended to stay a little bit angry with Wesley Fletcher. It was the safest way to combat a growing attraction to the good-looking ex-naval officer who seemed to be popping into her thoughts with alarming regularity. A man who lived his life according to regimens and schedules wouldn't complement Louise's more flamboyant style. More importantly, she wasn't staying in Bayberry Cove for long. Two months in this town was the only interlude she meant to have from her real life.

And last, she definitely intended to avoid legal matters of any kind. She was in the South, where everybody understood that the livin' was easy, and she was going to return to Oppenheimer Straus and Baker bathed in an aura of mint-julep cool if it killed her.

Unfortunately, each of these good intentions was blown all to bits on Tuesday evening.

Just two days after she moved into her little apartment, an unexpected event made her ignore every promise she'd made to herself.

Tired of reading, bored with dusting and totally disinterested in popping a frozen dinner into her microwave, Louise wandered down to the Kettle, where she'd eaten most of her meals the last couple of days. There was a good supper crowd gathered in the diner, but she found a small table and sat down.

After a few minutes Bobbi Lee came to take her order. "Hey, girl, how's it going?" she said, her red lips curving into a welcoming grin. "How's that place of yours working out?"

"Just fine, Bobbi Lee," Louise said. She and Bobbi had established a friendly relationship. In fact, Louise was now beginning to worry about how this steadily increasing bond with the waitress might translate into fat grams.

"What'll it be tonight?" Bobbi asked.

Louise folded the menu so she couldn't see the words *sausage gravy.* "Just a salad."

Bobbi sauntered off to place the order and Louise sat back and watched the people around her. Four women at a nearby table caught and held her attention. Occasionally the women's conversation was interrupted by boisterous laughter. But without fail, they quickly resumed a serious discussion once the joviality passed. Other sounds of the restaurant faded as curiosity made Louise tune in their voices. The ladies were obviously close acquaintances even though there was a wide range in their ages.

"All I know is that I couldn't afford to give up another day's wages at the factory to stay home with my son," a young, olive-skinned Hispanic woman said. "Thankfully he was well enough to go back to the baby-sitter today."

"Did you tell Justin why you needed to stay home?" an older woman with a long gray ponytail asked.

"I did, hoping he'd be sympathetic. He said, 'Go ahead, Miranda. Take all the time you need, but come payday—'"

"Wait, don't tell us," a slim woman with short blond hair interrupted. "He said, 'Come payday, your check might be a little less than you expected.'"

Empathetic laughter erupted around the table until the older woman lifted her iced tea into the air. "Let's drink one to Justin Beauclaire, in honor of his unending compassion for his employees and his sense of fair play," she said.

Something of an expert herself in the subtle deployment of sarcasm, Louise appreciated the old gal's admirable use of it. She smiled and raised her glass of iced tea in silent commiseration.

Four glasses met and clinked above the center of the table, and each woman took a long swallow. The older woman set down her glass, wiped her mouth with a napkin and gave her friend a serious look. "You know, Miranda, you could have brought Lorenzo to my house yesterday. It was my day off, and I would have watched him."

Miranda smiled in gratitude. "Thanks, Bessie, but you've got enough to handle just taking care of your husband. Besides, who knows what germs Lorenzo could have brought into your house? If Pete had caught something from him, his emphysema might have gotten worse."

"How's Pete doing, anyway?" a woman with coffee-brown skin asked.

"Not too well, Yvonne," Bessie said, "but thanks for asking."

"You've got to get some help," Yvonne said. "Between work and Pete, you're wearing yourself out."

"Without health insurance, I can't afford to get outside help," Bessie said. "Even if I could afford insurance, I doubt I could get coverage for Pete at this stage of his illness."

*Not an individual policy,* Louise agreed to herself. *But it would have been nice if you'd had family coverage provided by your employer when you started working.*

Yvonne, the African-American woman, shook her head slowly. "That's a shame. My sister's husband over in Raleigh got coverage for the whole family when he went to work for the paper mill...."

Louise nodded. *Right. That's the way it should be.*

"...and tight ol' Justin Beauclaire won't even provide coverage for his employees," the woman continued.

The blonde, the youngest by several years, downed the rest of her iced tea in one long gulp and curled her lips into a catlike grin. "Yeah, but we get all the candles we can steal," she said.

Candles? These women must work for the Bayberry Cove Candle Company, which Vicki had mentioned a couple of days ago. The factory was the town's largest employer.

The young woman unzipped a huge canvas purse sitting on the floor beside her chair and pulled out an eight-inch pillar candle. "I figure this pretty one will set the mood when Luke and I are alone at his place later."

"Shame on you, Darlene Jackson," Bessie said. "You took that from work?"

Darlene shrugged. "Why not? I haven't had

a raise in three years. I figure the company owes me."

Bessie sighed. "The last thing I want to see when I leave the factory every day is another candle."

"Yes, girl," Yvonne said, and then shook a finger at Darlene. "Especially when you're wasting it on Luke Plunkett. When are you gonna wise up and find yourself a nice fella?"

Darlene stuffed the candle back in her purse and frowned. "As soon as Justin Beauclaire pays me a wage that allows me to put a little away each week so's I can walk outta that factory for good. And you all know that's not likely to happen." She set her elbows on the table and cradled her chin in her hands. "Until I can afford to get outta here, Luke is about all I got to look forward to each night." She gazed at the ceiling, avoiding eye contact with her friends. "Besides, he can be nice."

Yvonne stared at Bessie and said in a conspiratorial voice, "Is it snowing in hell, Bess?"

Darlene stood up, dug into the pocket of a pair of skin-tight jeans and tossed a few bills onto the table. "I heard that, Yvonne," she said. "But even you've got to admit that a girl can't sit home with her momma and daddy every night on a big, lonely farm. And like I said, Luke can be nice."

She draped the purse strap over her shoulder and pushed in her chair. "I'm off to the Brew and Bowl. Luke will be wondering where I am." She straightened her spine defiantly and lifted her chin. "See you all next Tuesday night, I guess. And tomorrow at work."

Louise munched on the last of her salad and watched with the three other women as Darlene strutted from the restaurant.

"I don't know what will become of that girl if she stays with Luke," Bessie said with a shake of her coarse gray ponytail. "She's got a big heart, but I don't think that boy will ever appreciate the goodness in her."

Miranda ran a hand through her long dark curls and sighed. "I worry that Luke will get drunk and really hurt her. Deputy Blackwell has broken up a couple of fights between them, but one day Darlene won't be so lucky. She needs to get away from that devil before it's too late."

Yvonne smirked. "Not much chance of that as long as she's working for Beauclaire and earning minimum wage. She can't afford a place of her own."

Louise had heard enough. The problems at the candle factory were issues she understood well in her capacity as a corporate lawyer, though she'd never really studied them from the employees' point of view. Her promise to avoid work-related entanglements abruptly abandoned, Louise stood up and went to the table.

"Pardon me, ladies," she said. "I couldn't help overhearing. I'm Louise Duncan, attorney. Do you mind if I sit down?"

None of the women spoke, apparently too surprised to respond. Finally, Bessie pressed her booted foot on the leg of the chair Darlene had just vacated, and pushed it away from the table. "It's a free country," she said.

Miranda narrowed her dark eyes suspiciously. "Not to an attorney it isn't."

Louise dropped onto the chair and scooted close. She waved off the Hispanic woman's comment with a flutter of her hand. "Don't concern yourself with what you've heard about lawyer fees," she said. "If you ladies and I come to an agreement about some things, and I decide that I can help you, I'll take on this project strictly for the experience—and the fun of it." She smiled at the women.

"I know a little about corporate law, ladies," she continued. "And a thing or two about labor regulations." She looked at each woman. "If you three have a little more time this evening,

I'd like you to tell me all about the factory and your employer, Justin Beauclaire."

The two younger women looked to Bessie, who chewed her bottom lip a moment and finally said, "Girls, I can't see as it would hurt to talk to her."

# CHAPTER FIVE

WESLEY CAME AROUND the third corner of the town square jogging path and slowed to an easy trot, just as he'd done the last two mornings. He looked up at the three windows above McCorkle's New and Used Furniture Store on Main Street—just as he'd done the last two mornings. He knew his actions must be conspicuous, and he felt like a fool. If Louise were looking out one of the windows, she'd surely notice that he altered his pace each time he passed this particular part of the track.

She wasn't there. In fact, she hadn't shown her face since Sunday when, in front of half the population of Bayberry Cove, she'd hollered a greeting from her window and cheerfully wished him a good morning. And now it was Wednesday, and he hadn't felt nearly as cheery since. He waved at his grandfather, seated, as always, on a bench, and picked up his speed, heading into his second lap. "Forget about her, Wes," he puffed to himself on short, choppy bursts of air exploding from his laboring lungs. "Louise Duncan is the last woman on earth you should be interested in."

At the next corner, he ran faster. Louise was still in town. He'd heard that from several sources, including Jamie Malone. In fact, Jamie couldn't seem to talk about her without aiming a knowing grin at Wes.

Surely Jamie didn't think he was interested in Louise. She was about as alien to Bayberry Cove as nouveau cuisine was to the Kettle. If Wes ever did settle down with one woman again, it wouldn't be with an independent, wisecracking, beautiful city girl like Louise Duncan.

Jamie wasn't the only one in town who'd taken a liking to Louise. Bobbi Lee referred to her as "the princess" without the slightest hint of malice in her voice. Lots of folks in town seemed to like her. Wes wasn't at all sure how he felt about her, but as each day passed, he found himself wishing the warning bells in his head would cease their clamor so he could have the opportunity to decide how he did.

And then opportunity knocked—or dashed—right smack into his exercise regimen. In the middle of the long section of track opposite Main Street, Louise suddenly appeared next to him, jogging with all the vigor he had begun to lose. Long, lean legs extended from midthigh shorts and ended in sparkling white running shoes. She wore a red baseball cap low on her forehead, and a swath of raven hair swung from the opening at the back, reminding him of the tail of a Thoroughbred twitching at the starting gate.

"Nice day for a run, isn't it, Wesley?" she said, her voice even and controlled, and irritatingly unlabored.

He huffed out an answer. "A beautiful morning, Louise. I haven't seen you run before."

"I've indulged in entirely too much Southern cooking at the Kettle," she said, patting a tummy which, now that he looked, might be straining her zippers a little. "I run three days a week at home." She smiled at him. "Can't let myself go just because I'm on vacation."

Ordinarily Wes might have slowed as he approached the third curve for the second time. But he wasn't about to exhibit a lack of endurance in front of Louise. He sucked in his diaphragm, straightened his back and kept up the pace that somehow in the last minute he'd let her establish. "So how's that vacation thing working out for you?" he asked.

"Fine, but I'm counting on you to help make it better."

He stumbled on absolutely nothing. In disciplined military fashion, he covered his blunder and kept running. But he knew from the quick upturn of her lips that she'd seen him falter. "Oh?" It was all he could manage to say.

"I figured, who better to show me the sights than one of the town's most respected citizens." She cast him a sideways glance. "And from all I've heard, that's you, Commander."

The sun glinted off a silver medallion that bounced against her chest above the scooped neckline of her top. Wes couldn't take his eyes off it.

Her voice jolted him back from a dangerous place. "Wes? Are you interested?"

He snapped his eyes to hers. "Well, okay. Where would you like to go?"

"I thought we'd start with the candle factory."

The candle factory? He'd expected...deep down he'd *hoped* she would request a boat ride on Currituck Sound. In fact, he could picture her in his speedboat or the lively little skiff he'd brought out of dry dock and kept by the shore at the cottage. Or he thought she'd ask to see Bayberry Park with its thirty-foot waterfall, an anomaly in an area that boasted few attractions above sea level. But no, she wanted to see the candle factory.

As if sensing his confusion, she elaborated. "I love candles. I have dozens in my condo in Florida. What about this afternoon? I want to see the factory from the inside out, how candles are mass-produced, all the details I wouldn't get if I didn't go with someone who knows the territory."

Of course he could accommodate her. His father and the candle factory president, Justin Beauclaire, had been friends, fishing buddies and poker-playing rivals for years. The factory was certainly a safe place to take the bewildering Miss Duncan, but Wes's thoughts kept returning to a vision of a more intimate afternoon at the park or skimming over the crystal water of the sound. "Okay, the candle factory it is," he said, trying to hide a disappointment that surprised him with its intensity. "I'll pick you up behind the furniture store at two?"

They'd reached the path by Main Street again, and Louise veered off toward her apartment. "Great. See you then."

As soon as Wes was certain she couldn't see him, he stopped running, bent his knees and placed his hands on his thighs. He expelled a long, exhausted breath and heard his grandfather chuckling. Wes looked over his shoulder, frowned and said, "What's so funny?"

"I'm just sympathizing with you, boy," Mason said. "That woman can knock the wind right out of you."

HER LEGS ACHING, her heart pounding and her breathing as ragged as if she'd climbed a hundred steps instead of eighteen, Louise flung open the door to her apartment, grabbed a bottle of water from her small refrigerator and collapsed onto her sofa. "You idiot," she said. "Are you trying to kill yourself?"

Running a mile-long track around the square was nothing like hitting the treadmill for fifteen minutes at her Fort Lauderdale gym before getting a smoothie and a massage. She gulped the water and lay on her back, propping her head on the arm of the couch. Her gaze connected immediately with her coffee table and the single item sitting there, the blue candle.

"I just love candles," she said in a sing-song voice that mimicked her previous comment to Wes. "I have dozens in my condo." She flung her ball cap and hit the candle dead center, hiding it from view. "Candles!" she groaned.

The only ones she'd ever bought in her life had been skinny little things to stick into birthday cakes, and those she'd bought for someone else. Louise was a firm believer in electric light—bright, soft, romantic, whatever. As long as it illuminated without threatening to set the house on fire. But she was getting inside the candle factory, and she was going in on the arm of Wesley Fletcher.

BY TWO O'CLOCK that afternoon, Louise had showered, applied makeup and slipped into a coral shirtwaist dress.

He was waiting at the bottom of the stairs, wearing a pair of khaki shorts and a tan knit shirt that fit his military-sculpted chest as if it had been molded to him at the factory. He leaned on the hood of an immaculate dark green Jeep.

"Nice car," she said, figuring a compliment to his vehicle would go a long way with a guy like Wes.

He opened the passenger door, and she slid onto a spotless tan leather bucket seat. "It gets me where I need to go," he said.

He bolted to the other side, got in and started the engine. With one wrist draped over the steering wheel, he turned to her and asked, "You sure about this? You really want to see the candle factory?"

She swiveled toward him so her knees were mere inches from his thigh, and stared at the handsome, rugged face that had invaded her thoughts for the last few hours. "I've been thinking about this excursion all day." That was the truth. "I can't wait to see how candles are made." That was a lie. "I hope you can take me behind the scenes—you know, introduce me to the movers and shakers at the factory."

He laughed. "I'm afraid the only moving and shaking you'll see is when Justin Beauclaire walks across his office to the bar and shakes the martini pitcher." He pulled out of the lot and headed down an alley. "But whatever your pleasure..."

The factory was located a couple of miles outside of town on a two-lane county road that curved past the Brew and Bowl Alley, a few blue-collar businesses and three trailer parks. Louise recognized the name of the mechanics garage where Miranda Lopez's husband, Pedro, worked, as well as the Lazy Day Mobile Home community where the family lived.

Louise knew she might see the women she'd talked to the night before at the Kettle.

They'd all agreed that if they encountered each other at the factory, they would pretend to be strangers. Their association would be public soon enough, but for now, Louise was concerned with getting information, and her guise of being a tourist interested in candles was the best way of doing that.

Wesley parked near the double doors of the two-story colonial offices. This part of the building resembled a modest but gracious Southern mansion. The rest of the business, the production area extending behind the offices, was a long, single-story metal building with windows along the roofline.

Wes and Louise entered a lobby furnished in Wedgwood-blue wing chairs, Queen Anne tables and peaceful pastoral prints. And of course, candles. A half-dozen mahogany shelves displayed the products, which came in many shapes and sizes. The receptionist, a middle-aged lady, gushed over Wesley while Louise scanned the racks, picking up samples. One fact was abundantly clear. This company didn't miss a holiday sales opportunity or the chance to permeate the world with all sorts of intoxicating smells, from light floral to exotic spice.

After answering questions about where he'd been, how long he'd been home, and thanking the receptionist for expounding on what a handsome young man he'd become, Wes waved for Louise to follow him through a door that led from the lobby. "I called ahead," he told her. "Justin Beauclaire, the CEO of the company, is expecting us."

Louise walked beside him down a short hallway to an elevator. This was exactly what she'd hoped for. She whistled in appreciation. "Wow, are we getting a tour from the president?"

"Looks like it."

"I'm impressed with your contacts, Wesley."

"Don't be. This is a small town. Justin and my dad go way back."

They exited the elevator on the second floor and were met by a portly, balding man. He shook Wes's hand and introduced himself to Louise as Justin Beauclaire. While he openly admired his visitor, Louise gave him her sweetest smile, slipped her hand into her shoulder bag and discreetly turned on her tape recorder.

BACK ON THE MAIN FLOOR, Justin Beauclaire took his guests past offices on either side of a long hallway. They ended at a metal door. "Through here lies the pulse and energy of the factory," Justin said. "This is where tons of paraffin is turned into the beauties I hope you saw on display in the lobby."

"I did indeed," Louise responded. "I was truly amazed by the number and variety of candles produced here."

"We're trying new designs all the time," Justin said. "We have a research department entirely devoted to market analysis, product testing and nationwide sales." He opened the door and held it for Louise and Wes to precede him. "Ordinarily I don't allow any visitors into this part of the business," he explained. "Insurance issues, you understand."

She stopped just inside the warehouse and waited for Justin to close the door.

"'Course, I don't mind breaking the rules for old Wes, here," he said. "Even if I do remember wiping his nose a few times when he was just a little sprout."

Wes, clearly embarrassed, forced a snicker.

"We have a lot of expensive and sensitive machinery in here," Justin added. "Plus nearly every employee inside this building is working with wax in one form or another. In the beginning stages of candle production, wax can be tricky to handle. We melt ours to one hundred eighty degrees." He gave Louise a sly grin. "Can't have any novices poking their pretty noses, or fingers, into a vat of hot wax, now can we?"

Louise *tsked* in sympathy. "Certainly not. I promise to stay safely away from any bubbling cauldrons." She studied the huge metal tanks across the warehouse. Suspended above each were large circular racks, each holding dozens of taper candles of varying thicknesses. "Has anyone ever gotten badly burned?" she asked.

Justin waved off the question. "No. The wax isn't hot enough to cause blisters. Just smarts a little if it gets on the skin. Besides, we have all the required safety measures in place." He frowned. "Got no choice in the matter. We have government inspectors from OSHA breathin' down our necks every time we turn around." He clarified in case she didn't understand. "That's the Occupational Safety and Health Administration."

Louise nodded. "I see." She gestured toward one of the wheel racks that had just begun lowering its candles into a vat. "What's happening there?" she asked.

"That's one of our dipping wheels," Justin explained. "We have six of them operating sixteen hours a day. Each candle is dipped fifty times and cooled in between each lowering."

Louise remembered that Bessie referred

to herself as a dipper. She'd worked in that position for fifteen years. As if to validate that thought, the older woman walked out from behind a wheel and glanced at the trio of onlookers. Louise gave her a hint of a smile. A hairpin held between her teeth, Bessie nodded at her behind a pretense of rewinding her long gray mane into a knot at the crown of her head.

Justin next took them to where wax was molded into various shapes. Several women poured the thick substance from large tubes into metal forms, reminiscent of cake decorating on a grand scale. When Justin had explained the procedure, Louise asked how many people the candle company employed.

"We're the largest employer in the county," he said proudly. "Got one hundred and thirty-three on the payroll. We're just one big happy family here at Bayberry Cove Candle Company," he added. He poked Wesley in the ribs. "Even had Wes working for us at one time. Remember the summers after your junior and senior years of high school, boy?"

The question produced an involuntary flinch, as if Wes was trying to erase the memory from his mind. "How could I forget?" he said. "I left here every afternoon smelling like a bouquet of roses."

Justin hooted before explaining to Louise, "Wes worked in the scent department. He was a good employee. We could have made a junior chemist out of him if he'd stuck around."

Louise cast a sideways grin at Wes. "You mean instead of the junior plumber he's become?"

Wes rolled his eyes. "Never mind, both of you."

"How many positions are there in the candle factory?" Louise asked.

Justin stared at the ceiling. "Let me see, now. We've got dippers and packers, cutters and polishers, dyers, mixers, machine operators...too many to list. And then, of course, we've got our office, research and sales force in the main building, where you first came in."

As they'd walked the hall earlier, Louise had glanced into each office. "I noticed mostly men behind the desks," she said. "Don't you have any women in management positions?"

"Not really," Justin answered unabashedly. "We mostly hire women for the production jobs." He walked ahead of her to a rear entrance and turned around before leading the way outside. "Women seem to take to the repetitious tasks better than men. Guess it comes from all that diaper changing."

Gratified to hear Wes blow out a breath of air in a quiet whistle, Louise bit her lip before answering. "Well, of course, all that diaper training is good preparation for employment."

Justin held the door as she stepped into the paved lot of the factory's loading area, the apparent end of the tour. "You're right there, Miss Duncan. You got any young 'uns yourself?"

"No, not yet. Got to find me a good man first," she said with a flippant tone she figured Justin wouldn't notice even though his narrowed eyes were giving her a close scrutiny.

"From where I'm standing," he said, "there's probably a few fellas in this town who wouldn't mind applying for that job. You staying here long?"

"As long as it takes," she answered. "Now, if I can just ask you a few more questions…"

TWENTY MINUTES and at least as many questions later, Wesley walked around from the passenger side of the Jeep, climbed behind the wheel and slammed his door. He was angry. He'd been had. Duped. Plain and simple. This woman who'd professed with a

saccharine smile to love candles had taken
him on a merry chase.

He stared across the space between them
and scowled. Fiddling with the contents of her
shoulder bag, Louise pretended not to notice
his emotional state. Or maybe she really didn't
notice, and that was probably worse. One
thing was certain. This lady, with her pretty
dress, her high-heeled sandals and well-toned
body, cared as much about seeing candles
made as she would digging oysters out of the
muck of Currituck Sound.

He started the engine, thrust the gear shift
into reverse and backed out of the parking
space, spitting gravel from his rear tires. And
then, because that was childish and stupid, he
reined in his anger and put the Jeep through
its gears until they were retracing their tracks
to town at a safe speed.

But he'd gotten her attention. Out of
the corner of his eye he saw her arch her
eyebrows in question. "Something wrong,
Commander?" she said.

He clenched his teeth, tightening his jaw
muscles. "What were you doing back there?"

She concentrated on her purse again. "What
do you mean?"

"I mean that you grilled Beauclaire like he
was in front of a congressional hearing."

"I did no such thing," she said. "I was merely trying to learn as much about candles—"

"Let's cut through the scum and get to the clean water underneath," he said. "What are you up to, *Counselor*? And why did you feel it was necessary to involve me?"

Her shoulders sagged as she sighed deeply. "You already are involved, Wesley," she said. "You live here. You worked there. Nearly everyone in this town is involved to some degree."

"In what, Louise? Do you see some sort of conspiracy that no one else has noticed in the last thirty years?"

"No, not a conspiracy." She emitted a most unladylike snort. "That almost makes it worse. What's happening at the candle factory is out in the open for all the world to see… and ignore!"

He gripped the steering wheel and stared at her. "What are you talking about?"

"The injustices perpetrated by your buddy, Justin Beauclaire, every day. The man virtually laughs in the face of the EEOC…that stands for Equal Employment Opportunity—"

"I know what it stands for," he answered curtly.

She had the decency to blush. "Sorry.

I don't mean to be condescending. But Beauclaire simply doesn't give two hoots for his employees."

"That's ridiculous. There are people who have worked in that factory since I was a teenager. If conditions were so horrible, why are they still there?"

"Why are they still there? Why, in this depressed economy with our nation facing the highest unemployment rate in decades, would anyone stay in a dead-end job?" She expressed her dismay in an openmouthed stare. "Have you truly been in the navy all these years, Wesley, or have you been on the moon?"

He yanked the wheel to the right, pulled off the road and jerked on the emergency brake. His anger was palpable. He felt it beating in his heart and trembling in his hands. "You know something, Louise?" he sputtered. "You've got a mouth on you. And something of an attitude."

Her cheeks turned the color of her dress and she looked up at the overhanging tree limbs. "So I've been told," she answered with something resembling genuine contrition. "I'm sorry. That was uncalled for."

The boiling in his stomach became a slow simmer. "It sure was."

She turned to face him. "Do you know Bessie Granger? She works at the factory."

He thought a moment. "I'm sure I'd know her if I saw her."

"You did see her. About a half hour ago. She was standing by the candle dipping rack she's operated for fifteen years. In all that time she's had three pay raises, and she now earns a whopping seven dollars and thirty-five cents an hour. Would you like to know why she stays at the factory?"

He shrugged, refusing to admit he was curious.

"Because she's fifty-seven years old, and her husband has advanced emphysema and diabetes. That's why she stays. She has no health insurance because the company doesn't offer any, so she maintains his well-being as best she can at home. The state of North Carolina pays for his insulin."

"I see."

"And there's Miranda Lopez. She and her husband are Mexican immigrants who ran out of money in Bayberry Cove before they reached New Jersey and relatives who have since reneged on a promise to help them. They're lucky to have jobs at all. Miranda has two little boys she sends to a private baby-sitter who charges her more than Miranda can afford. She makes minimum wage.

"And Yvonne Richardson, a single mom who barely makes do, and Darlene Jackson, who actually loves candles and would be a great sales rep if only—"

"Okay, I get your point," Wes interrupted. "It's not a perfect world. But why single out the candle factory in this campaign of yours to right the evils in society?"

"Because I can," she said. "I have the time, the expertise, and I don't need the money these women can't afford to pay me, anyway. For once in my life I can do something for purely altruistic reasons." She looked out the windshield, her gaze focused on a butterfly fluttering in front of the Jeep. "I might have reconsidered and kept my—" she lowered her voice and slipped into Beauclaire's Southern drawl "—*pretty nose* out of this town's problems. But then I realized that Justin Beauclaire is a self-indulgent chauvinist and a braggart.

"I think my mind was made up when he boasted about the golf vacations three times a year to Hilton Head. He charters private planes to take his front office people for three days to one of the most expensive resorts in the country."

Wes winced inwardly. He'd known about the lavish expenditures for years. In fact, his father often went along.

"Do you realize," she continued, "that even a small percentage of the money from one of those weekends would keep Miranda's two boys in private schools until they were ready for college, and there would still be enough left over to pay their tuition?"

Wes checked his side mirror and eased the Jeep back onto the road. He couldn't very well argue with Louise against motherhood and education. But he knew she would be butting her head against a brick wall if she tried to take on the candle factory.

In a few minutes he pulled behind the furniture store to let her out. "I don't suppose you'll take any advice," he said.

"I've never been particularly good at it. But maybe someday I'll take yours." She looked at him, her expression unreadable. "I'm sorry I used you today, Wes. It was dishonest. But unfortunately, I've got to do it again."

He gave his head a quick shake. Had he heard her correctly? "What?"

"I need an appointment with your father. He's the only attorney in town, and I can't pursue this case on a legal level without aligning myself with a recognized North

Carolina attorney. Haywood Fletcher seems the logical choice."

Wes might have laughed out loud, but Louise wouldn't understand the depth of the irony in her request. Instead he gave her his most sincere look. "Here's my first piece of advice, Louise, whether you're ready to accept it or not. Consider it a warning of sorts. Don't even think about seeing my father."

She lay her hand on his arm. He stared at slim fingers tipped in polish. "You're sweet to worry about me, Wes, but don't. I think I can convince him of the validity of my commitment." She squeezed his arm. "Please, just call him and tell him I'd like to see him in the morning. And tell me how to get to that mansion of his."

She was just a bit too cocky. Too self-assured. She'd ambushed him this morning and now she was completely ignoring his warning. So he wouldn't explain the folly of her decision to visit his father.

Instead, he nodded and gave directions. "I'll tell him to expect you at ten o'clock tomorrow."

"Good. Now, what about dinner Friday night?"

"Dinner?"

"Sure. I owe you for today and tomorrow.

And besides, Commander, you're not half-bad to be with. Dinner would be a bonus for both of us." She took a small tablet out of her purse. "What's your number? I'll call you."

A voice inside him warned that spending more time with this woman would only lead to disaster. The emotional kind, and the physical kind, because after she'd seen his father, she might end up lacing the bonus dinner with arsenic. Despite all that logic, and the fact that Louise wasn't his type at all, Wes heard himself recite his phone number.

She got out of the Jeep. "Okay. See you Friday."

She was halfway to the building when the back door opened and Suzie McCorkle came out. The woman's surprised expression changed to one of sincere enthusiasm as she took a couple of steps toward the Jeep. "Hi, Wesley. Welcome home," she said.

That was about all anyone could expect from Suzie at any one time, and Wes called back an equally succinct greeting.

"How are you, Suzie?" Louise asked.

The woman looked up over her wire-framed glasses and stuck out her hand. "Fine. I was going to leave this candle by your door."

"How nice," Louise said. "I did enjoy the blue one you gave me."

Suzie gave her a beatific smile. "See, this one is violet and meant to soothe your inner spirit. When you light it, a sense of calm permeates the room and encourages peaceful self-development. The scent is very delicate."

Wes listened to the exchange with a sense of awe. He'd never heard Suzie speak more than one sentence.

Louise took the candle. "Thank you, Suzie. I'm sure I'll love it."

Wes pulled out of the parking lot. *You'd better enjoy your soothed inner spirit tonight, Miss Duncan. Your peace and calm is about to be blown to bits when you visit Haywood tomorrow morning.*

# CHAPTER SIX

SECTIONS OF Haywood Fletcher's house appeared through groves of budding trees as Louise drove down a curved driveway from the ornate front gate. She caught glimpses of angled rooflines, fieldstone exterior walls, sweeping multipaned windows. But none of these architectural hints prepared her for the mansion that sat with all the splendor of an English country manor in a sea of green grass and expertly manicured shrubs. "The pride of Bayberry Cove. Yes indeed," she said to herself.

At precisely ten o'clock, the exact time she was expected, the new, never-tardy Louise Duncan stopped in front of the massive double doors and cut the engine of her BMW. "So this is where you could be staying, Wesley," she said to his imaginary presence. "Instead, you chose that dinky little cottage, *my* cottage. To each his own, my friend, but it seems to me that years of living on destroyers and battleships would have sent you scurrying to Daddy's humble estate."

Walking to the door, she smoothed her navy-blue midthigh skirt and buttoned her hip-length tailored jacket. The V neckline was accentuated with a simple white silk scarf. Louise was thankful this morning that she'd packed one of her designer business suits. The argument that she wouldn't need it in North Carolina had been proved wrong.

She lifted the impressive brass knocker, but the door was opened before the lion's head ever sounded against its heavy metal plate. Louise looked into the chestnut-brown face of an older gentleman whose halo of coarse peppered hair matched straight, evenly groomed eyebrows. Dressed in an immaculate black jacket and charcoal-gray pants, the butler lacked only a pair of white gloves to complete the picture of Southern elegance.

"I'm Louise Duncan," she said simply.

He took her offered hand and introduced himself as Rudy Williams. "Mr. Fletcher is expecting you," he said. Opening the door to its fullest extent, he admitted her to a large entry hall. "If you'll follow me, please…"

Haywood's office was in the rear of the house. Louise's first impression of the dark-paneled room was that it was saved from dreariness by wide windows overlooking a terraced back lawn interspersed with colorful gardens.

The butler's voice drew her from the picturesque scene to a large desk in the corner. "Mr. Fletcher, this is Miss Louise Duncan."

Haywood stood up, slipped one pudgy thumb under a wide suspender and came around the desk to shake her hand. She looked into Wesley Fletcher's blue eyes, but all similarity between the two men ended there. While Wes was tall, lean and wiry, his father was medium height with most of his weight centered at his waistline. His abundant white hair was combed back from a prominent forehead and tamed with oil. His eyebrows were thick, with errant hairs spiking over a narrowed, keen gaze.

"How do you do, Miss Duncan," he said.

"Just fine, Mr. Fletcher. I appreciate your taking an appointment on such short notice."

He dismissed her gratitude with a flick of his fingers. "No thanks necessary. When my son called and said you wanted to see me, I was happy to honor the request."

He excused Rudy and indicated Louise should sit in a plush upholstered chair. Then he returned to his position behind his desk. "I assume this has nothing to do with that bit of unpleasantness you and I found ourselves in a few months ago with regard to Jamie Malone's divorce papers."

Good. The sly old fellow had brought their past involvement into the open right away. He knew he'd fabricated a reason to keep Jamie from signing the perfectly executed divorce settlement she'd drawn up for her friend Vicki. And he knew Louise was well aware of his bluff. There was no reason to pretend otherwise. "Certainly not," she said. "All's well that ends well, and I think we would both agree that Jamie and Vicki's relationship has ended quite satisfactorily."

"Indeed it has," he declared. "So what brings you out here this morning?"

Louise sat back in the chair and crossed her legs, noting that Haywood watched her movement with masculine interest. "I've decided to represent a group of workers in Bayberry Cove," she said. "I've discovered some inconsistencies with regard to certain federal labor regulations in one of the businesses in town. I think I can help my clients to better their positions within their working environment."

He rubbed his thumb and forefinger along a slack jawline. "Would this business be the candle factory, Miss Duncan?"

She wasn't surprised that the news of her visit to the candle company had reached him. "Yes, it is. Some of the policies of the EEOC seem to have been ignored or at least manipulated to suit the purposes of the company's president, Justin Beauclaire. I'm willing to represent the employees on these issues, but I need to align myself with an attorney in town."

Haywood nodded slowly, exhibiting what she took to be astute interest. "As you know," she continued confidently, "an out-of-state attorney can be admitted to practice locally on a temporary basis for a particular case. But for me to be admitted pro hac vice, I need to be sponsored by a North Carolina attorney. Naturally, knowing your son, I came to you first."

"Naturally. Besides, I am the only practicing attorney in this town."

"Yes. That too."

He stared at her over the wide expanse of the desktop and finally grinned in an almost fatherly way. "Let me tell you something, Miss Duncan. You don't want to do this."

"What?"

"This employer-busting campaign isn't necessary in a town like Bayberry Cove. It isn't necessary and it isn't suitable." He picked up a pencil and rolled it between his hands. "You're only visiting our town, isn't that correct?"

"Yes, but I don't see what difference—"

"I'd advise you to forget about legal matters and find something else to occupy your time while you're here."

She sat up straight. "Forget? I will not, Mr. Fletcher. I would advise *you* to reconsider. There are serious issues…"

The pencil twirled, clicking against a thick ring on Haywood's right hand. "I don't need to reconsider," he said. "I'd made up my mind even before you stepped into this office." The grin was back, but now it lacked any warmth. "Truthfully, it didn't take much internal debate on my part."

"How did you know why I was coming here?" She had the answer as she asked the question. "Of course, your son told you."

Haywood cocked his head to the side. "You're wrong. He didn't say anything besides asking me to meet with a visiting attorney. Though from your obvious distress at his possible betrayal, I realize that he knew why you were coming." He sighed. "I must speak to that boy."

"Then how did you find out?"

"Justin Beauclaire and I are old friends. He

called me right before Wesley did. Justin may not be the brightest firefly in the park, Miss Duncan, but he did, eventually, suspect an ulterior motive on your part. When he told me about your extensive questioning, I put two and two together. And then Wes called. He's a well-intentioned fella, my son, but he should have advised you against pursuing this."

Louise frowned. Okay, she couldn't blame Wesley. "He did advise me against it," she admitted. "But I refused to listen to him, just as I'm going to refuse your counsel."

He shook his head. A low chuckle came from his throat. "Well, you won't get any sponsorship from this office. No, ma'am. You seem like a nice enough gal, but you shouldn't get involved with this." He stared at her expensive suit, her pricey shoes, and swept that stupid pencil in an arc that encompassed her entire appearance. "You aren't what folks around here are used to. We're simple, uncomplicated citizens who are comfortable with the status quo. If you come into town making all manner of insinuations with your big-city whereases and heretofores, all you'll end up doing is antagonizing a lot of good people."

Louise's fists clenched around the arms of the chair. How dare this self-righteous bag of wind attack her appearance, her credentials? She stood up. "I'm sorry I took up your time, Mr. Fletcher. It's obvious we're on opposite sides of a fence that runs right down the middle of your status-quo-loving town." She headed for the door but turned around before leaving the room. "But if I may leave *you* with one piece of advice. You might want to warn certain *good* people that there will be some antagonizing in the near future."

LOUISE'S PLAN TO EXIT Haywood Fletcher's house as quickly as possible was thwarted when she ran into a plump, redheaded lady who was lurking in the hallway.

The woman took her elbow and forced her to assume a more modest pace toward the front of the house. "Dear, you act as if the devil himself is chasing you."

Louise glanced over her shoulder. "He wouldn't dare," she said. "Surely even *that* devil knows he's done enough evil for one day."

The woman laughed, a soft tinkling sound like ice in a crystal glass. "Oh, he's not really so evil, once you get to know him. Though I admit that's not such an easy thing to do."

Louise stared at the pleasant-looking woman. Her Irish accent was almost musical, soothing to Louise's offended sensibilities. "I know who you are," she said. "You're Kate, Jamie Malone's mother."

"That I am."

Remembering her conversation with Vicki and Jamie the other day, Louise couldn't help adding, "Your son and daughter-in-law told me about you and Haywood. And, Kate, you have my sympathy as well as my admiration."

Kate looped her arm through Louise's and guided her down the hall to an expansive kitchen. "I've just put the kettle on. Would you like some tea?"

Louise wasn't a tea drinker, but she knew that Vicki considered the brew something of a miracle. "Sure, why not." She sat in one of eight sturdy chairs surrounding a thick pine table and watched as Kate prepared two cups and brought them over. Louise thanked her and added, "You are the only evidence I've seen that Haywood Fletcher has a heart. According to your son, you have somehow managed to snag it."

"He does indeed have a heart, though he tries his best to hide it, even from me sometimes. But after seeing you in such a state, I'm wondering what happened to his manners." Kate took a sip of tea. "I apologize for his behavior, Miss Duncan…."

"Call me Louise." She raised her cup, swallowed and released a deep sigh. "You and I could be friends, Kate."

"I'm sure we'll get the chance to find out," she said. "Jamie tells me you're staying in town awhile."

"That's right."

"And from what I heard through the opening in the door just now..." She winked at Louise. "It's the way I keep abreast of things around here. Anyway, I heard that you've found a way to keep busy."

"Yes, and your fella didn't discourage me one little bit."

"Good for you. A woman should be true to her convictions." Kate appeared to concentrate on her tea for a moment and then said, "There is something you should know, however."

"Oh? What's that?"

"The real reason Haywood refused to sponsor you." Kate fisted her hand, settled it under her chin and leveled a green-eyed gaze on Louise's face. "He owns thirty percent of the candle factory. Next to Justin Beauclaire, Haywood is the least likely person in Bayberry Cove to want to see any changes in the way things are run down there."

Louise felt her jaw drop at the information.

"You don't say? Well, that explains a lot, but it doesn't change my mind."

Kate shrugged. "I didn't expect it would. I just thought you should know."

Louise suddenly remembered an earlier conversation she'd had with Wesley. Her hand shaking, she set her teacup on its saucer. "Does Haywood's son know that his father has an interest in the factory?"

"Of course. Wesley is the executor of Haywood's will. He's knowledgeable about all of his father's holdings."

So Wesley wasn't above exacting a little revenge himself, Louise thought. He'd warned her not to meet with his father but he hadn't explained *why* the old guy wouldn't be receptive to her suggestion. *I'll bet he's having a big laugh thinking of me....* Louise forced the thought from her mind and stood up. "You'll have to excuse me, Kate. I have an important errand to run. And it involves a visit to Buttercup Cottage."

KATE MALONE MARCHED down the hallway to Haywood's office, letting the sound of her determined footsteps announce her arrival. The door was still open, so she crossed the threshold and stopped just inside. Haywood looked up, frowned and returned to the document on his desk.

She headed toward him. "Haywood Fletcher, I'll have a word with you," she said, crossing her arms on her chest.

He peered up at her over the clear lenses of his reading glasses. "Now, Kate, don't start—"

"I'm not thinking of *starting* with you, Haywood. I'm thinking of finishing."

He took off his glasses and stared at her. "You don't mean what you're saying...."

"I'm saying that it's time you put a stop to rude, bullish behavior."

"Listening at keyholes again, Katie?"

She shook her finger at his smug face. "Never mind that, mister. Have you no manners at all? The way you treated that young woman. You ought to be ashamed."

He scowled. "It's a legal issue, Kate. You should stay out of matters that don't concern you."

"Decency concerns me, Haywood. And fair play. You could at least have told her why you can't involve yourself in the candle factory's problems."

He raised his bushy eyebrows in shock. "What problems? There are no problems at the factory. Beauclaire has things running like a fine Swiss clock down there."

Kate placed her palms on the desk and bent at the waist until her face was very near Haywood's. "You think that, do you?"

"I do indeed."

"You sit here in your ivory tower, collectin' your profits without ever knowin' how they come to you. What do you know of matters at the factory? What do you know of the lives of the people who help you to live like a king up here on the hill?" She sat heavily in a chair and took a deep breath. "I'm just sayin', Haywood, you could have heard the woman out instead of suggestin' that because she's not like the women from around here, she's somehow unsuitable for the task. I'm surprised at you, I am."

"I was merely giving her some good advice, Kate. You heard her. She has a big-city attitude that doesn't play well in Bayberry Cove, along with a cocky, take-charge air that doesn't suit folks around here. And you saw her in that outfit."

Kate narrowed her eyes. "I see you did give the woman a second thought, or look, after all."

Haywood chuckled, stood up and came around the desk. "Yes I did, Kate. And a third, if the truth be known." He walked to her and nuzzled her neck, letting his mustache tickle her ear. "And found her wanting when compared to you."

She swatted him away. "Don't try to sweet-talk me into letting this go, Haywood."

"I wouldn't for the world, Katie. I know you too well."

She rose and faced him squarely. "You mind what I say. That girl is not about to give up. She believes there's more to that factory than candle glow and sweet smells. And my guess is she'll make Justin Beauclaire sit up and take notice."

Haywood wrapped his hands around Kate's arms. "She wouldn't be the first pretty face to make a man do that." He grinned with something very much like boyish mischief. "As you well know, Katie, the men of Bayberry Cove are especially susceptible to fine-looking women."

Despite the thirty pounds she wished she could shed, and despite the fact that her last birthday cake had sixty-two candles, Kate knew that she still blushed like a young girl whenever Haywood tossed her an admiring phrase. She couldn't help loving him, though one of his faults was a stubborn refusal to make her his lawful wife.

She reached up and straightened the knot of his already perfect tie. "Enough of your blarney, Haywood. It's time for you to go to court. But you show those other men down at the factory that you're better than they are. You're willing to listen to your woman."

He picked up his briefcase and headed for the door. "I wouldn't dare not listen to my redheaded Irish girl." He glanced over his shoulder. "We'll see what happens, Kate. Miss Duncan wouldn't be the first woman who's all smoke and no fire."

Kate watched him go and shook her head. Speaking softly to herself, she said, "There's fire comin' all right, and maybe it's due."

LOUISE ROARED OUT OF Haywood Fletcher's driveway and sped down the county road that led back to town. She spotted a pay phone in a parking lot. On impulse, she parked, entered the booth and began flipping through the yellow pages. In South Florida, the Attorney section took up about a hundred pages. In this part of the country there were only about fifty listings total.

She started with the A's and held her finger under the name of Lawrence Aaronson. He listed labor regulations as one of his specialties. She dialed his number on her cell phone, spoke to his admin assistant and was put through to his office.

"What can I do for you, Miss Duncan?" he asked.

It was a short conversation, and considering the random selection process, a lucky conclusion. She told him about her interest in helping the women at the candle factory, and mentioned her unsuccessful meeting with Haywood Fletcher. Mr. Aaronson agreed unconditionally to sponsor Louise in her representation of the workers. He knew very little about the factory or its policies, so his decision was not influenced by any convictions. But he did know a good deal about Haywood Fletcher.

It seemed that two weeks previously at Spring Tree Downs in Raleigh, a three-year-old Thoroughbred named Lightning Strike, owned by Haywood Fletcher, had bested Larry's Luck, owned by Aaronson. In addition to the generous purse that went to Fletcher, the gloating winner collected an additional five thousand dollars from a costly side bet he'd goaded Aaronson into making five minutes before the start of the race.

Louise smiled as she disconnected the call. Amused by this very personal aspect of small-town politics, she said, "Let's see how we do in this contest, Haywood. I can't wait to see which one of us turns out to be the horse's behind this time."

She pulled out of the lot and continued toward Main Street. She wasn't going to stop at her apartment, however. As she'd told Kate, she had an errand to run. Her confidence restored, and her desire for satisfaction at its height, she drove toward Sandy Ridge, the road that led to Buttercup Cottage.

WES CHECKED THE WATER temperature in the third of his large aquariums, as well as the salinity, sediment textures and nutrient balance. Once he'd recorded his findings, he adjusted the air conditioner he'd installed in the shed behind the cottage so the temperature closely resembled actual outdoor conditions.

This morning, as always, he'd headed out from shore in the trim twenty-two foot Aquasport powered by a smooth-running two hundred horse Mercury outboard. The National Oceanic and Atmospheric Administration had provided the boat to facilitate his research. Once he'd gathered semi-salty samples from Albemarle Sound, brackish water from Currituck and fresh water from the heads of the North and Pasquotok Rivers, he'd returned to his dock and added his newly collected specimens to the tanks in the shed. Then, as he routinely did, he had a light breakfast before going into town for his run.

Wes had spent most of his life adhering to strict regimens, so he found this routine of living in Bayberry Cove on the edge of the sound well-suited to his needs. And today, as he'd jogged, he'd been able to concentrate on the track instead of the second-story windows of McCorkle's Furniture Store. He knew Louise Duncan was meeting with his father.

Now with a last look at the sea life populating his tanks, he closed the door to the shed and slid the bolt across. Immediately he heard the sound of an engine racing and tires spewing gravel on his driveway. Coming around the corner of the cottage moments later, he saw—and heard—Louise rapping on his front door.

He halted several yards away and watched her draw her shoulders up rigidly with an impatient breath. It didn't take a psychologist to read the woman's body language. She was angry, and he was probably the reason.

"Nobody's in there," he said before she could split her knuckles on the weathered wood of the old door.

She spun around and glared at him. "Are you hiding from me, Wesley?"

He tried to fight a grin and lost. "No. If I were hiding, you wouldn't see me right now. I'd be somewhere else. I'm better at hiding than this."

"Very funny."

He continued to the front door, wiping his damp hands on the soft jersey of his shorts. "This is a nice surprise, Louise," he said. "I thought our date was for tomorrow night."

She smirked. "I'm starting to think that it's less of a date and more of a second round."

"Oddly, they both have a certain appeal." He stepped around her and turned the knob. "The door's hardly ever locked. You might want to remember that the next time you try to break it down." With a sweep of his arm, he invited her in.

She marched ahead of him, stopping to notice the arrangement of the items in the room. Wes tried to see the place through Louise's eyes. It was significantly different from when she'd been there a week ago. Two easy chairs were spaced an equal distance from the sofa. The desk occupied a spot exactly in the middle of the window to catch the best sunlight. The chair fit neatly between the double pedestals. Writing utensils were arranged in rows on the surface. Magazines that had been scattered haphazardly around the room were now stacked in squared-off piles on the coffee table.

As much as he appreciated uniformity, Wes found himself thinking that it looked a bit sterile.

With a toss of her head, she said, "I love what you've done with the place. So cozy." She ran a finger along the top of an end table, leaving a slight smear in the fresh polish. "If I'd been lucky enough to descend from Mason Fletcher's family tree and gain possession of this cottage, I'd at least have left enough dust to write my initials on the furniture." She gave him a hint of a smile. "I'm very territorial underneath my easygoing exterior."

He chuckled at her obvious misrepresentation and walked toward the kitchen. "You're probably going to hate my cupboards," he said. "My canned goods are in alphabetical order."

She followed him. He opened the refrigerator door, revealing an assortment of drinks lined up like little soldiers on one shelf. "Soda?"

She glanced at her watch. "Why not. It's eleven o'clock. Give me one from the second row. It starts with a *C*."

He tossed her the Coke and opened one for himself. She sat in the chair she'd occupied during her first visit. He sat opposite her. She took a long swallow from the can and licked her lips before a drop could fall to the lapel of a navy-blue jacket that was probably standard business attire in the city.

"I suppose you know why I'm here," she said.

Right then he wished he could suggest a reason without getting slapped. "It'd probably be better if you told me," he said.

"I just came from your daddy's." She tapped the can with a long nail. "Nice guy, that Haywood."

"All the Fletcher men are known for their charm. I'm glad Dad didn't disappoint you."

She grinned in a feline way, without showing any teeth. "Actually, I plan to disappoint *him*. But I didn't come here to tell you that. I came to make a simple accusation. You could have told me."

Wes pretended ignorance. "Told you what?"

"That your father owns a third of the candle factory. We did spend a couple of hours yesterday ambling through the quaint little business. Did that fact skip your mind?"

"No. Facts rarely skip my mind."

She snorted. "That I believe. So, you could—*should* have told me."

He leaned back in his chair and matched her grin with his own. "Fair is fair, Louise. You should have told *me*."

"What, exactly?"

"That we were going to the factory to put poor old Justin Beauclaire on the hot seat. That up your pretty pink sleeve yesterday you were probably packing a tape recorder and a detailed report intended for the EEOC."

She had the decency to blush. "That's different. I…" She paused as if she'd started an argument that she knew couldn't be defended.

He lifted his can in a toast. "So why don't we call it a draw, and you can tell me how your meeting went with Dad."

Her gaze drifted from the can to his hand and up his arm to his bare shoulder. He'd put on a T-shirt with the sleeves cut off. It wasn't like him to wear nonregulation clothing, but now that he saw the interest in Louise's eyes, he wasn't sorry.

"Okay, it's a draw. And since you asked, the meeting went pretty much as you expected, I'm sure. Haywood didn't want any part of sponsoring me. He even had a few choice words of advice."

Wes nodded. "Tough break."

She idly revolved the soda can between her hands. "Not really. I found another attorney to sponsor me. Quite an enthusiastic supporter, I might add."

Once again she'd surprised him. She worked fast. "Are you going to tell me who? Dad's the only attorney in town."

"But not in the county. Lawrence Aaronson is my sponsor."

Wes whistled in admiration. "Top drawer. Does he believe in your case?"

"He doesn't have to. It's enough that he dislikes your father. Besides, I don't know exactly what my case will be yet. Maybe I won't find anything significant to submit to the EEOC." She took a swallow of soda and set the can down. "On the other hand, maybe I'll really shake things up in candle land."

"Maybe you will." He slid his can around in the little water spot on the table. "What about dinner tomorrow night? Is that still on or have you passed the sins of the father onto the son?"

She finished her drink and stood up. "Of course it's still on, but I've decided on a change of plans. I'll bring dinner here."

"Here?"

"Sure. I want to see what the sun looks like

setting over the cottage that was almost mine. And I want to see you freak out when your kitchen counters get a little messy."

"Okay. Buttercup Cottage it is."

His cell phone rang, and he dug in his pocket to retrieve it. "Sorry."

"No problem. I've got to go, anyway. I have a shingle to hang next to the entrance of the furniture store." She gave him a little wave and left through the front door.

Wes read the number on the digital screen of his phone and punched the connect button. "Yeah, Dad, what is it?"

The voice that responded was gruff and impatient. "Wesley, I want to see you this afternoon."

"What about?"

"I'll tell you when you get here. Make it three o'clock."

"See you then." He disconnected and went into the living room. From his front window he watched Louise's car pull onto Sandy Ridge Road. "Something tells me this meeting has everything to do with our town's new lady lawyer," he said to himself.

## CHAPTER SEVEN

HAYWOOD FLETCHER SET DOWN his glass, glanced around the room to make sure the other three men were paying attention, and smiled at his son. "At ease, Wesley. I'm not going to give you a demerit."

The others chuckled, no doubt because they were expected to. "That's right, Wes," Justin Beauclaire said. "This is your father's house, not a court-martial."

Realizing he had been standing at attention, Wes allowed his shoulders to relax and his knees to unlock. It wasn't that these men intimidated him. He'd known Justin for more than thirty years and Hatch Winslow, vice president of personnel at the candle factory—or human resources, as it was now called—almost as long. The youngest of the trio, Warren McGovern, had been VP of marketing for nearly five years. Still, Wes thought, as he took the last remaining chair, he'd not been summoned here to engage in a friendly father-son chat. These men obviously had a serious matter on their minds.

"So what's this all about, Dad?" he asked, though now that he'd seen the cast of characters, he knew the answer.

"We need to talk, Wesley, about that little foray you instigated into the candle factory yesterday."

Wes shook his head. "Foray? Come on, Dad, it wasn't a military maneuver."

"Maybe not to you. But your participation's upset ol' Justin plenty. I think you owe all of us an explanation as to why you cooperated with Miss Duncan's snooping around the business." He put his grin back in place and added, "'Course, now that I've seen her face-to-face I can understand your interest in playing along with her scheme—to a degree." He snickered and waited for responses from his companions. "But I'm just wondering how much you knew about her motives beforehand."

Wes crossed his ankle over his opposite knee and tried to appear casual. His father's insinuation about Louise, and Wes's attraction to her, rankled, but he supposed the best way to handle the situation was to tell the truth.

"What did I know of her motives?" he repeated. "Nothing. She told me she wanted to see the factory, and I took her there. What did I hope to gain?" He smiled. "Community goodwill. You gentlemen can understand that. Two of you are on the town council, aren't you?" He stared pointedly at Justin and Warren.

"Then you didn't know she was a lawyer?" his father asked.

"Well, yes, I knew that. But I believed she was a lawyer on vacation who was fond of candles." He shrugged one shoulder. "Now, like all of you, I realize Louise Duncan is much more than that."

Haywood raised his hands palms up and looked at each of the factory executives. "Now there, you see? I told you Wesley wasn't a party to this woman's shenanigans. He knows where his loyalties lie…" he patted the breast pocket of his jacket "…and his bank balance."

Wes sat forward and curled one hand over his knee. "Thanks for the vote of confidence, Dad, but right now my loyalties lie with the National Oceanic and Atmospheric Administration and a shedful of experiments I'm conducting thanks to their generous funding. So if all you gentlemen are satisfied, then I guess I can get back to business."

He started to rise, but his father's outstretched hand stopped him. "Not so fast,

Wes. It's good to know that you were an unwilling party and that you were taken in by this city lawyer just like Justin here, but…"

Wes looked at Beauclaire. "No offense, Justin, but I actually had her figured out by the time we got to the specialty candle department. I just wanted to see how far she'd go."

"But," his father repeated more emphatically, "our meeting is not concluded. It occurred to us—" his hand swept toward the group of men "—that this female could possibly stir up something of a ruckus. Not enough to matter, really, but enough to cause an interruption in the operation of the factory."

"I understand what you're saying, Dad." Wes scanned all four faces. "You guys are scared of her. Maybe you should be."

Haywood scowled. "We're not scared of her, son. But I've never been one to underestimate an opponent. And she identified herself to me this morning as just that." He blew out a breath. "That was a mistake on her part, but Miss Duncan's got moxie, and we've got to be ready with a counterattack if need be."

This time Wesley did stand up. "That's up to you, Dad. I think Louise can handle her end, so you gentlemen plan whatever you need to. I'll be interested to see how it all turns out."

Haywood leaned forward and pounded his fist on the desk. "Wesley, you're not taking this seriously. We need a lawyer on our side, and you're it."

He dropped back into the chair. "What?"

"Well, I can't represent the factory. Because of my shares in the company, it'd be seen as a conflict of interest."

"Then get somebody else."

Justin Beauclaire took a step forward. "We don't want anybody else, Wes. You're a hometown boy. You care about Bayberry Cove. You're one of us."

"Oh, sure. Justin, just because my current address is within two miles of your house does not mean you can still wipe my nose."

Haywood's eyebrows knitted in warning. "Son…"

His father was right. The remark was uncalled for. "Look, Justin," Wes said more calmly, "I can't represent the factory in this. I just told you that I'm working on a grant from the NOAA. I have responsibilities to that organization."

"This won't take much of your time," Haywood argued. "A few hours at most. You know we can't let that woman come here and turn everything upside down. You've worked at that factory. You've seen that nobody's mistreated. Everybody gets honest pay for honest work."

"Even if that's true, I'm not your man. I served in the Judge Advocate General's Corps. I look at everything from a military perspective."

"Your specialty was civil cases," Haywood pointed out. "And you're still recognized by the North Carolina Bar Association. This little matter would be a piece of cake for you."

"And we'd never find another lawyer who would care so much about Bayberry Cove and the values we believe in," the aspiring mayor, Warren McGovern, said.

"Mostly, son, this will just be a matter of signing your name to a few documents," Haywood added. "I'll be advising you all the way. It'll take hardly any time away from the fish and seaweed you've got down in the shed."

"It's a matter of principle, Wes," the previously quiet Hatch said. "We can't let this woman come in and tell us how to run our business. We've been doing a bang-up job of it till now and it wouldn't be right if some big-city lawyer came in and made us look bad."

Wes gazed at the ceiling and gathered his

thoughts. He truly didn't know what Louise had in mind. But he figured she had enough confidence and old-fashioned grit to pursue her goals.

He addressed the four men waiting for his reaction. "What if she's right?" he asked. "What if things do need fixing down at the factory?"

"Aw, son, you don't believe that," Haywood said.

"I don't know...."

"Tell you what. If she finds a thing or two that we can change without much fuss, then we'll do it. But once you start digging into labor regulations you'll see that we follow the letter of the law."

Wes sensed the trap closing. "Once *I* dig into regulations?"

"You, me, whoever," Haywood corrected. "Come on, son, make me an even prouder father than I already am. Come to the aid of your community. Don't let this thing get out of hand. Tell us we can count on a Fletcher to stand by us. Show this community that you're thankful for all the support these people have shown you over the years."

Wes sighed. When he'd decided to take partial retirement from the navy, he certainly hadn't planned to enter the legal game again.

He thought of his aquariums, his experiments, his plan to keep Currituck Sound safe from development. And then he looked at the men who represented the people he'd grown up with. "And you'll do most of the work?" he said to his father.

"You'll be a consultant, that's all. It's just your name instead of mine on the paperwork, to keep things aboveboard."

"And you'll change a few things if Louise is successful in pointing out some shortcomings?"

"I said we would, didn't I?"

Even as he stood and said the words, Wes feared he would regret them. "All right. But—"

He never had the chance to finish. Four hands simultaneously slapped his back, and he began to cough.

Haywood beamed. "Wait till that gal hears we got the best lawyer in all of North Carolina."

Wes cringed. He'd already thought about how she would react to hearing the news. "Actually, Louise doesn't know I'm a lawyer," he said. "At one point she thought I was a plumber, and not a very good one."

Haywood hooted. "She doesn't know? Then this will be a real sweet surprise."

Wes walked out of the office thinking of his date the next night. It would probably be the last one he would have with Louise Duncan, and that was really for the best, especially now that they were on opposite sides of a legal debate.

BEFORE MCCORKLE'S New And Used Furniture opened for business on Friday morning, Louise was in the shop. She climbed over a pair of tapestry living room chairs, skirted around an end table and two floor lamps and got down on her knees in the front display window.

"Here now, what's going on? What are you doing up there?"

Startled, she retraced her steps and jumped down from the platform. She clasped a plastic document holder to her abdomen so Evan McCorkle couldn't see what was inside. "Good morning, Evan. I'm just waiting for Suzie. She's bringing some decorations…."

"Here they are," Suzie called from across the room. She waved a garland of silk pansies as she traversed the aisles of sofas and dinette sets.

"What are you doing with that thing?" her husband asked.

Suzie presented the string of flowers to

Louise. "I told Louise that these would make her sign stand out in the window."

"Sign? What sign?"

"Her lawyer sign, of course."

Louise tried to smile to combat the frown on Evan's lips. "It's just a small sign, Evan. Just so people know I'm here. I'm putting one in my window upstairs as well." She showed him the clear plastic frame she'd picked up at Cove Stationers that morning. The shop owner had also printed the sign that identified Louise Duncan as an attorney. And when Louise had paid her bill, the woman, who'd said she was a friend of Bessie Granger's, had wished her luck.

Evan groused at his wife. "Now, Suzie, this is a furniture store. Our windows advertise our own stock. I don't think I like announcing to everyone who walks by that we've got a business operating right upstairs. As you know, I don't even like putting up notices of the Girl Scouts Jamboree."

"I know you don't, Evan, you old grouch. But this sign hardly takes up any room at all. And besides, I told Louise she could put it here. How else will all the ladies know exactly where her office is located?"

His cheeks flushed scarlet. He apparently

wasn't used to chastisement from his wife. "All what ladies?"

Louise climbed back into the window. She chose a spot for the frame and began arranging the garland around it. The flowers were strictly Suzie's touch, but Louise wasn't about to tell her they weren't necessary.

"That's the other thing I was going to mention, Evan," Suzie said. "Louise is having a meeting in her apartment tomorrow morning. Several of the women from the candle factory are coming."

Evan belched, the evidence of his distress. "Now, see here, Suzie…"

"I don't think there will be too many ladies," Louise offered. "And why don't you give me a bunch of those flyers advertising this week's specials in the shop? I'll hand them out to everyone who comes and encourage them to stop downstairs and look around before they leave."

Suzie clasped her hands under her chin. "How thoughtful of you, Louise. See, Evan, isn't that nice?"

"I don't like this, Suzie," he said. "I've heard grumbling around town about this woman shaking things up. Some of the men don't like the sound of it."

"Oh, who cares, Evan?" Suzie said. "If you

ask me, those fellas down at the hardware store need some shaking up."

He huffed loudly. To preserve his dignity, however, he straightened his spine and nodded. "I'll let it go this one time," he said, "and I'll just get those flyers."

Louise's hastily prepared shingle sat in the morning sun in the window of Bayberry Cove's only furniture store with a string of colorful spring flowers drawing attention to its existence. Out on the sidewalk with Louise, Suzie sighed. "It's beautiful. All we need is a candle garden to set it off." And she scurried inside to get one.

AT NOON ON FRIDAY, Jamie Malone copied statistics onto a tablet as Wes relayed them from the detailed charts by his tanks. "Do you really know what all this means?" Jamie asked when they'd finished.

"I hope it means that I can intelligently argue in front of the North Carolina State Legislature this fall that the high-rise construction slated for this county needs to be reconsidered."

Jamie set the tablet on a counter and leaned over to study the fish and plants in the largest of Wes's tanks. "I know you think Currituck

Sound is being affected by increased building, but these guys all look fine to me," he said.

"Yes, they do, right now, but subtle changes are happening in our waters that will only get worse if contractors continue tampering with the shoreline." He looked at Jamie. "I can explain it in more detail if you're really interested. A lot of variables are involved, including wind speeds, current changes, even the flow of the Gulf Stream...."

Jamie laughed. "Hey, buddy, you've got my vote if it ever comes down to it. I'm trusting your brain to sort all this out. Right now I'll settle for a soda and a sandwich."

"Sure. It's the least I can do after that dinner you and Vicki fixed Wednesday night." He smiled. "Have I mentioned that you've got a great girl there?"

"I think she was worth fighting for," Jamie said.

The two men left the shed and walked to a pickup where Jamie whistled for Beasley. The dog jumped from the cargo area and lumbered toward them. He then flopped down in the middle of a patch of sea oats by the shore, curled himself into a pretzel and fell asleep.

"That's some dog," Wes said. "I might actually consider getting one to share the cottage with me if I thought I'd find one as uncomplicated as Beas."

Jamie followed Wes into Buttercup Cottage. "Yeah, he's pretty easy to please most of the time. But he sheds. I can't see you fighting the battle of dog hair every day."

Wes pulled pristine plastic bags of salami, cheese, tomatoes and lettuce from his sparkling refrigerator. He set two hoagie rolls on a cutting board and two cans of soda on the table. "Why does everybody think I'm such a neat freak?" he asked.

Jamie raised his eyebrows, glanced around the kitchen and said, "Duh."

Wes laughed, washed his hands and began slicing the rolls. "Point taken."

Jamie sat in a chair, popped the tab on his can and said, "So Vicki tells me you've been seeing a lot of Louise."

Wes looked over his shoulder. "It depends what you mean by 'seeing.' I've run into her a couple of times, and she suckered me into taking her to the candle factory under false pretenses."

"I heard about that. My guess is you're not the first guy to be led down the primrose path by that gal. Vicki thinks Lulu's serious about representing the workers over there."

Wes snickered. "Oh, she's serious all right. But that's not the worst part."

Jamie picked up the thick sandwich Wes set down in front of him. "Oh? What's the worst part?"

"Louise doesn't know it yet, but she's not the only one who's suckered me into something lately. My dad and his cronies from the factory talked me into representing their interests if Louise actually files complaints with the EEOC."

Jamie stopped the sandwich halfway to his mouth. "You're kidding? You said yes?"

Wes nodded.

"Couldn't you think of a way out?"

"Actually, I tried and then I figured maybe it wouldn't be so bad. Dad assured me the factory will make some changes if the issues warrant it. And I really do owe something to this town. Those old boys down at the factory gave me jobs, wrote letters of recommendation to the Academy when I was applying, sent me Christmas cards every year no matter where I was. And besides, I don't think conditions are all that bad at the factory. I think Louise may be stirring up trouble where none exists."

"Maybe so, but buddy, siding with the enemy is no way to further a blossoming romance. Louise is not going to like hearing that you're the counsel for the opposite side."

"That's no problem," Wes replied. It was time to set Jamie straight. "There's no romance between Louise Duncan and me."

Jamie grinned. "Yeah? Vicki seems to think there might be. I don't mean to pry into your business, Wes, but isn't Louise coming over here for dinner tonight?"

Sudden heat infused Wes's neck. Stupid small town. "Yes, she's coming here, but only to make up for tricking me into taking her to the factory."

"That's what she said, huh?"

"Yes, exactly."

"Okay, buddy, but if you ask me, a combination of good food, moonlight on the water and a great-looking woman like Louise means anything can happen."

Wes had been having those same thoughts all morning, and liking them too much. But, emotionally and intellectually, he'd made up his mind that he was strictly opposed to any sort of relationship with Louise. Maybe convincing Jamie would be a good start. "I'm not interested in anything like that with Louise."

He stared at Jamie's skeptical expression

for several seconds before emphasizing again, "I'm not. Not in any way. And you know why."

His friend slowly nodded his head. "Donna."

"Right. I've been down this road before with a woman like Louise. And it was too bumpy a ride."

"Louise isn't your ex-wife, Wes."

"No, but she's close enough to sound alarm bells in my head. She's independent, determined, bossy...."

"Yes, she's all those things. But Donna, from all I've heard, was self-serving, conniving and ambitious. You were lucky she took off."

All that was true—and the reason Wes hadn't had a serious relationship with a woman since his divorce fourteen years ago. And part of the reason he'd come back to Bayberry Cove. If he ever hoped to find a woman suited to him it would be here, where he'd grown up, where Mason Fletcher had made his fortune and given his beloved wife a cottage by the shore.

Wes wasn't opposed to marrying again. In fact, he often thought it would be nice to have a future with the right woman. But this time he'd pick a simple girl, straightforward and honest, who'd put their life together above everything else. Wes's wife—if he was lucky enough to find one—would have roots as deep as his and wouldn't spend the better part of their marriage trying to dig them up.

She certainly wouldn't be Louise Duncan, who manipulated the world to suit her needs.

Wes snapped out of his reverie when Jamie waved his hand in front of his face. "Wes, come back, buddy."

"Sorry. I was just thinking about what you said."

"I've been thinking, too," Jamie said. "And I think I've figured out why you took your dad's offer, why you're representing the factory."

"I told you. I owe these guys—"

"Nope, that's not it. Deep down you agreed because accepting that job is a sort of insurance policy for you."

"Insurance policy? For what?"

"To keep the biggest natural hazard in your life from attacking you on all vulnerable sides. You agreed to be your daddy's lawyer because you knew Louise wouldn't like it and she'd lose interest in you immediately. It's a sure way to keep the boundaries clear between you."

Jamie stood and pushed his chair under the table. "And buddy, I hope you know what you're doing, because it just might work better than you anticipated. You might have maneuvered yourself into a position that is a whole lot safer than you really want it to be."

Wes smirked, but for a moment he didn't trust himself to speak. His mouth had suddenly gone dry. "You're a psychologist now?" he finally managed to say.

"Nope. Just a man. I know how we think when we're scared. I know about the walls we build. And I've also been scared of Louise. Pleasantly so, but scared just the same—until I realized that anyone Vicki would care about so deeply must have a whole lot of soft spots beneath her sharp-edged exterior. She's a lot of woman to handle. But I think you may have found the way to avoid having to do so."

Jamie headed for the back door. "I'd tell you to have fun tonight, but I don't think the odds are in your favor. But, hey, that's what you want, isn't it?"

Jamie left, and Wes sat in the silence of the empty kitchen for several minutes. His old friend might just be right. Maybe those charitable reasons about community loyalty were nothing more than smokescreens hiding the real reason Wes had agreed to his father's demands. Maybe he *was* protecting himself from letting his feelings for Louise get out of control.

He stood up and took the dirty plates to the sink. "Well, so what?" he said. "I can't imagine a worse combination than me and Louise Duncan."

LOUISE SPENT PART of the afternoon preparing for her meeting with the women factory workers the next morning. She drove into Morgan City to consult with Lawrence Aaronson and to use his extensive legal library. Her research on federal labor law provided factual material she was anxious to share with the Bayberry Cove ladies.

She accomplished what she needed to in order to have a successful meeting despite the fact that her mind kept wandering to the dinner plans she'd made with Wesley for that evening. She couldn't stop thinking about him. He was a fascinating combination of inflexibility and unpredictability. He built his life around schedules and order; yet he somehow amazed her with his ability to adapt to situations that might catch other men off guard.

He'd refused to give in on the cottage issue, and he'd stood his ground when she'd accused him of withholding information about his father's investments in the candle factory. He seemed interested in her as a woman, yet only marginally affected by those characteristics that usually enabled her to win any contest between the sexes. He didn't appear uncomfortable around her as many men did. Yet he hadn't made any advances that would indicate he wanted to pursue her. Maybe all that would change tonight.

In men Louise usually gravitated toward bold, assertive types. However, since meeting Wes, she was finding the quiet, yet indisputably confident man more appealing. Handsome, well-built, intelligent, Wes piqued her interest on almost every level. She could certainly envision having a romantically satisfying relationship with him once she broke down his barriers. She didn't doubt for one minute that underneath that crisp, disciplined military exterior, Wes Fletcher could be wild and fun and quite a pleasant diversion for the next two months.

# CHAPTER EIGHT

WHEN LOUISE KNOCKED, Wes took a fortifying breath and mentally rehearsed his plan to keep the evening short and uncomplicated. Then he opened the door, and Louise waltzed in, leaving a trail of gardenia fragrance in her wake to assail his senses and send his thoughts on a course far different from his goal. She gave him a bright smile and said, "Hi. I figured you for a seafood man."

"You figured right."

"Good. I'll just fire up your oven so I can warm some things."

She strode into the kitchen, set a basket on the table and began familiarizing herself with the contents of his cabinets. "I hope you're hungry," she said.

"Starved." He watched her remove foil-covered dishes from the basket. His mouth was watering, but he wasn't at all sure it was the food producing the pleasant sensations in his body. He tried to find something he didn't like about her appearance. It wasn't her hair, which fell in a glistening black wave below her shoulders. It wasn't that face with expressive lavender eyes framing a cute little nose. It wasn't lips tinted light coral and just full enough to tempt any man to kiss them.

"You're going to be impressed with this meal, Commander," she said, sliding dishes into the oven. "I debated about telling you I prepared it myself, but I decided to put my best foot forward, and not tell any more lies. Our relationship is strictly on the up-and-up from now on."

The ex-plumber-turned-candle-factory-attorney tried to ease a smile onto his face. It probably came across as a smirk. "Honesty between us. That's quite a change."

She passed by him on her way to the table and tweaked a button on the shirt he'd just picked up from the dry cleaners that morning. "I'm hoping honesty will have its rewards," she said.

He gulped.

His plan had been to eat, talk a little about not much at all and say farewell. Of course, he could still make that happen. All he had to do was wait until she'd had enough food in her stomach to mellow out a bit, and then tell her he was legal counsel for the candle factory.

That information would ruin this evening like a bomb dropped in the middle of the kitchen.

"Want some wine?"

He snapped his attention back to her and was reminded of the famous line that started, "The best-laid plans…" No, he would not be led astray by one very beautiful woman pretending with an oven mitt and spatula to be a domestic goddess. Goddess, yes. Domestic, hardly. "Yes, please."

She filled two glasses and handed one to him. When she raised hers in the air, she said, "To an evening that begins with the score tied between us and ends with…well, no one can predict the future, right, Commander?"

Wrong. He knew how the evening would end. If he stuck to his guns.

"We have to wait a half hour or so for the food to heat," she said. "What kind of music do you have?"

He thought of his limited music collection and was suddenly self-conscious that his tastes weren't more eclectic. "Mostly 1970s stuff."

"Jim Croce? Eric Clapton?"

She had him pegged. "Yeah. My iPod's on my coffee table in the living room. You can pick out something while I hook up the player in here."

A couple of minutes later they were listening to the blended tones of Simon and Garfunkel crooning "Bridge Over Troubled Water." Louise walked to the back screen door and looked out on the sound. "It's nice here." She smiled over her shoulder at him. "I would have liked living in this cottage."

"No, you wouldn't have. The electricity only works part-time. Water pressure's terrible. Most days they forget to deliver my mail. And sand gets into everything." He looked at his Jeep, which sat under a pine tree and was protected from the elements by a bumper-to-bumper canvas cover. There had been no room in the shed for the vehicle once he set up the tanks.

She tucked a windblown strand of hair behind her ear. "Sorry, Wes, but you haven't discouraged me." Then, as if reading his mind, she said, "What's in the shed over there?"

"Nothing you'd be interested in. I've set up some experimental biology tanks. I'm keeping track of water conditions, marine life, things like that."

"Show me."

"You want to go to the shed?" He'd figured the words *biology* and *experimental* would have been a sure turnoff.

"Absolutely. I'm a sucker for any dark, mysterious place, including a…" she gave him a seductive smile accompanied by a horror-movie growl "…la-bor-a-tory." She flounced away from him, burst through the door and took a direct line to the shed. She knew he'd follow, and he did—wordlessly.

He slid back the bolt and ushered her inside. Lights on top of each tank illuminated the water with what approximated a soft infusion of moonlight. The fish seemed to glow as they darted among plants that had taken on an olive hue in the artificial dusk he'd created.

Louise stood in the middle of the room between tables that held jars, thermometers, testing equipment, all the tools of his current trade. Aerators emitted their continuous subtle hiss. Bubbles squirted from air lines under the floor of his manmade sea beds and plopped softly at the surface. All teasing now absent from her voice, she whispered, "Wow."

He stood behind her, close enough to put his hands on her shoulders if he'd let himself. He didn't. "It's kind of overwhelming, I guess."

"It's amazing. What do you do out here, Wesley? What are you trying to accomplish?"

How could he tell her what he'd spent years studying, exploring and now attempting to safeguard? How would anyone comprehend the depth of his commitment? How would this woman, especially, understand why he would give up everything else to live a solitary existence by the sea in the company of creatures with scales? "It's complicated," he ended up saying. "I couldn't explain it in the little time we have."

She teased him with a flutter of dark lashes. "Come on, Wesley, in a hundred words or less. Try me."

And so he told her about the unique characteristics of the marine habitats of Currituck Sound and the Outer Banks. He explained about coastal swamps and estuaries and barrier islands, and how the distinctive qualities of each combined to create one of the most intricate and unusual marine environments on the planet. And when he determined that her eyes had not glazed over, he told her that it was vital to the North Carolina coastal region to preserve the wetland and the essential fish habitat.

She actually asked questions, interesting ones, and he answered with more detail than he was sure she expected or needed. And when he paused and looked at his watch, forty minutes had passed.

He gave her a guilty smile. "I'm afraid your dinner might be blackened by now."

She leaned over and watched a small fiddler crab burrow into the sand. "I wouldn't worry about that. I suddenly feel guilty offering you anything fishy at all. You're going to feel like you're eating pets."

He laughed. "Not at all. That's what I was going to explain to you. We need to safeguard this environment so that the fishermen and—"

She put a finger to his lips. "Wes, if it's really okay that we eat the food I brought, then let's do it."

She removed her finger but did not step away from him. She remained in close proximity to his body, her face inches from his, her eyes like amethyst crystals in his manufactured moon glow. Her lips turned up in an insinuating smile that any normal man would recognize as an invitation to kiss her— and only an idiot would resist. He clenched his hands at his sides until the blunt nails bit into his palm. He swallowed, retreated. "Well, then, let's go eat," he said, and went to open the door.

The idiot was saved.

TAKING DOWN THE WALL around Wesley Fletcher was going to be harder than she thought. During dinner conversation, he'd been attentive, complimentary and polite. The problem was, he'd shown more enthusiasm for a tankful of fish than he had for her.

When they'd finished the gourmet dinner, Louise picked up the dishes and stacked them in the sink. She turned on the hot water and let it run while she reached under the counter for detergent.

Wes came up behind her, took the plastic bottle out of her hand and set it beside the sink. He turned off the water. "No way. You fixed the meal. I'll do the dishes."

"Well, okay. Would you like more wine?"

He waved his hand. "None for me, thanks."

"Coffee?"

"I guess coffee would be all right."

She plugged in his automatic drip machine while he took a canister from the cupboard. Then he chose a Bee Gees album from his iPod and hit play.

She found the cream and sugar, asked him if he wanted either, and prepared his coffee. He remained distant, but she was convinced he watched each move she made. What was with this man? she wondered. Was he shy? Or just afraid to express what was on his mind? She could read the interest in his eyes, see it in the anxious way he kneaded the back of his neck. So why did he avoid getting close to her?

She handed him a mug. "Let's take our coffee outside. I'd like to look at the water, listen to the waves."

He raked his fingers through his hair, which had grown since he first arrived. "I don't know about going outside," he said.

"What's wrong with that?"

"It's late. There could be mosquitoes."

"Wes, it's nine-thirty. And there's a breeze. Mosquitoes don't land when it's windy." He still looked so uncertain she almost took pity on him. "Do you want me to leave?"

"No!"

The conviction of his answer startled her, and she blurted out a bark of laughter. "All right, then, I'll stay."

"Unless you have something you have to do," he countered.

"I don't."

He walked to the back entrance and looked out. "I guess it won't be too bad out there." He held the door for her. "You might as well see what Currituck Sound looks like at night."

She stepped over the threshold and smiled back at him over her shoulder. "My thoughts exactly. Everything's different at night, don't you think?"

They walked down to the water's edge, where an outcropping of boulders provided a convenient platform for viewing the waves. Louise climbed over the first one with Wes's help and settled on the higher rock next to it. She set her mug down and slid over to make room for him.

A half-moon winked down at them and shimmered on whitecaps that rolled to shore. A few feet away from her canvas shoes, waves crashed on the smaller boulders and retreated back into the sound. Louise leaned against Wes's shoulder. "It's beautiful."

"Yeah, it is. No matter where I've gone, I always come back. And always with a sense of anticipation that's hard to explain. This part of the country calls to me somehow."

She looked to her left a few yards down the beach, where a dock jutted into the sound. She identified vague shapes bobbing in the scant moonlight. "Are those boats yours?"

"One is, the little Hobie with the single sail. I've had it since I was a teenager. The other one is a speedboat. It's on loan from the National Oceanic and Atmospheric Administration."

She gave him a quizzical look and he explained. "They're funding my experiments. They have an office in Norfolk where I was stationed for a couple of years. I visited there a lot and talked about Currituck Sound and what I wanted to do here. I suppose I made a pest of myself."

"I doubt that," she said. "I'd say you made an impression."

He smiled. "Maybe."

"So where do you go in the speedboat?"

"All over. To the head of the sound, up the Pasquotok River, into Albemarle Sound. Sometimes when I need especially salty samples, I go all the way to Pamlico, where there's a major inlet from the ocean. All the bodies of water feed into each other. Yet, at their heart, they each maintain their own unique characteristics."

She looped her arm through his. His biceps contracted and relaxed. "Will you take me with you sometime?"

"Those are working trips I make out there," he said. "I have cages in certain locations so I can retrieve live samples. So, I would take you—"

"Good. When?"

He laughed, the first truly relaxed sound she'd heard him make since he'd played professor in the shed. He knew she wasn't going to be put off, and he seemed okay about it, and even pleased. "You don't take no for an answer."

She smiled up at him. "Sometimes I have

to. But mostly I just don't let other people say it." She smoothed the palm of her hand along his bare forearm, then wrapped her fingers around his wrist. "Tell you what, Wesley. I'll give you a chance to say no to me, and I'll accept it."

He glanced at her out of the corner of a narrowed eye.

"Your skepticism is showing," she teased.

"A little, I suppose. But go ahead, ask what you want to."

"Okay. Do you like me, Wes? Even a little?"

He blew out a slow, long breath and looked out at the water.

"Is it that hard to answer?" she said.

"No. Sure, I like you."

She moved her fingers and grazed the palm of his hand with her nails. The tendons in his wrist flexed. "But?"

"No *buts*. Despite the fact that we don't have much in common, and despite the fact that you tricked me the other day into taking you to the factory, and even though you soaked me with dirty water from the cottage faucet, I still like you." He grinned a little. "Now that I think about it, I probably shouldn't, but I do. Still, you are a little pushy."

Everything he'd just said was negative, and yet Louise's spirit soared. He did like her. She heard his affection in his tone of voice, saw it in the smile he tried to hide. And she planned to take full advantage of that affection now. "Some men need a little pushing," she said.

"What do you mean?"

"Wesley, we've been together a lot lately." She picked up the silver medallion that lay against her chest and slid it back and forth along the chain she wore around her neck. She was pleased when he followed the movement with his eyes. "In case you haven't noticed, I've put forth considerable effort to make you aware of me. And deep down I think you are. But it's time for you to act on your feelings."

He drew his eyebrows together in a frown and looked away from her. "Louise, in all fairness, you can't possibly know what my feelings are."

"No, but we have connected on a level that goes deeper than just friendship. I can feel it, and I'm pretty sure you can, too. Are you going to say that you aren't attracted to me? That you haven't wondered what it would be like to, well, to get to know each other a little better?"

He exhaled, rubbed the back of his neck again. "Louise, even I have to admit that you are hard not to notice. But frankly, while you've crossed my mind a time or two, I've been too busy with my experiments, catching up with family and old friends, trying to make the cottage livable."

She removed her hand from his arm, laced her fingers together and angled her body so she faced him squarely. Despite the limited confines of the rock ledge, he managed to put a few more inches between them.

"Wes, you said the other day that we should cut through the scum and get to the clear water underneath. I think that was good advice, and we should follow it right now."

"Okay. And?"

"I think you should kiss me. I can't think of a better time or place than right now, in your backyard with the surf rolling in and moonlight filtering through hazy clouds. As you say, I can't possibly know what your feelings are, but I can tell you that kissing you is what I want right now. And I'm hoping it's what you want as well."

His gaze moved over her face. He seemed to study each of her features one by one until he let himself stare overlong at her mouth. He moistened his lips.

Her breath hitched in her lungs. If ever a man was preparing to take a woman in his embrace and kiss her senseless, it was Wesley Fletcher. Louise leaned close to him, so close her mouth nearly touched his. Her skin tingled as she anticipated his arms around her. She closed her eyes, breathed deeply and waited. And waited.

After a moment she forced her eyes open and looked into cool blue eyes that had lost their desire and had assumed a steely resolve.

He turned away from her and focused on the far horizon. "We shouldn't be doing this," he said. "It's not as simple as it may seem to you."

Louise's appetite for Wes Fletcher evaporated as if she'd just eaten a seven-course meal of humiliation. "It's not brain surgery, Wes. It's not even plumbing. It's a kiss. And you're making too much out of it. Either you want to kiss me or you don't. And it's obvious now that you don't."

He drew his knee to his chest, threaded his fingers together and wrapped his clasped hands around his leg. "I agreed to something yesterday, and I think you should know what it is."

She felt almost dizzy from this abrupt change in conversational direction. "Okay."

"I agreed to represent the factory in the event you bring charges against Justin and the executives with the EEOC."

This made no sense at all, and Louise

felt herself lose patience. How could Wes represent anyone? "What are you talking about? Beauclaire is going to need a lawyer if I decide to do this, not a marine biologist—"

*Oh no.* She halted midsentence, suddenly struck speechless with the significance of his confession. Then she stated the obvious conclusion. "You're not a marine biologist, are you, Wes?"

He gave her a serious look that quickly mutated to a sheepish grin. "No. Not technically. It's an avocation only."

"And your vocation?"

"I was a naval lawyer."

Louise struggled with a range of emotions that ran from shock to betrayal to a condemnation of her own naiveté. She should have known that Wesley, smart, knowledgeable, well-spoken, was more than a career navy man who sailed the seven seas studying radar screens and thinking about fish in Currituck Sound. Of course, in her own defense, he'd failed to mention that rather important detail of his life. She bit her bottom lip and tried to gather her thoughts. Finally she said, "Those gray bars and embroidered gold leaves on that cap you were wearing the day I found you at the cottage…?"

"Judge Advocate General's Corps. Sixteen years."

"I see. No wonder your repertoire of lawyer jokes was lacking that day."

The corner of his mouth lifted in a small grin. "I still know a few."

"That's not all you know, Wes," she said, standing up and dusting off her shorts. "You're an expert at spoiling a perfectly wonderful evening, and at dashing a woman's expectations."

She turned away abruptly and climbed from the rocks without any help from him.

NOW WHAT WAS HE supposed to do? Go after her? Let her vent her anger by stomping back to the cottage alone? He'd done the right thing. He'd been honest and told her that he was counsel for the candle factory.

And he'd saved himself from stepping onto the dangerous quicksand that would never have supported a relationship between him and Louise. It hadn't been easy for him. She'd been close enough for him to smell the citrus scent of her hair.

Even when she'd offered him the taste of those full coral lips, he'd survived the challenge of giving in to a gorgeous woman who was all wrong for him. He should be patting himself on the back. Instead, like a crab on steroids, he was climbing over the rocks to reach her.

He caught her arm at the back door. She whirled around and glared at him. "Let me go."

He didn't. "Look, I'm sorry," he said. "I shouldn't have blurted it out like that."

"Why not? Would the significance of the moment been any different if you'd told a joke first to soften me up?"

"Well, no, but you were so…"

She stared at him while he struggled for words, and then she finished his sentence for him. "So what, Wesley? I was so willing to see if a human heart actually beat under that solid chest wall of fine, upstanding military bearing?" She twisted her arm free. "Don't apologize, Commander. You did us both a favor. You pulled the bandage off quickly. In the end, that's the best way."

She stormed into the house, grabbed her purse off the kitchen table and kept going. At the front entrance, she yanked on the knob, but he slammed his hand against the door. "Come on, Louise, don't go like this."

She spun around. "Like what, Wes? Like a woman scorned? Like a lawyer deceived? Like a friend betrayed? Well, sorry, but that's what I feel like and that's how I'm going." She pushed at his hand. He kept it right where it was. She exhaled loudly. "Besides, I really do have things to do tonight. I have an important meeting with my clients in the morning."

It was subtle, but it was definitely a threat. "This business with the candle factory doesn't have to get ugly, you know," he said.

She stopped pushing at him and leaned against the door. He placed his other hand on the wood panel beside her face, trapping her between his arms. She ducked. He lowered his arms in a childish game of cat and mouse. She rolled her eyes to the ceiling.

"I don't intend for this business to get ugly at all," she said. "I know the difference between what's business and what's personal, and right now it's the personal stuff between us that's not very pretty."

Her chest rose and fell with each labored breath. Her face was flushed, just as it would have been if he'd kissed her the way he'd wanted to out on the rocks.

His hands curled into fists and it was all he could do not to pull her to him. He felt his reaction to her all the way to his toes, though it was definitely centered halfway down his body. He tried to look away from her but his eyes wouldn't move. And so he said, ineffectually, "I know you're upset...."

"That's right, I'm upset. But not as upset as you're going to be."

She was threatening him again? Only this time it was ridiculous. He had her pinned to the door. She couldn't budge, and yet she was trying to intimidate him. "What do you mean by that?"

She reached out with one arm, wrapped her hand around the nape of his neck and pulled his face down to hers. Their lips met with a blinding, crushing force that nearly buckled his knees. It was the most terrifying, exquisite kiss he'd ever experienced, full of fire and passion and anger. His blood rushed to his ears. His lungs felt as if they might explode. Even when she drew back, he forgot to breathe. And he dropped his arms.

She yanked the door open and stepped effortlessly outside. "Think about *that* when you go to bed tonight, Commander."

## CHAPTER NINE

THOUGH SHE'D HAD a restless night, Louise
was ready for her meeting at eight forty-
five Saturday morning. She felt relaxed and
comfortable in jeans and a white T-shirt with
Key West Florida printed across the front in
glittery pink paint. She gathered her hair into
an elastic wrap at her crown and then lit the
lime-green candle Suzie had brought upstairs
to the apartment fifteen minutes before.

"Lime candles are known for eliminating
discord," Suzie had said. "It's the color you
use when you're facing obstacles to settling
a dispute."

Louise regarded the flame flickering on her
coffee table. "You've got your work cut out
for you, Candle," she said. "After last night, I
feel like my whole world is in discord. Luckily
for the ladies of the Bayberry Cove Candle
Company, I'm infinitely more qualified to
handle the problems at the factory than I do
the ones in my own life." She waved her hand
as if the gesture would put Wesley Fletcher

out of her conscious thoughts once and for all, but she knew it was hopeless. His obstinate, handsome face refused to go quietly to a dark corner of her mind.

A knock at the back door sent her scurrying to answer it. Bobbi Lee waltzed inside balancing two large boxes in her hands. She was followed by a busboy who carried a tray loaded with six thermal jugs and packets of cream and sugar. "I've got your order," she chirped.

"Thanks a lot, Bobbi," Louise said. "I know Saturday mornings are busy at the Kettle. I hope you didn't get in any trouble bringing all this stuff up here."

"Trouble? Are you kidding? Max is as happy as can be with this order. He'd have carried each pastry up one by one himself and presented you a tab dipped in gold leaf for this kind of money."

Louise pictured the congenial owner of the Bayberry Cove Kettle and smiled. "I hope he's not the only person in town I can help this morning," she said.

Bobbi Lee opened the boxes and placed a stack of napkins on the table. "I know you'll help the girls at the factory," she said. "I've been friends with most of them for years, and it's about time somebody stood up for them."

After the busboy left, having received a tip from Louise, the waitress sidled up to the kitchen counter, leaned her hip against the sink and gave Louise a sly grin. "But I'm interested in more than candle company news this morning," she said. "So tell me. How'd it go last night?"

The fiasco at Buttercup Cottage was the last topic Louise wanted to discuss, but since she couldn't be rude, she settled for evasive. "You were right. The food from the Seafood Station was wonderful. Thanks for the recommendation, Bobbi."

"You're welcome, but that's not what I'm asking about and you know it. How did things go between you and the handsome sailor?"

Louise knew Bobbi wanted to hear some gossipy news about a budding romance. Louise wished she could fulfill her expectations. Unfortunately, the truth still hurt. She shook her head slowly. "Not so well. It looks like Commander Fletcher and I have many more differences than similarities."

"So what? That just makes gettin' to know each other all the more interesting." Bobbi smiled. "Don't you get discouraged. And don't give up on Wesley. I've known him since we were kids, and he's always let his codes and his morals get the best of him. That fella never cut up once in his life that I know of." She chuckled at a memory. "We used to call him Mr. Stick in the... Well, you know the rest. 'Course, we all liked him and admired him just the same. Even when he married that out-of-towner, Donna VanFleet. We all knew she wasn't right for him."

That was the second time Louise had heard a negative reference to Wes's first wife. She couldn't deny her curiosity. "You and I need some girl time together," she said to Bobbi. "There's a lot I don't know about the commander, and I'll bet you could fill me in."

"Anything you want to hear, I'll tell you," she said, and headed for the door. "Now have a good meeting. I figure you're going to find out that Wesley isn't the only mule-headed man in Bayberry Cove. The gals comin' up here today will give you an earful."

Bobbi left and a few minutes later Bessie Granger arrived with five middle-aged women from the candle factory. "Looks like I'm the official shuttle service for us blue hairs," Bessie said with good humor. "I saw to it that we arrived first so we wouldn't have to subject our old bones to sitting on the floor."

"How's Pete doing?" Louise asked, after she'd been introduced to Bessie's coworkers.

"Pretty well right now. I'm taking him

into Morgan City for his treatment after the meeting."

Miranda Lopez arrived next with two other women, both young, and both with children at home. Yvonne and four others came next. Darlene was the last of the original group at the Kettle to show up. She ambled in, grabbed a pillow off Louise's bed and plopped down on the floor near Bessie. A huge yawn served as her greeting when Louise welcomed her. "I don't know why we had to start this meeting at the crack of dawn," she said. "Besides, I don't see what any of this can do for me."

Bessie reached down and patted the girl's arm. "You won't know until you listen to what Louise has to say." She frowned, cupped Darlene's chin and angled her face to get a good look at her. "Darlin', were you out all night with Luke Plunkett again?"

"Where else would I be? And you can quit examining me like you were Doc Penderghast. Luke was a gentleman."

"That'll be the day," Bessie snickered.

Three others came to Louise's apartment though none of them were directly involved with the candle factory. Suzie arrived, grinning jubilantly. Louise remembered her promise to Evan and handed out the flyers advertising the week's store specials.

Vicki Malone came to show moral support for her friend, and introduced herself to the women she hadn't yet met. Then she sat to the side, looking very feminine in a ruffled maternity top.

The last woman to appear—and the one who created the biggest stir—was Kate Malone. She breezed in under her cloud of bright red curls, kissed her pregnant daughter-in-law and pretended to ignore the murmured comments about her unexpected attendance. She grabbed a Danish and sat in the middle of the group.

Louise was delighted to see Kate. Bessie Granger, however, was skeptical. "What are you doing here, Kate?" she asked. "This isn't your fight. I hope you're not going to run back to Haywood with information."

Kate bristled. "What a thing to say, Bessie. I'm here as a woman of Bayberry Cove who wants to see fair play down at the factory." She gave Bessie a chiding glance. "If it's spies you're expecting this morning, you'd best take your search elsewhere. You'd easier find one of your own husbands on a ladder outside these windows." She smiled up at Louise. "Do you think I'm a spy, dear?"

"Kate stays," Louise said. "I trust her."

And so the first meeting of the Bayberry

Cove Women's Movement for Employment Opportunities officially began. And of all people, it was Suzie McCorkle who came up with the lengthy name and volunteered to make a BCWMEO canvas banner on the old sewing machine she used to repair seams in sofa cushions.

Two HOURS LATER, the coffee carafes were dry, the pastry boxes were empty and Louise had taken fifteen pages of detailed notes.

"So what do you think, Louise?" Bessie asked. "Do we have legitimate complaints that you can file with the EEOC?"

"Oh, I have enough here to bring a representative from that organization to Bayberry Cove on the next bus," Louise said. "But I have to address Bessie and Miranda and Darlene first, since I've spoken to you three more than any of the others."

The three women sat up with attention. "What more do you need from us?" Miranda asked.

"I've heard a number of violations from all of you today," Louise said. "Many of them are repetitions of the ones you three ladies have encountered, and are indicative of the ways the company has kept some employees from advancing. But I can't possibly expect the EEOC to consider each and every instance where a violation has occurred. I need test cases that will represent the company's infractions."

Bessie looked at Miranda and Darlene. "And you think the three of us will make good test cases?"

"Yes, I do." Louise flipped through her notes to the appropriate page. "Bessie, you have clearly been the victim of age discrimination according to the Equal Pay Act. You reported that recently a man who'd never worked a day at the candle factory and who is half your age was hired to supervise your department after you repeatedly applied for the promotion yourself. And he is being paid half again as much as you currently make."

"That's right," Bessie declared.

"And Darlene, every year you've filled out the proper paperwork to be considered for the marketing and sales apprenticeship program."

The blonde nodded. "Yes, I have. And each time I've had to go back to Human Resources to ask why I wasn't picked. And each time ol' Hatch Winslow tells me to apply again next year and that somebody with 'more potential' was chosen for the program. This year Newt

Parker got in over me. A slug has more potential than Newt if you want my opinion."

There was a titter of laughter as all the ladies agreed with Darlene's evaluation of the man.

"That's also discrimination," Louise confirmed. "Title VII provides for equal opportunity in training programs."

"And Darlene would be great at marketing and sales," Bessie stated. "She could go to trade shows all over the country and sell candles better than any other employee I know of. She actually likes candles more than anybody else in Bayberry Cove—" Bessie broke off and fixed a guilty grin on Suzie. "Except maybe you, hon." Turning back to the group, she continued, "And Darlene would love to travel, and, in my opinion, needs to get out of this town."

Louise understood the implication. Everyone who cared about Darlene wanted her to get away from her destructive relationship with Luke Plunkett.

"And Miranda, you say that Justin Beauclaire made you take a leave of absence six months into your last pregnancy?"

The Latino woman shook her head, sending her dark, spiral curls dancing. "Yes, he did. He said I was a safety hazard, that I might fall or catch my loose clothing in the scent vats. I told him I would switch positions, but he told me to stay home. I lost three months pay, not counting the time I nursed Mateo after he was born."

"And you've been at the candle company for four years without a raise in pay?"

"That's right. None of the female Mexican workers have had raises."

Louise folded her tablet and laid it on an end table. "I have plenty to take to the commission, ladies. I'll use these three cases as examples of violations that occur regularly at the factory. And hopefully, by bringing these issues to light, we can initiate changes that will improve conditions for everyone." She looked at each of the three women and raised her eyebrows in question. "So, are we agreed? We'll go forward?"

Miranda squirmed on the rug, where she sat on a pillow. "Will our names be used?" she asked.

Louise wasn't going to make these ladies think their fight would be an easy or an anonymous one. "Yes, Miranda. That's a condition of filing."

"Could I be fired?"

"I don't think so. If there is any harassment or retaliation as a result of you coming forward, it would be another case to bring before the EEOC, or even take to court as a full-fledged lawsuit. I can't guarantee there won't be some type of retribution, something petty, perhaps. But I don't think the executives at the factory would risk a lawsuit."

Bessie was the first to speak out. "I say let's go for it."

"I'll stick with Bessie," Darlene said. "She's got the most to lose, and if she's got the guts to do this, then I do, too."

Miranda chewed her lip. "I have children to think about. I can't get fired...."

Bessie reached down and took her hand. "Think about those kids now, Miranda. Think what you getting a raise could do for them. I think we should take the chance Louise is offering us."

Louise studied her worried expression. "Tell you what, Miranda. If it's okay with Bessie and Darlene, I'll concentrate on their complaints first and use yours only if we need it."

Miranda managed a small smile of relief. "Okay. Then count me in."

There was a round of applause before Bessie asked, "What's the next step?"

"Bring me any documentation you have," Louise said. "When you were hired, the approximate dates you were denied promotions and apprenticeships, recent incidents of salary loss due to personal emergencies, pay stubs from the last few years and written reports of the violations, in your own words. I'll take it from there and file the appropriate papers."

"Wow, this is the most exciting thing that's ever happened in this town," one woman said as the group filed out of Louise's apartment. "Imagine taking on Justin Beauclaire and the candle factory!"

When everyone but Vicki had gone, Louise smiled at her friend. "The excitement's just beginning," she said.

Vicki scraped icing from the bottom of one of the pastry boxes onto her finger and licked off the sweet confection. "You know, Lulu, I was impressed seeing you in action this morning. You're a terrific leader."

Louise swept around the room picking up empty cups. "You've seen me in court before."

"Yes, but this was different. More personal, I suppose. You seem committed…."

Louise laughed. "Maybe I should *be* committed, you mean."

"Not at all. I'm amazed by you, my friend. You could be sitting at the beach in Fort Lauderdale doing nothing, or drowning your resentment every night at a bar, but you're not. You're helping these women. You care about them and their problems, and I'm proud of you."

Louise halted her cleaning spree and stared at Vicki. Her friend's words just then meant as much to her as any hefty retainer from a corporate executive. "Well, thanks," she said with a humility that felt alien, but good.

Vicki smiled and abruptly changed the direction of the conversation. "But speaking of commitments, how did it go with Wesley last night?"

The adrenaline rush Louise had experienced during the meeting vanished. She had to address the Wesley issue one more time, and it wasn't any easier to discuss now. "Not well. It turns out the sailor I'd set my sights on is actually an attorney. And he's going to represent the candle factory if I submit violations to the EEOC."

Vicki frowned in sympathy. "I heard. Jamie told me last night. That really stinks, Lulu, but maybe you can't blame Wes. I hear his father can be pretty convincing."

Louise stuffed the cups into her trash can, tied the ends of the bag and carried the garbage to the back door. "His father is a lot of things. Convincing is only one of them.

Anyway, I'm not thinking about Wesley today. I've got more important things on my mind."

"But you're not giving up on him?"

There was his face again, with its strong chiseled features and bright blue eyes, popping into her mind with all the clarity of the sun in a cloudless sky. Louise settled a fist on her hip. "When have you ever known me to give up after one defeat? I'm simply shelving the subject of Wesley Fletcher until I can truly concentrate on what to do about him. But one more evening like last night, and I may switch him to the hopeless column."

Further discussion of Wesley was forgotten when shouting from the back parking lot drew the attention of both women. "What's going on out there?" Vicki asked.

"I don't know, but it sounds like Darlene's voice."

Louise opened the back door and stepped onto a wooden platform that led to the staircase. The parking lot was empty except for her BMW, an older model Japanese car and a black pickup truck. Darlene and a tall, rangy man in a cowboy hat were standing near the pickup. He had his hand wrapped around her upper arm, and she was struggling to get free.

"Let me go, you big ox," she shouted. "You had no right to come here."

"I've got every right," the man hollered back. "Especially when you lie to me. You said you were going to your sister's this morning. I don't like being lied to, Darlene."

She yanked her arm away and took several steps back from him. "You make me lie to you, Luke, by always telling me what I can and can't do. I'm sick of it."

He closed the distance between them and held up a fist. "Get in the truck, Darlene. We're going for a ride."

"I'm not going anywhere with you when you act like this…."

"That's right," Louise shouted from the platform. "You come up here with us, Darlene. And you—" she shook a trembling finger at Luke "—you make tracks, buster."

Luke stomped over to the stairs and glared up at her. "Who are you? Oh, wait, I know. You're that lady attorney who's been creating a ruckus around here."

"I'm also Darlene's friend. And it's your misfortune that I happen to be the one friend who can put you behind bars for a few years if you lay a hand on her."

Luke put one booted foot on the first step. "You don't scare me, lady."

Darlene grabbed Luke's arm and pulled him away. "Just go, Luke, please. I don't want any trouble. And you sure don't need any more."

For one long, frightening moment, the man appeared to weigh his options. He narrowed his eyes first on his pickup, then Darlene and finally Louise. She held her breath and stared back at him.

And then a Jeep Wrangler came down the alley and pulled into the parking lot. Wesley stepped out, looked at all the parties, who were now standing in silence, and said, "What's going on here? Luke, what are you up to?"

Luke yanked his hat off and slapped it against his thigh. "Nothing's going on, Wes. Nothing at all." He delivered a last blazing look at Louise and Darlene and said, "I was just leaving." He stomped to the truck, climbed in and sped out of the parking lot. Darlene got into her car and drove off in the opposite direction.

And Louise let out the breath she'd been holding.

"Thank goodness," Vicki said from behind her.

Wesley watched the dust settle from the pickup's wild departure and then approached the stairs. "Good morning, ladies," he said. "Do either of you know what got into Luke?"

Louise smirked. "I don't know, Wes. Maybe the men of Bayberry Cove just don't know how to treat their womenfolk." After experiencing a slight jolt of satisfaction at seeing him cringe a little, she said, "But more to the point, what are you doing here?"

He went back to the Jeep and lifted her picnic basket from the passenger seat. "I was just out for a drive and thought I'd drop this off. You forgot it last night."

"How thoughtful of you, Counselor," she said. "But I can't see myself using it again in the near future. Suddenly I don't have much interest in picnicking, and I know I won't have the time."

He brought the basket to the stairs, acted for a moment as if he might ascend to the second floor, but stopped before climbing up. Instead, he set the basket on the bottom step. He rubbed his hand along the nape of his neck and said, "So how'd your meeting go?"

She gave him a stiff smile. "Swell, thanks."

"That's good." He shifted from one foot to the other, as if waiting for an invitation. When none was forthcoming, he added, "I guess I'll be going then."

Louise nodded. "Bye."

"Nice seeing you again, Vicki," he said.

"Same here, Wesley."

"I'll see you later, Louise."

She flicked her fingers in an offhand wave. "No doubt."

Once he was in his vehicle and heading away, Vicki released a long, audible sigh.

"What's that for?" Louise asked.

Vicki gave her a silly grin. "I just get all squishy inside when I see love in bloom. That guy's crazy about you, Lulu."

"Right." She retrieved the basket, carried it upstairs and put it on her kitchen counter. "He probably thinks I left it at his house on purpose so I'd have an excuse to see him again."

When Vicki didn't respond, Louise turned around to look at her. The silly grin was still in place. "What now?"

"Did you?" Vicki asked.

"Leave the basket on purpose?"

"Yeah. Because if you did, I'm proud of you for the second time this morning. It's a little obvious, but that's all right. It still shows that never-give-up determination of yours that I've grown to admire."

Louise started taking items from the basket. Everything had been washed and packed carefully, and she smiled at one aspect of

Wes's personality that was truly predictable. "Of course I didn't mean to leave it there. Don't be ridiculous."

But had she? Louise remembered how she'd picked up her purse from Wes's table, never once thinking of the picnic basket. The subconscious worked in strange ways.

ONCE SHE SAW Haywood's car in the driveway and realized he'd returned from his golf match, Kate drove around to the back of the house and walked into the kitchen through the rear entrance.

"That you, Katie?" Haywood hollered from his office. "I've been waiting for you. What's for lunch?"

"I don't know yet, Haywood," she said, regretting that she hadn't made her usual Saturday-morning trip to the grocery. "How does a can of soup sound?"

"Like we're running a nursery school," he called back. "A man needs real food, Kate, not something he can slurp with a straw. What did you buy today?"

"I didn't go grocery shopping," she said.

Relieved when he didn't comment, she found some stew and inserted the can into the electric opener. And then she squealed in fright and leaped away from the counter when she heard Haywood growl right behind her, "What do you mean you didn't go shopping? You always go to the grocery store on Saturdays."

She whirled around and shoved him away. "You scared the wits out of me, Haywood. Don't sneak up on me like that."

"Okay, but where were you this morning?"

"I went to a flea market in Wrightsboro." Though she knew her anger was mostly unreasonable, she dumped the stew into a pot and snapped, "If that schedule doesn't suit your needs, you can drive yourself to McDonald's!"

He raised his hands. "Whoa, Katie. I was just asking."

She tried to be more pleasant. "I'm sorry, dear. I'm a little jumpy I guess."

He sat in the large chair at the head of the pine table. "I could do with that stew, I guess."

She realized she was feeling more guilty than angry. She'd never lied to Haywood before.

"So what did you buy?" he asked as she handed him the stew.

"Where?"

"At the flea market. You always come back with an oddity or two when you go to one of those."

What was this? An inquisition? Kate dipped her hands under the spigot of running water and spritzed drops of water onto her warm face. This was no time for a hot flash, or a guilt flash, or whatever it was. "Well, not today, Haywood," she said. "Didn't see a thing I wanted."

"Did you happen to get downtown this morning?" he asked around a mouthful of beef and potatoes.

She turned the water on full force and filled the dirty pot. "Downtown? Why would I go downtown? I told you I didn't go to the supermarket."

"Yes, I know, but the strangest thing happened. My father finally learned to use his cell phone. He called me from the square today and said there was a flock of women going into that lady lawyer's apartment."

Kate scoured the pot until she feared the Teflon lining might come off. "My, that is strange. I didn't think Mason would ever catch on to that cell phone."

"That's not the strange part, Katie, and I think you know it. He said he saw your car on Main Street."

She slammed the clean pot loudly on the drainboard and faced him. "What's this,

Haywood? Now you've got your father spying on me?"

"No. I'm just curious about why you lied to me."

She threw up her hands. "All right. I was at that meeting. And I'm not sorry I went."

He stood up, came to the sink and completely surprised her by wrapping her in a huge bear hug. "Neither am I, Kate. I'm pleased as punch to hear it." He kissed the tip of her nose. "Now tell me what you found out, you clever woman."

"I'm not going to tell you anything."

He stepped back from her as if she'd suddenly grown a forked tail. "What?"

"I went there to support the women in this town, Haywood. Anything that happened at that meeting you'll find out soon enough, but you won't hear it from me."

His eyes bulged under bushy white brows. "You can't be serious."

"I'm all that and more. I'm proud of the women I was with this morning. They're showing great courage in the face of…the bullies at the factory. And I admire that young lawyer who's standing up for them."

Haywood pounded his fist on the counter—just once, and just loudly enough to command attention. "Kate, I demand you tell me what those females are cooking up. Your loyalty is to me and this house. I *own* this house!"

He had gone too far. Kate knew it and read in his eyes that he knew it, too.

"I'm well aware that this isn't my house, Haywood," she said. "I've lived in it for more than five years without benefit of license or title. Maybe it's time I found more suitable accommodations elsewhere."

"Aw, Katie, come on now..."

He took a step toward her, but she stopped him with one look. She tore off her apron, crushed it into a ball and shoved it into his hands. "Here, you'll need this when you fix your supper."

On the way out of the kitchen, she ripped the grocery list from the magnetized tablet on the refrigerator door and thrust that at him as well. "And you can do your own shoppin'. Won't you be the dandy fella down at the Piggly Wiggly squeezin' melons!"

Haywood sank into the nearest chair and stared at the doorway. A few seconds later, Rudy entered the room with a backward glance over his shoulder.

"What's goin' on with Miss Kate?" the butler asked. "What did you do?"

Haywood shook his head. "Who knows,

Rudy. All I said was, 'What's for lunch?' I think the women in this town have all gone mad."

## CHAPTER TEN

FOR THE NEXT FOUR DAYS Wesley successfully avoided Louise. He jogged along the shore of Currituck Sound instead of the town square track even though the uneven, sandy terrain was not kind to the soles of his feet. He stayed away from the Kettle except for breakfast on Monday morning, when Bobbi Lee acted as if taking his order was as unpleasant as getting a root canal.

"You won't see her here this morning," Bobbi Lee had smartly informed him.

Of course he pretended he had no idea what she was talking about. "Won't see who?" he'd asked.

"Don't play ignorant with me, Wes Fletcher," she'd snapped at him. "I remember your high school grade point average." And then she'd smugly told him that Louise was in Morgan City conferring with her legal team, which included one Lawrence Aaronson. Wes had laughed at the whole idea. He was quite certain that Louise didn't need a team of any sort nor any help beyond her sponsorship.

During his infrequent trips to town, Wes realized something else as well. The ladies of Bayberry Cove had obviously heard who was acting as counsel for the factory. The cold shoulder he'd received from Bobbi Lee was pretty much the same reaction he got from most of the women in his hometown. People who normally waved and smiled at him from passing automobiles now pretended they didn't see him. Even the checker at the supermarket swept his purchases over the scanning window without so much as a "How are you today?"

He found out that circumstances weren't much better for his father. By Wednesday night, when the isolation of Buttercup Cottage was making him stir-crazy, Wes accepted an invitation to eat with his dad at a chain restaurant on the freeway a few miles from town. Besides questioning Wes about what he knew of the secret meeting on Saturday morning, Haywood complained that his relationship with Kate had turned as cold as a winter frost.

"That lady attorney is turning my life upside down," he grumbled. "So what has she got on us, son?"

"I don't know, Dad. Maybe you should tell me."

Haywood covered a belch with his napkin and dipped his twelfth chicken wing in spicy barbecue sauce. "Nothing. She's got nothing. Justin Beauclaire tells me we're clean as a scrubbed blackboard."

"That's not the impression I get from half the women in town. I feel like my female neighbors have suddenly taken sides and I've assumed the identity of a Yankee."

Haywood leaned over the table and spoke in a whisper. "Do you think she's filed any complaints with the EEOC?"

Wes took a long swallow of soda. "Well, Dad, she said she would, and I don't think she's the type to make idle threats. She's not afraid of any of you boys, and she's set herself up with Aaronson. So, yes, I'd say she probably has, or will as soon as she gets enough documentation."

"This is just what I need to hear with Kate treating me like a flea off a dog's hiney." He stared down at his empty plate with a look of disgust. "I haven't had a decent meal in nearly a week. Or even so much as a hug!"

Wes held up his hand. His father's dating life, or lack thereof, wasn't a topic he wanted to discuss. Wes didn't need to hear how a few days deprivation was making his father grumpy. "Let's keep to the legal issues, okay?" he said.

"So what are you going to do? How are you going to handle this situation?"

Even after forty years association with Haywood Fletcher, Wes could still be knocked over by the sheer nerve of the man. "How am *I* going to handle this? Dad, have you forgotten that I'm just your consultant? I'm supposed to sign my name on the paperwork *you* prepare, remember?"

Haywood brandished his fork in the air. "Don't throw my words back at me, Wesley. I'll help you, but you're the legal eagle in this case. You've spent the last sixteen years studying contracts and interpreting civil law. I'm counting on you, son."

Wonderful. Wes should have known that his father would pass the whole job of defending the factory on to him. "I'll do what I can, Dad. But I can't promise anything. If it looks like Louise has chosen obscure, even insignificant violations, then I can argue on the side of the company. Admit to innocent negligence if I have to. But if—"

"Well, of course she's scraping the bottom of the barrel! Petty stuff. That's all she's got.

The kind of things that every company in America gets away with."

Leaving his steak half-eaten, Wes searched the restaurant for their waiter. The first signs of indigestion rumbled in his stomach as he waved the boy over and asked for the check.

BY THURSDAY MORNING Wes gave up pretending to himself that he was enjoying every minute of his simple, uncomplicated life at Buttercup Cottage. He was in this quagmire of a legal dilemma up to his waist and sinking lower. The case of the women candle workers versus the factory executives wasn't going to go away. And neither were the nagging thoughts of the dynamite attorney who represented the other side.

Circumstances being what they were, he'd have to see her again. To keep this candle factory business from getting out of hand, he decided to try and make things right with Louise. He was a grown man with a firm control on his emotions and actions. He could see her in social situations and act like the gentleman he'd always been.

Besides, he could see Louise again now that he'd admitted honestly that she fascinated him on several levels. One of those levels was a safe, intellectual one. She was interested in his studies of the wetlands, and he could keep their personal relationship grounded on that common interest.

He'd invite her to go out on the Aquasport. She'd said she wanted to, and it would be the perfect way to break the ice that sat between them like a polar glacier.

After tending to his experiments on Thursday morning, Wes drove over to the Malones' houseboat. He accepted the cup of coffee Vicki offered him, talked a little with Jamie and then stated bluntly, "Vicki, I need her phone number."

A smile spread across her face. "Lulu's?"

As if there was any other phone number on the face of the earth he could possibly be asking for. "Yes, Lulu's."

"She only has her cell phone. It's a Florida number. Long distance."

"I'll figure the added expense into my budget," he said.

Vicki jotted the number on a piece of paper and handed it to him. "It's about time."

Jamie gave him an enigmatic smile and a shrug that seemed to say, *Why resist the inevitable?*

Wes went home and dialed the number.

She answered on the third ring. "Louise Duncan."

Her voice was crisp and cool. Businesslike. No doubt the majority of her phone calls were related to her business affairs these days.

"Louise. It's Wes."

There was a pause, and for a moment he thought she might hang up. "Well, my. Wes. What can I do for you?"

To the point, slightly aloof but thankfully not antagonistic. "I'm calling to see if you're still interested in going out on the boat with me. I thought you might like to learn how I collect my samples. I'm going all the way to Pamlico Sound tomorrow. It would be a good chance for you to experience our marine environment."

*Boy, Wes, could you make it sound any more boring?* "It's supposed to be a beautiful day," he added, hoping that extra perk would compensate for his lackluster invitation.

"I see." She paused again, showing a command of the element of suspense. "Will I need a life jacket?"

"I have them in the boat already. I always recommend—"

"It was a joke, Wes. Though subtly aimed at determining if we're going as friends."

He smiled. "Absolutely." *Friends who can have a platonic relationship despite the legal issues between them.*

"Okay. I'll go. Shall I drive to your place?"

"That would be great. Can you be here by seven? I like to visit my collection sites before the waterways get too crowded with pleasure craft."

"All right. Seven o'clock it is."

"I'll have a thermos of coffee."

"And I'll bring doughnuts from the Kettle."

Wes stared at the phone for several seconds after they disconnected. He felt energized, more enthused than he had in days. Since Friday night's dinner if he were truly honest— even though that experience had ended disastrously. Louise was fun. And didn't he deserve to have a little fun?

WHEN HE HEARD THE SOUND of a car engine on Sandy Ridge Road, Wes looked up from the deck of the Aquasport where he was readying the boat for the morning's trip into Currituck Sound. Louise's dark BMW slowed and turned into the drive of the cottage.

Wes noted the time on his wristwatch. Six-fifty. A guy had to admire a female who didn't keep him waiting. She came around the corner of the house and Wes decided a guy had to admire even more a woman who looked like she did at this hour. Dressed in shorts and a sleeveless top, her hair bound in a kerchief, her stride eager, her face luminous in the morning sun, Louise was so striking he nearly lost his grip on the thermos he was stowing in a cup holder.

"Hey, Commander," she called. "Everything shipshape?"

He noticed the white sack from the Kettle. "It will be once I have a doughnut."

She tossed him the bag and climbed into the boat as if she'd been sailing every day of her life. "Any particular place you'd like me to sit?" she asked. "I wouldn't want to throw off the balance of this thing and send us toppling overboard."

With that statement he realized she hadn't been sailing much at all. He indicated the seat next to the captain's position. "That will be fine. Your life vest is stored under the seat cushion."

"Good. That answers my next question."

He laughed. "You can put it on now if it makes you feel better."

"No. Just promise you'll give me enough time to fasten it before we capsize."

"No problem. I'm known for my slow rollovers." He filled a marine-style coffee cup hinged at the sides to keep liquid from spilling over, and held it out to her.

She took the warm mug, settled in her

seat and slipped on a pair of dark-framed sunglasses. "I'm ready when you are."

He turned the ignition key with the engine in neutral and felt the steady, assertive vibrations. Louise stowed her cup in a holder and grabbed the sides of her seat.

"You're going to love this," Wes said, thrusting the throttle to its forward position. The boat shot away from the dock, banked in a tight turn and raced into Currituck Sound.

She squealed before shouting through a cool, brisk wind that whipped her hair around her shoulders, "If you say so, Commander."

HE WAS RIGHT. She loved it. Once her breathing returned to normal and she decided they weren't going to become an artificial reef for future scuba divers to explore, Louise reveled in the performance of the speedboat.

She'd been on cruises, of course. She'd sailed on large, lavish ocean liners fitted for two thousand passengers. She'd taken dozens of pictures of glass-enclosed elevators outlined in sparkling white lights, and buffet tables that stretched the length of a basketball court. But none of it compared with the exuberance of racing across the sound with the sun at her back and the watery world shimmering to the horizon.

After about fifteen minutes, Wes slowed the boat as it approached a red plastic ball bobbing in the current. "We're here already?" she asked.

"This is only our first stop. I identify my research sites with these floats so I can find them again." He dropped an anchor over the side and let the boat drift to the marker. Then he reached under the ball and pulled on a chain.

"I know we talked about your experiments a little the other night," Louise said, "but what is it exactly that you hope to prove?"

"I'm trying to show that development of Currituck Sound in any major way, such as with high-rise apartments, luxury hotels and so on, will upset the delicate balance of the North Carolina marshes and wetlands. I gather specimens from the various water types— salt, fresh and brackish—and demonstrate in the tanks in my shed what would happen to sea life if waters with such diverse salinity levels intermixed too rapidly."

"And development would do that?" she asked.

"It already has." He continued coiling the chain onto the deck of the boat until he pulled up a wire cage with a funnel-like device on one side. He left the cage in the water while he finished explaining. "Development causes change in the salinity of the water from such things as dredging, waste material dumped from the shore, even, believe it or not, human viruses being introduced. Changes in salinity affect aquatic vegetation, which in turn affects the life cycles of the creatures who feed on it. All these changes would be disastrous to our water industries like fishing and shrimping."

He lifted the cage, causing water and sand to run from the sides. When he settled the contraption on the deck of the boat, Louise observed several creatures scurrying or flopping about on the bottom tray. "How do they get in there?"

"That's what the funnel's for," he said. "Fish and crabs go in the wide opening but can't find their way back out."

"Are you taking these guys back to your shed?"

"Yep." He raised the lid on top of the cage and began transferring the creatures to a larger tub of water inside the boat. He seemed pleased when he picked up one fish behind its gills and held it up for close inspection. "This is an interesting specimen."

"How so?"

"This is a shortnose sturgeon. He spends most of his life in saltwater, only going to fresh to reproduce, which he shouldn't be doing at this time of year. You're kind of lost, aren't you, buddy?" he said to the fish before putting it into the tub and returning his attention to Louise. "He's a perfect example of specimens who get comfortable in an environment that's exactly where they should be, and then new stimuli move in when the salt levels become inconsistent. The sturgeon loses his way and doesn't know if he's coming or going."

*An interesting analogy,* Louise thought. "You'll pardon me for saying so, Wes," she said, "but it seems as if you understand what this fish is going through."

He closed the lid of the tank and leaned back on his haunches. The look he gave her was both thoughtful and amused. And incredibly intense. After a moment he said, "Maybe you've got something there, Counselor. Maybe I do understand this guy's dilemma." He stood up and returned to his task. "It will be interesting to see if he survives the new environment of my tanks as I alter the salinity and nutrient levels."

She smiled at him. Poor Wes. Nineteen years in the navy characterized by regimens and codes and a lifestyle that didn't change much from day to day. And all he'd hoped for was a simple life of scientific accomplishment in Bayberry Cove, perhaps with an uncomplicated woman in blue jeans and a gingham shirt waiting by the back door of Buttercup Cottage. But what did he get after a week of retirement? A major legal role in an EEOC investigation, and quite possibly some weird, unwanted attraction to a woman who was about as far from his ideal as anyone could be.

"I have a prediction about that fish, Wes," she said. "He seems like the hardy sort. I think he'll figure out what he has to do to stay alive…and swim happily along."

"You could be right, Louise," he said as he secured the cage again and dropped it over the side. Back in business mode, he returned to his seat and pushed the throttle into gear. "Keep your eye open for the next red float," he said. "We've got four more cages to find."

LOUISE HAD BEEN A GOOD sport about everything. She'd even picked up a couple of blue crabs from one of the cages and, with their jointed appendages wiggling madly, had transferred them to the temporary tank in the boat. At one point in Pamlico Sound she took over controls of the boat, punched the speed up to its maximum and whooped with the enthusiasm of a rodeo rider. But when they returned to Buttercup Cottage around noon, she was the first one out of the boat, racing toward the house and the conveniences inside.

Wes introduced his new specimens to the aquariums in the shed and secured the boat and its equipment. When he entered the cottage a few minutes later, he found Louise standing at the kitchen counter with various utensils spread out in front of her. She'd abandoned the kerchief around her hair, which hung straight and long, past shoulders that were tinged pink from the sun.

"You hungry?" she said.

"I could eat an octopus."

She grinned. "Sorry. You're fresh out. But I did find some ham and cheese in the refrigerator, and I'm making sandwiches." She found a tomato and a head of lettuce in the crisper and slathered mayonnaise onto thick slices of bread.

She looked so natural performing this domestic task that Wes sat down at the table and simply watched her. Many times the last few days he'd wondered what she'd been doing, but he'd never pictured her in a kitchen looking as if she belonged there. He stretched his legs under the table and said, "Do you like to cook?"

Keeping her attention on the tomato she

was slicing, she said, "Sorry again, but no. I bought my current condo in Fort Lauderdale based on the variety and accessibility of take-out food in the neighborhood."

The answer disappointed him, though logically it shouldn't have. Why would it matter to him if Louise enjoyed cooking? "So what do you do in your spare time?" he said. "Do you garden?"

She laughed. "Wes, I said 'condo.' As in 'no lawn, no flowers, no shrubs.' I have a beautiful silk tree in the corner of my living room that I tend lovingly with a feather duster and a damp cotton swab." She set two plates and two sodas on the table and sat across from him. He took a large bite from his sandwich.

"Now that your mouth is full I guess it's safe for me to ask if you have any other questions," she said.

Maybe he was probing a bit too much into her personal life, but now that he'd gone this far, he decided to plunge ahead. He washed down the sandwich with a swallow of soda. "I don't mean to be nosy, but—"

"Yes, you do."

He grinned. "Well, maybe. You must have a hobby. Do you knit? Do needlework? Make things?"

Her eyebrows shot up in amusement. "Make

things? No, Wes, I don't make tea cozies or twig wreaths. But I can file efficiently, and I type sixty words a minute. So if this is a job interview, you might want to consider me for any position other than that of the next Mrs. Wesley Fletcher."

He choked on soggy bread and took another gulp of his soda. "What in the world are you talking about?" he said when he'd caught his breath. "I wasn't even remotely suggesting—"

She shook her head, took a dainty bite of sandwich and swallowed. "Calm down, Commander. I know I'm not a suitable candidate."

He stood up, walked to the door and looked out at Currituck Sound. "You really amaze me with the things you say sometimes."

"Just like you amaze me with the ones you *don't* say." Her voice came from directly behind him, and he spun around to see her standing within inches of him. "I know you and I would make a terrible old married couple, Wes. But I'm still tickled that you're searching for some little facet of my character that might make me even moderately acceptable to your Bayberry Cove standard of womanhood."

His skin started to heat up. "That's ridiculous."

"I don't think so. The other night you said you liked me. You couldn't understand why exactly, but you did. I was happy to hear that—despite how the evening turned out—but now I think I need a few specifics. I don't grow things or sew or bake." She took a step closer to him.

His knit shirt suddenly felt too tight. He pulled at one sleeve, trying to stretch it out around his biceps.

"So what *do* you like about me, Wes?"

"This is silly. You've put me on the spot."

"Good. It's where you should be. Name one thing you like about me. My hair? My figure? My brain?"

He rolled his eyes. Actually, he liked the first two a great deal. The third was a little scary.

She clasped her hands behind her back and lifted her face up to his. "I play a pretty fair game of tennis," she said, "and believe it or not, I once bowled a perfect three hundred. I'm an excellent driver and I have a double-jointed thumb." She gave him a tight-lipped grin that came across as a dare. "Have I mentioned anything yet that you really like?"

If she meant to intimidate him, it wasn't working. If her goal was to fire every red-blooded cell in his body, she was doing a good job. At the same time, he was beginning to figure Louise out.

He flexed his shoulders, answered her grin with one of his own and stared down at her until she was the one who seemed uncomfortable. Amazingly, his voice was calm as he said, "Yes, there is something. I like the fact that you bowl. I think we can build on that."

Her eyes grew so wide that for a moment all he could see was the sheer lavender brilliance of them. And then a deep, rich chortle came from her throat. "Now we're getting somewhere," she said. "But know this. I will never, *ever,* let you win. We'll go all the way to the tenth frame each time if we have to."

"I don't doubt that you'll make it a worthy contest, Counselor."

She unclasped her hands and crossed her arms in front. *Watch yourself, Wes. Not with this woman. You're about to step off an emotional cliff, and while the fall may be a thrill, you still have to face hitting bottom.*

"Just so we understand each other, Wes," she said. "We're not just talking about bowling anymore, are we?"

She was testing him to the limit, and it was inhuman to try and resist her. For right now, just this once, he would silence the controlling forces in his head and deal with the consequences later. He grasped her elbows and pulled her into close, intimate contact. "No, Louise, I don't think we are."

He lifted her to her toes and crushed her against his chest. When his mouth covered hers, his blood raced through his veins until the voice of his conscience was drowned out. He'd wanted to kiss her from the first moment he'd seen her. And now she was soft, pliant and willing in his arms.

Maybe Louise Duncan was the last woman he needed in his life, but right now, she was the one he most wanted to be with. Forget everything else.

SHE'D KNOWN IT ALL ALONG. Underneath that polished military exterior, Wes Fletcher was an amazingly passionate man, and she was enjoying discovering this far more than she should. *You've got to stop, Louise,* she said to herself. *If you're not careful this could turn dangerous.*

She made herself listen to the ticking coming from above her head. She looked up and saw an old schoolhouse clock mounted to the wall. Two o'clock. She squeezed her eyes shut and released a long, frustrated groan against the mouth that still threatened to send her over the edge.

Wes leaned away from her. "What's wrong?"

She lay her forehead against his chest. "It's two o'clock."

He kissed the top of her head and rubbed his hand down her back. "So? I can't think of anything else I have to do."

"Well, I can, and you're not going to like it." And neither did she. All morning she'd been aware of her afternoon appointment. She hadn't intended for a little playful flirtation to get out of hand.

Soon she had to leave to meet with a representative from the Equal Employment Opportunity Commission.

Louise didn't have a problem separating the activities of her legal life from the activities of her personal one, but she knew Wes would. She sighed, admitting to herself that putting his feelings first was something new to her.

She walked away from him, picked up the dirty plates and carried them to the sink. That way she didn't have to face him as she said, "I have a meeting at two-thirty."

"With anyone I know?"

"His name is Christopher Tenant, and he's with the EEOC."

There was a moment of uncomfortable silence until Wes said, "He's coming to Bayberry Cove to meet with you on a Friday afternoon?"

"Yes, but I didn't know about it until late yesterday. He received my paperwork on Thursday, and since I mentioned that I'm pressed for time on these cases, he made an adjustment in his schedule and called me right away."

She turned to face him. "I'm sorry, Wes."

He stared as if he weren't really seeing her. His eyes were as bleak as a winter sea. "Don't be sorry. You were right to put the brakes on what was happening here. It was crazy. I don't know why…" He stopped, rubbed the back of his neck. "I guess you'd better go, then."

"Yeah." She picked up her purse and headed for the living room. "It was a lot of fun," she said as she left the kitchen.

He went to the sink and picked up where she'd left off, putting his tidy world back together. "Right," he said. "Fun. We'll do it again sometime."

# CHAPTER ELEVEN

LOUISE STEPPED HARD on her brakes and swerved into a parking space a few yards from her apartment. She'd made the trip from Buttercup Cottage in six minutes flat, which was not nearly as much time as it should have taken. She'd never looked at her speedometer. Wouldn't have cared if she'd gotten a ticket. She felt that lousy about what had just happened, and more confused than she'd ever been about her feelings for Wesley Fletcher.

And now she only had fifteen minutes to pull herself together for the meeting with Christopher Tenant. "At least I've got one thing going for me," she said as she got out of her car. "Tenant's a government employee. He won't be early."

She hurried up the sidewalk. Her foot was on the first step to her apartment when she heard her name being called. "Miss Duncan? Young lady?"

Turning away from the stairs, she peered

across the street to the town square. Mason Fletcher was waving at her. She and the old guy had gotten to be pretty good friends. She could always count on him being at his familiar bench, and he always seemed eager to talk to her. "Hi, Mason," she called back. "I don't have time to chat now. I'm running late."

He pointed to a man sitting next to him, and Louise noticed the stranger for the first time. "I know ya' are," Mason said. "And this young fella's waiting for you."

Christopher Tenant. It had to be. The guy whose head was the target of Mason's pointer finger was definitely an out-of-towner. In tan chinos, a dress shirt and tie, he was Raleigh all the way.

"Well, nuts," Louise said under her breath. She made a quick repair to her appearance, tucking her blouse into her shorts, smoothing her windblown hair and pressing her lips together before she remembered that any lipstick that might have remained from this morning had been thoroughly kissed off. She plastered a smile on her face and crossed the street, wishing she could make a better first impression on the man who would decide the fate of the women candle workers.

She stuck her hand out when she reached the bench. "Mr. Tenant?"

He stood up and shook her hand. "That's right."

"Louise Duncan. I'm sorry you had to wait."

He appraised her with cool gray eyes that probably assessed her none-too-proper business attire. "It's no problem," he said. "I'm early, and I've only been here five minutes." He glanced at Mason, who was studying Louise with equal intensity. "This gentleman has kept me entertained, and informed."

She narrowed her eyes at Mason. "I'll just bet he has. I hope you didn't prejudice the case against my clients, Mason."

"He couldn't do that, Miss Duncan," Christopher said. "It's my job to judge each case with an unbiased eye, and I take it very seriously."

So Mr. Tenant was all-business. When Louise returned her attention to him, he was still staring at her, holding her hand and smiling. She noticed that his tie was loosely knotted and hung at an awkward angle on his chest. He wasn't perfection, after all. She extricated her hand and smiled back. "Call me Louise. And if I could ask a favor of you, Mr...."

"Chris. And ask anything at all."

"There's a café just down the street called

the Bayberry Cove Kettle. Could I buy you a cup of coffee while I run up to my apartment and change? I don't normally conduct business in the same clothes I wear on a speedboat."

"You look fine to me, Louise," he said. "But sure, I could go for a cup of coffee. You take your time."

She pointed the way to the Kettle and Chris set off. Before she'd taken two steps toward the furniture store, Mason chuckled and said, "You've been out with my grandson, haven't you?"

She shot him a stern look over her shoulder. "That, Mason, is none of your business."

"All right, young lady, you can sass me all you want. I'll just ask someone else."

She shook her head and kept walking. *Small towns!*

Louise showered and changed in record time. She and Christopher Tenant ended up conducting their meeting in a corner booth of the Kettle. The EEOC rep reacted to Louise's findings pretty much as she'd anticipated.

"I think you've got some legitimate charges," he said over his third cup of coffee. "After some in-depth research, I'll take my conclusions back to Raleigh and see where we should go with this. I'm sure that mediation will be suggested at the very least."

Louise sipped her iced tea. "What other research do you have in mind?"

Tenant's professionalism slipped a notch as he flashed her what she figured was supposed to be a winning grin. "I'll need to go over these reports again for starters. Are you free for dinner?"

"I've got to eat," Louise said, her feminine instincts on alert. "If you'd like to make it a working meal, I have no objection."

"Great. Is that your apartment over the furniture store where I saw you earlier?"

She indicated it was.

"I'll pick you up at seven. You choose the restaurant."

Louise gathered her papers together. "Fine. Obviously we'll need one with a good source of light."

"IT'S LOVELY OUT HERE," Louise said Saturday evening when she and Vicki sat on the front porch of the houseboat. The women had returned from a shopping trip to Morgan City. Louise had been amazed at how much stuff a baby needed. Now she was enjoying the cool, dry air that drifted off the sound and stirred the flames of citronella torches that kept the insects away. From the living room, a sportscaster's voice droned on about scores of the day's baseball games. Jamie was inside, giving the women the privacy they needed.

Vicki poured tea from a china pot into two cups and slid containers of sugar and milk to her friend. "Now, what's going on with you and Wes?" she asked.

Louise swirled milk into her tea. "It's hard to explain. Wes isn't like anyone I've ever dated."

Vicki responded with a knowing grin. "I thought so. Our handsome commander is getting under your skin."

"I'm not sure. Maybe."

"But you are dating?"

"That's just it. I'm not sure about that, either. We're like two dogs growling across an alley at each other one minute, and sharing the same string of spaghetti the next."

Vicki smiled at the Disney reference. "Except that Wes is no tramp, and most of the time you, my good friend, are no lady."

Louise accepted this honest appraisal from her closest friend without feeling insulted. "That's true, Vic, and it's part of the problem. From the first minute I saw Wes, I was attracted to him. Tall, muscular, with enough earthiness to hold my interest..."

"So what's the problem? He's obviously attracted to you, too."

"Yes, I think he is, reluctantly so. Ordinarily, if this were Fort Lauderdale and if Wes were any other guy, I'd be pursuing him with every feminine weapon I possess. But this is homey little Bayberry Cove, and I have to tread more carefully. Each time I start to, well, get close to him, I get this horrible attack of guilt."

Vicki huffed an incredulous breath. "You, my take-no-prisoners friend, feel guilty?"

"Yes, and it's the pits. I can talk myself out of any kind of guilt most of the time. Except not now. Wes is just too..." The right word failed to come to mind.

"Noble?" Vicki suggested.

"Okay, yes, and..."

"Trustworthy?"

"Yes."

"Uptight?"

Louise laughed. "Definitely that, though maybe not as much as when I first met him. It's just that he's so...good. Every instinct I have screams at me to kiss him, but my conscience butts in and tells me to behave myself." She sighed. "What am I going to do, Vic?"

Vicki put her elbows on the table and gave

her friend an earnest look. "Lulu, I can't believe I'm saying this, since for the last fifteen years you've continually shocked me with your outrageous behavior, but I honestly believe you're analyzing too much. You're letting Wes Fletcher intimidate you, subtly but surely, and the Lulu I know and love wouldn't let that happen. You're who you are, and despite some of the things I've said to you in the past, I've always admired the woman you dare to be. And a lot of men have responded pretty favorably, as well."

Dear Vicki. She could always find the best in any situation. And she was right. Men usually reacted to Louise in positive, flirtatious ways that she normally encouraged. But it was time to clear up a misconception that Vicki had been living with for too long. Louise leaned forward and clasped her hands on the table. "I've got to tell you something, Vic, and I hope it won't burst any bubbles you may have about me."

"There's nothing you can't tell me," Vicki said with a little grin. "Though maybe there are still things that could shock me."

"This probably will. The truth is, Vic, where my exploits with the opposite sex are concerned, I've often talked a bolder game than I've actually played."

Vicki's eyes opened wide with surprise, but Louise sensed it was mostly for show. "You mean you've lied to me?" her friend asked.

"Not lied so much as exaggerated a few times. I decided long ago that when you work in a man's world, it's best to create an aura that makes them think you have the upper hand, both in and out of the workplace. But," she added, "to my knowledge, I've never really hurt anyone. I've always maintained certain ground rules where men were concerned, and I played fair."

That's why this relationship with Wes, whatever it was, had become so disturbing, she thought. Maybe her rules no longer applied. Maybe her attitudes were changing since she'd come to this quirky little town where everyone knew his neighbor's business and really cared about it.

Now it was time to tell Vicki what was really troubling her. "Here's the truth, Vic," she said. "Deep down I know that Wesley Fletcher doesn't really want me. I'm not his type and I never will be."

Vicki jumped to her friend's defense. "That's silly, Lulu. How do you know what Wesley's type is?"

"Because he practically told me so yesterday. He actually questioned me about my domestic skills. What a laugh, huh? He asked if I cooked or quilted or did anything homey."

Vicki sat back in her chair. A look of genuine shock crossed her face. "He didn't!"

"Yeah, he did, the poor guy."

"Well, then, that proves it. Wesley Fletcher doesn't know his type himself. Because, Lulu, I've seen his eyes when he's talked about you, and honey, you're his type."

"But he doesn't want me to be. And even if he did, he knows that anything that might happen between us can only last a few weeks. I'm not staying, remember? I'm going home once I figure I've become the nice person Roger Oppenheimer wants me to be."

A mischievous twinkle lit Vicki's eyes. "Then I'm not worried, because that will never happen. Besides, look at me. I never thought I'd be living in Bayberry Cove." She rubbed her belly. "And living for two."

"And it's fine for you." Louise laughed softly. "But imagine *me* living in Bayberry Cove!"

"Well, what if it works out between you and Wes?" Vicki asked.

"It won't. That's what I've been telling you. I've never been really serious about any man. I live by my own standards, which certainly aren't anything like Wes's. And besides, we're on opposite sides of a legal battle. This is probably not the best time for us to get involved."

"Oh, pooh," Vicki said. "I know you're committed to helping the women at the candle factory, and that's fine. But it's not like you and Wes are arguing Roe versus Wade here. You probably won't even go to court over these issues."

"No, but I'm pretty sure that if it ever came down to serious dating, Wes's ethics would kick in at the last minute and he'd run like the wind. Remember, he is solid, moral, not to mention what you said—uptight."

Vicki reached across the table and covered Louise's hand. "My dear Lulu, Wes Fletcher is forty years old. He's responsible for his own decisions, and if he kissed you again, it would be because he wanted to. I'm sure he's quite capable of bearing the consequences of his actions." She smiled with a coyness Louise hadn't seen before. "Here's what I think, my friend…"

Louise smiled back at this woman who had been her confidante and support for more than a decade. "What *do* you think, Vic?"

"I think it's time to loosen Wes up a bit. The candle factory case won't last forever, anyway. Maybe he needs to learn that it's okay to separate business from pleasure. And who better to teach him than you? My guess is he'll thank you for it."

Jamie came around the corner of the houseboat. "I hear you ladies plotting to snare Wes."

"We're not plotting anything," Vicki said, giving Louise a knowing look her husband couldn't see.

"Don't get me wrong. I'm all for it," Jamie said. "Wes has been running from women since he broke up with Donna. It's time he let one catch him." He jerked his thumb down the side of the houseboat. "You can start chasing right now. He just drove onto Pintail Point."

## CHAPTER TWELVE

As Wes drove up the causeway, he was relieved to see lights still burning in the Malones' houseboat. It was almost ten o'clock, late to be calling on friends even if it was a Saturday night. And too, married people seemed to live by a different clock than single ones.

He pulled his Jeep alongside Jamie's pickup, got out and walked to the boat. Beasley lumbered around from the bow and stood staring at him from the catwalk.

A few feet from the narrow bridge that connected the boat to land, Wes crouched down and whistled softly. "Hey, Beas, how ya' doing?" The dog crossed over and rolled to his back. Wes took the hint and scratched his belly.

Jamie came out to greet him. "Wesley, my lad, what brings you to the *Bucket O' Luck* tonight?"

Wes stood, followed Jamie and Beasley

onto the boat. "I hope it's not too late," he said. "I have a favor to ask."

"Of course it isn't too late. Wait here." Jamie ducked inside the boat and returned with a couple cans of beer. "Let's go on the porch."

Jamie walked ahead to the deck at the bow. Just when Wes rounded the corner, Jamie made the announcement he should have made before there was no turning back. "Vicki and I have company tonight," he said, as if that simple statement weren't designed to rattle Wes to his toes. "I'm sure that's all right with you." He held out a beer.

Wes stood like a statue, the cold can sweating in his hand. Both women stared at him, Vicki with an amused expression on her face and Louise with something near horror on hers. Vicki scooted a chair to the table with the toe of her sneaker. "Hi, Wes. Sit down."

The scowl he leveled on Jamie was wasted. His friend was enjoying this. Still, he showed a modicum of commiseration by handing him the second beer. "Here, I figured you could use both of these," he said under his breath.

Wes set one can on the table and popped the top off the other. Seeing no alternative, he settled into the chair next to Louise.

"Jamie, why don't you see what's in the kitchen," Vicki said. "Are you hungry, Wes?"

"Couldn't eat a thing. I just came from that big Italian restaurant by the interstate. My dad bought one of everything on the menu."

"I'm surprised," Jamie said. "My mother doesn't usually eat Italian food."

Wes frowned. "Kate wasn't there, and I wish to heaven she had been. This separation or whatever it is she's forced on my dad is driving me crazy. He's probably gained ten pounds since Kate quit cooking for him. And I've gained five."

Vicki nodded dramatically. "Isn't it silly how this whole candle factory business is making everyone in town so edgy?" She took a sip of tea. "Pure nonsense if you ask me. Anyone should be able to see that whatever happens at the candle factory shouldn't affect personal relationships."

Wes gaped at Vicki while Louise coughed and seemed to shrink in her chair. Jamie affectionately patted his wife's hand. "Didn't I get me a wise ol' gal here," he said, and then turned his attention to Wes. "Now, then, what's that favor? Assuming you can ask it in front of the ladies."

Grateful that the conversation was now on a safe topic, Wes drew a normal breath. "I need you to check on my aquariums in the shed for a while. I won't ask you to do anything too complicated. Just see that the temperatures remain at a constant level, check a couple of gauges, that type of thing. I'll leave a chart."

Louise sat forward in her chair. "You're going away?"

"For a few days. I've been called to Newport."

"Why?" Jamie asked.

"When I took semi-retirement, one of the conditions was that I'd be available to teach classes in civil law at the Naval Justice School in Rhode Island. One of the regular staff is ill, so they called me in."

Out of the corner of his eye he caught Louise staring at him. "When are you leaving?" she asked.

"Monday. I'll be back next Saturday night."

"Oh." The single syllable was soft, almost childlike.

Wes rolled his can between his hands. "You're not sorry to see me go are you, Counselor?"

She put her confident grin back in place, and he felt a little disappointed. "You know what they say about small towns, Wes. The loss of one person diminishes us all."

"Funny. I've never heard that one." He looked at Jamie. "So, can I count on you?"

"You can indeed." He winked at Vicki. "Remind me to buy extra tartar sauce at the market this week, love. With me watching the gauges, I've a hunch we'll be having fried fish."

Louise stood up. "Now that that's settled, I have to be getting home."

Without thinking, Wes blurted, "Your car's not here." *Idiot! Now she knows you actually looked for it when you drove up.*

"Very observant," Louise said. "Vicki drove tonight. We were in Morgan City doing some shopping." Louise picked up her purse from the deck. "Ready to take me home, Vic?"

Jamie gave Wes a pointed stare. "I won't have you two women driving along Sandy Ridge in the dark. I'll take you myself."

"Don't be ridiculous, Jamie," Louise said. "It's perfectly safe—" She stopped abruptly and frowned down at her friend. Wes had seen the exchange under the glass-topped table. Vicki had just kicked Louise's leg.

Several seconds went by before Wes said the line he supposed had been scripted for him by the Malones. "Never mind, Jamie. I haven't touched my drink and I should be going anyway. I'll take Louise home."

Louise gave them all a look that would have made the most stubborn jurors quake in their boots. "Well, I don't mean to put anyone out."

Jamie jumped up and tugged on the back of Wes's chair. "You're not putting Wes out. Like he said, he's got to go, anyway. Why have two cars out on Sandy Ridge, when one will do quite nicely?"

Wes stood, swept his arm toward the catwalk of the boat. "Okay, then. Miss Duncan?"

He followed her to the Jeep, marveling at how he'd been roped into this. And thinking how much he'd rather be taking her anywhere but home.

LOUISE WAS THANKFUL the top was down on the Jeep. The vast expanse of Carolina night sky gave her plenty of excuses to keep her eyes off the man beside her. She glanced through the front window, then out the side toward Currituck Sound. She laid her head back and pretended to study the stars. Despite the spectacular panorama of nature, it was still difficult to ignore the rugged profile of Wes Fletcher just a couple of feet away.

They drove slowly down the half-mile causeway. "So you and Vicki were shopping," Wes said after a moment.

"For baby things." She focused on the gravel roadway. "Not that I was much help."

He didn't respond. Of course he wouldn't. They certainly couldn't repeat a conversation about her lack of domesticity.

"So what did you do today?" she asked.

"Actually, I did something I haven't done in months. I played golf."

She stared at him then. Yes, she could picture him on a golf course, his long, lean body silhouetted against a background of carpet-soft green grass and moss-draped willow trees. She could visualize the subtle arc of his muscled right arm as he raised the club over his shoulder, the power of his left arm, straight and sure as he drove the ball confidently down the fairway. She almost shivered at the image of athletic perfection.

"I'm really lousy at it," he said. "I never could get the rhythm of the swing."

She burst out laughing as her vision shattered.

He gave her a self-effacing grin. "What's so funny?"

She waited while he braked at the end of the causeway in preparation for the turn onto Sandy Ridge Road. "I guess you should have gone bowling," she said, knowing he would remember their conversation from yesterday.

He thrust the gearshift into first while he gripped the steering wheel with his other hand. His gaze never wavered from her face. "I thought about bowling today. Too much, probably. A guy shouldn't think about bowling when he's trying to smack a golf ball to impress his father's cronies."

She looked down at her clasped hands, away from his penetrating blue eyes. "No, I suppose not."

They sat at the juncture of the Pintail Point causeway and Sandy Ridge Road. The Jeep's engine rumbled patiently, waiting for direction. If Wes turned left, they would be heading toward Buttercup Cottage, and soothing sounds of the sea cloaked in the sweet-scented darkness of isolation. If he turned right, they would go to Main Street of Bayberry Cove, populated with folks feeling the energy of a small-town Saturday night.

She squeezed her hands together until they hurt. *Turn left, Wesley, please turn left.*

He turned right. Okay, so she wasn't telepathic. Maybe Suzie had a candle for that.

Ten minutes later he pulled into a parking place in front of the furniture store. Several doors down, the Kettle bustled with late-night activity. A small group of people came out and strolled by the Jeep. A few of them stared into the vehicle, and then mumbled in reaction to seeing Wesley and Louise together.

"I probably should have pulled around back," Wes said.

"It doesn't bother me," she stated. "But then, I'm not really one of them."

"Lately I've been wondering if I am, either."

"Look, Wes, there's something I should tell you."

He curled his arm over the steering wheel and stared at her. "Louise, every time either one of us starts a sentence that way, it turns out badly."

"I know, but that's not going to stop me."

"I didn't think it would."

"Christopher Tenant. Remember that name. He's the rep from the EEOC...."

"Okay. What about him?"

"He's going to request personnel files from the candle factory records. He's doing an in-depth study on a couple of cases, specifically Bessie Granger's and Darlene Jackson's."

"Then I suppose I should warn my golfing buddies."

"Probably, although this is standard procedure."

"I know that, but the old boys still should be given the chance to stock up on antacids.

Plus I'll have to tell them that a sudden unexplained fire would look a bit suspicious."

"I'm telling you this so you can go in tomorrow and make copies of the files for yourself. You should know what you're up against."

"Well then, thanks for the heads-up, Counselor."

"It's only right, Wes." She unbuckled her seat belt and reached for the door handle. "Thanks for the ride, and you take care of yourself up there in Newport, Commander. Don't let those JAG students leave a toad in your desk drawer."

"You take care in Bayberry Cove, Louise."

She got out and closed the door. Before she walked away, he said, "And don't go bowling without me."

THE NEXT MORNING, Wes walked into his father's office at the Fletcher estate, eyed the imposing man who was just hanging up the telephone, and wished he were anywhere but here. This wasn't going to be easy. "Got a few minutes, Dad?"

Haywood stood up from behind his ornate rosewood desk, placed his hands on his hips and said, "What a coincidence, son. I just happen to have a question for you."

"Oh? What's that?"

The old man glowered at him. "Have you gone crazy, Wesley Fletcher?"

Wes strode across the room and sat in a plush leather chair. "Good morning to you, too, Dad," he said. "And to answer your question, before I took semi-retirement, a naval doctor gave me a psychological examination, and he didn't find anything particularly disturbing."

Haywood pointed an accusing finger at the telephone. "Then he hasn't heard the rumors I've been hearing lately." He came around the desk and stared down at Wes. "You've been cavorting with that lady attorney, haven't you?"

It was all Wes could do to stifle his laughter. Yet when he recalled that magnificent kiss Louise had delivered at his front door last Friday night, and this past Friday when he'd nearly lost his head over her in the cottage kitchen, he decided he probably had been guilty of a little "cavorting." He smiled. But since he wasn't about to admit any of this to his father, he said, "It depends what you mean by cavorting, Dad."

"Dudley Boggs's son Chester was on the shrimp boat Friday morning, and he saw you and a brunette take off from Buttercup into the sound. And then last night, Hatch Winslow's wife was escortin' her grandkids out of the ice-cream parlor in town, and she saw you and Miss Duncan sittin' for all the world to see in front of the furniture store." Haywood's bushy eyebrows came together in a scowl. "What do you have to say to that, Wesley?"

"I'd say that ten-thirty at night is awfully late to have two little kids at the ice-cream parlor." Wes settled one leg over the opposite knee and matched his father frown for frown. "And I'd say that where I was last night is none of your business."

Haywood huffed in frustration. "You're going to ruin us, son. You can't make nice with the woman who's trying to tear down the very fabric of this community."

"Oh, come on, Dad. Where are the dramatics coming from? If you want to look at Louise as the enemy, that's your problem. As I see it, I drove a lady home last night. Big deal. It just so happens that lady is trying to help out the female employees down at the factory. I hardly think that constitutes the total annihilation of everything we consider sacred in Bayberry Cove."

Wes's explanation was amazingly simple, and he surprised himself by believing for a moment that his relationship with Louise could actually be viewed in such an uncomplicated context.

Haywood pounded one fist into his opposite palm. "That's because you don't own one-third of the candle factory. And at this rate you likely never will! Once those women get their way they'll be pushin' for day care centers and birthday parties, and who knows what all."

Wes knew his father was genuinely concerned. While the Bessie Granger and Darlene Jackson cases wouldn't change the course of history, they likely would have a noticeable effect on Bayberry Cove. As far as Wes could remember, there hadn't been any significant change in town for years. Bright red geraniums still bloomed all summer in the town square flower beds, and the same people still worked the same jobs at the candle factory and elsewhere. He'd just never realized that not everyone was happy with the situation.

His father gave him a pleading look. "Tell me you're not getting serious about that woman."

"Relax, Dad. No, I'm not serious about her. And even if I were, she's not the least bit interested in staying in Bayberry Cove. This is just a stopover for her."

Haywood's expression grew even more grim. "That's right. You don't need another gal like Donna who'll put her career above everything else. This one's cut from the same cloth. She's stoppin' by long enough to wreak havoc, and then, like that hurricane last year, she'll breeze off, leavin' the mess for the rest of us to clean up."

*Hurricane Louise.* That was an impression Wes's imagination could grab on to. He'd certainly considered that Louise had the power to leave his life in a mess when she took off. And like a hurricane, she sure created a thrill while she was around.

He was about to tell his father that he hadn't come to talk about his past marital mistakes when Kate scurried by the open door, her bright red hair a blur in her determination to avoid the office. Nevertheless, she'd obviously noticed Wesley, because she reappeared a second later, keeping her hand on the door frame.

"Hi, Kate," Wes said.

"Hello, Wesley. I didn't mean to ignore you. As we all know, I can't abide rudeness in any form."

"Except when you direct it at me," Haywood mumbled.

"What's that, Haywood?" Kate asked.

"Where you off to now, Kate?" he replied, ignoring her question.

"I'm going to Bessie's." She held up a canvas sack. "I went to the store today and picked up a number of movies for us to watch. I'll let Bessie and Pete pick what they want to see."

Haywood snorted in displeasure. "Woman, that beats all. When's the last time you watched a movie with me?"

"I honestly can't remember, Haywood. We've seen all the John Wayne movies." She dangled the sack to irritate him. "There's not a war movie or Western in here."

He waved her off with a flick of his hand. "Then go on and watch your sissy movies. I'll just fend for myself *again*." He gave his son a slap on the back that was apparently meant to seem jovial but practically knocked him out of the chair. "Where do you want to eat tonight, Wes? How 'bout that build-your-own-burger place? They hand you a half pound of raw meat and you cook it yourself."

Wes's stomach did a flip. "Actually, Dad, I thought I'd go back to the—"

"Yessir, the burger place it is," his father

announced with finality. Kate frowned at the two of them and flounced off.

Wes stared up at his father with a look meant to convey his impatience. "Why don't you just ask the woman to marry you? You're obviously miserable without her."

"Am not. I wouldn't ask her now, anyway, not the way she's been acting. She treats me like the flea—"

Wes sighed. "I know. You told me. She's only doing that because she's trying to get through to you. She wants permanence in her life. She's tired of just dating and being your housekeeper—"

"I know what she wants." His father leaned against his desk and released a long sigh. "And I've given her an option in that regard. She knows I'm never going to marry again without having safeguards in place…"

"What kind of safeguards? You can't mean a prenuptial agreement."

Haywood's cheeks flushed with what might have been uncharacteristic embarrassment. "You know my track record of picking the wrong women," he said. "I've lost small fortunes!"

"Dad, Kate's not the wrong woman. I know that and so do you. Just trust her and you won't be sorry." When another thought occurred to

Wes, he added, "Or maybe you're afraid she'll turn you down after all these years."

Haywood scoffed at the notion. "No. She'd grab my hand in marriage quick as a glowworm's twinkle..." he strode to the window and looked out "...despite being the finest piece of Irish frippery ever to come across the Atlantic."

"Then swallow your pride, or whatever it is that's holding you back, and ask her."

Almost as if he'd stopped listening, Haywood's voice became calm, reflective. "That Kate...she's pretty as a shamrock, feisty as a Thoroughbred and beautiful as a siren. And what made her perfect was that she needed me. She was grateful for every little thing I did." He turned back to Wes as the ends of his mustache lifted in a grin.

Haywood paced in front of his desk. "And now, since that lady attorney came to town, Kate's acting like the Queen of Sheba—givin' orders and steppin' out. It puzzles me, Wes. It puzzles me something fierce."

Wes suppressed a grin. "So, she's the queen, and all of a sudden you're something less than king."

Haywood grimaced at the reference. "I suppose."

"You'll figure it out, Dad. You're a smart man."

"I won't figure anything out on an empty stomach. Let's go eat. You drive."

"Wait a minute, Dad. I came here to tell you something."

"Well, out with it."

Wes told him about his upcoming trip to Newport to fill in at the Naval Justice School. Once he'd convinced Haywood that, yes, the navy really could command his presence in spite of the controversy in Bayberry Cove, Wes delivered the next bit of bad news. "There's a man in town," he said. "His name is Christopher Tenant, and he's with the Equal Employment Opportunity Commission in Raleigh."

"And he's trouble."

"Maybe. I don't know. But he is going to request some specific personnel files from the factory. And Justin Beauclaire has to give them to him."

Haywood shook his finger as if it were a metronome. "Justin won't do it. He'll burn the things first. I know how he thinks."

"Well, he'd better not. If I hear that Mr. Tenant encountered so much as a 'No sir' or a 'Can't find them' from anybody at the factory, I'm off the case. And tell Justin not to tamper with anything in those files. I made copies of them today, which I'm taking with me to Newport to study, so I'll know if he changed even a decimal point."

Haywood scowled. "Whose side are you on, Wesley?"

"Not to sound corny, Dad, but I'm on the side of justice. And if I can achieve that and still save the factory's reputation, then I'll have done my job. We're going to have some wiggle room on some issues, but you've got to let me handle it."

"Like you're handling that Duncan woman, I suppose."

"Dad…"

"Okay, okay. Have you met this Tenant fella?"

"No, but he's probably just doing his job, too. Remember, give the guy a break while he's here."

"All right. I'll behave myself. Now, can we eat?"

MERCIFULLY, the restaurant Haywood chose offered a grilled chicken breast sandwich. It was still early when Wes dropped Haywood off at the estate, and he didn't especially want to go back to Buttercup Cottage. His packing was all done. The aquariums had been set up so Jamic could monitor them. If he went home, there was nothing to do but try to find a decent television show among the twelve channels he could pick up with the cottage antenna.

He drove toward town and let an impractical thought take root in the often-ignored part of his brain that resisted logic and common sense. He actually considered stopping by Louise's apartment. But reason prevailed and he avoided making the worst possible decision a lonely guy could make. Instead he pulled into the parking lot of the Brew and Bowl and went inside.

It wasn't crowded on this Sunday evening. Wes spoke to a few Bayberry Cove old-timers and took a seat at the bar. He'd watch a little baseball and head home. Unfortunately, the game didn't keep him from thinking about Louise. He figured she'd have a laugh if she knew he was at the bowling alley thinking about her.

He pushed Louise to the back of his mind and tried to imagine what the EEOC rep, Christopher Tenant, was like. Probably a methodical, middle-aged government geek who was even more compulsive about his habits than Wes himself was.

Nothing at all like the thirty-something

fella in blue jeans and a golf shirt sitting next to him. Wes noticed the man because he was talking on his cell phone, and making no attempt to keep his voice down.

"Don't expect me back in Raleigh anytime soon," he said into the phone. "If you could see this lady attorney who's filing for the workers, you'd understand."

Wes's ears perked up instantly. He glanced at the man's profile and watched a huge grin form on his face.

"Hot? You bet she's hot. Star quality all the way. I can just picture her in one of those bikinis like the models in *Sports Illustrated* wear."

Mr. Subtle glanced over at Wes and kept the grin in place. If he expected a fellow male to appreciate his hormonal tirade, he was going to be disappointed. Wes smirked at him and stared at the television.

Undaunted, the man continued his conversation. "Right now she thinks I'm all-business, but I'm having dinner with her again tomorrow night. If I have my way this time, we'll give the case studies a quick going-over, and spend the rest of the night with a bottle of wine, good music and the pursuit of happiness."

Wes hadn't been tempted to punch anyone's

lights out since his senior year in high school. But his right hand itched to knock a few teeth out of Christopher Tenant's stupid grin. Not that Louise needed his help. She could wipe the floor with a guy like Tenant, just as she'd nearly done that day with Luke Plunkett. But would she want to? That was the question that would bug Wes for the next week.

Going to the bowling alley had turned out to be a bad idea. So had telling his father to cooperate with the jerk the EEOC had sent from the capital. Wes left the bar. Getting away from Bayberry Cove was the best thing he could do right now. And the worst.

## CHAPTER THIRTEEN

LOUISE TURNED ONTO Route 17 North and reached for the handwritten directions lying on her dashboard. "The costume shop is on Lansing Street in Norfolk," she said.

Vicki took the sheet of paper from her hand. "I'll read. You drive." After a few seconds she said, "It's easy. Lansing is just inside the Norfolk city limits."

Louise wiggled in her seat, adjusted the rearview mirror, tugged on her seat belt and fidgeted in general.

"Will you relax?" Vicki said.

"I still can't believe I'm doing this," Louise responded. "And I can't believe that you encouraged me."

"Are you kidding? This is about the best idea you've ever had."

Allowing a hint of pride to influence her response, Louise said, "I suppose it is, and it's not like it's totally out of character...."

Vicki let out a snort of laughter. "I should say it isn't."

Louise tried to appear offended. "I was about to say that it's not *totally* out of character...but playing dress-up is a little crazy—even for me."

"Quit worrying. Wes will love this."

"I hope you're right."

"I am right. Wesley is the kind of guy you need to jolt into motion, and this plan will do that. And remember what I keep telling you, Lulu. Wes is a big boy. He can handle himself and make his own decisions—which means you are wasting good energy worrying that you're somehow trapping him. Trapping implies action that is cunning and calculating. You're romancing him, and that's fun. Big difference. And Wes is a guy. There's no guy alive who wouldn't be totally flattered by what you're going to do. So don't even think about backing out."

"I'm not going to back out," Louise assured her. "Wes Fletcher is driving me crazy, and he's not even here. I can't sleep, because I'm always thinking about him. I can't eat. I've never let a man invade my space like this, and it's only Thursday. He left three days ago, yet it feels like he's been gone forever. And we're not even dating."

Vicki gave her a coy smile. "Not yet, anyway."

"Not ever, and you know it."

"I don't know any such thing, and neither do you. You're both mature adults. You're obviously enormously attracted to each other. But you need to know if you're compatible in every way."

What was happening here? Louise always advised Vicki in matters of the opposite sex. Now the tables were turned. "This from a woman who was married for thirteen years before she ever made love with her husband," Louise said.

Vicki frowned. "No fair! You promised you'd never bring up the marriage-of-convenience issue again. And besides, when I found Jamie after all that time, I knew at once he was worth waiting thirteen years for."

"You get no argument from me on that."

"And you could be just as happy with Wes."

"Not when I'm litigating in Fort Lauderdale and he's collecting fish in Bayberry Cove." Suddenly uncomfortable with the topic, Louise said, "Can't we talk about something else?"

"Sure. How are you going to get into Buttercup Cottage?"

"That's not another topic, Vic, but I'll tell you anyway. Wes hardly ever locks the door, but when he does, he told me he hides the key under a rock by the front steps."

"Okay, so that's solved. Now tell me, how'd everything go with Chris Tenant?"

Louise wasn't too keen on this subject, either, but at least it was a change. "He's a strange guy," she said. "Professionally, I guess everything went well. He requested some files from Justin Beauclaire on Monday, and we met to discuss them over dinner Monday night."

"Again?" Vicki said. "I can tell there's more to this story."

"Right. We ate and came back to my apartment to discuss the particulars of the cases. A few minutes after he arrived at my place, I think he was coming on to me."

Vicki gave her a blasé look. "There aren't too many guys who don't come on to you, Lulu."

"But this particular guy shouldn't have. He's here to perform a government service. And besides, he was much too obvious about it. When he got out of his car and came up the stairs to my place, he had a bottle of wine in each hand."

"What did you do?"

"I thanked him for the wine and put it in a cupboard. And then I offered him a cup of coffee. About an hour later he moved over to the sofa where I was sitting and snaked his arm over the back cushion. I got up to get a glass of water. When I came back, I spread out the papers we were studying on the coffee table and handed him a pencil. Then I sat on the floor."

"The poor guy," Vicki said.

"Poor misguided guy, you mean," Louise said. "I would never prejudice a case by dating the person who decides its outcome. That really would be misconduct."

"So where is Tenant now?"

"He went back to Raleigh. He said he would put together the appropriate charges against the candle factory once he checked his statutes. I just hope that when I poured cold water over his libido, I didn't extinguish his enthusiasm for settling this quickly."

"I hope you did," Vicki said. "If Tenant stalls, that means you might have to stay in Bayberry Cove longer than you anticipated."

"I'm afraid that's not going to happen," Louise said. "I'm going back to Fort Lauderdale in five weeks, assuming Oppenheimer calls me. Tenant knows that. If everything's not wrapped up by then, I'll handle it from my home office."

"But you have to be here for the Fourth

of July. Jamie says Bayberry Cove goes all out for the holiday. There's a parade and banners on the downtown shop windows, and a picnic…."

The flippant remark Louise might have tossed out a few weeks ago never came because she actually agreed with Vicki that an old-fashioned Fourth did sound appealing. "We do celebrate the holiday in Fort Lauderdale, too," she finally said, "even though I've never participated."

"Well, we'll see," Vicki said smugly. "The first step is getting to Norfolk and making our purchase at Sophie's Costume Shop."

LOUISE HADN'T HEARD from Wes all week. But she hadn't expected to. They weren't in a call-me-from-out-of-town relationship. They weren't in any definable relationship at all. But he had phoned Jamie to inform him when he expected to be back in town. He was driving all day Saturday and would arrive about eight o'clock. That schedule gave Louise a lot of time to prepare.

At five o'clock on Saturday she packed a few gourmet goodies into her picnic basket and put the food, her costume and a few decorations into her car. She was about to leave when—on impulse—she entered the furniture store and waited for Suzie McCorkle to finish with a customer.

"Hi, Louise," Suzie said. "You look real nice. Going out tonight?"

*Going out? More like breaking in.* She certainly couldn't tell innocent Suzie what her plans were. It was enough that she was going to shock Wesley in a few hours. "Thanks," she said. "I am going out and that's why I stopped to see you."

"What can I do for you?"

"I thought you might have a candle that's meant to stimulate..." She stopped and stared at Suzie's beatific features. How could she explain to this sweet-natured woman what she wanted this candle to do?

She tried again. "I'm looking for a candle that encourages a man and woman to, well, take their mutual attraction to the next level. What I mean is..."

"Romance!" Suzie clasped her hands under her chin. "You want a romance candle."

Louise tried to conceal her surprise. "Ah... exactly."

"Wait here." Suzie scurried into the back room and returned with an eight-inch pillar candle wrapped in black cellophane and tied with a silver cord. She slipped the knot on the ribbon to expose the top of the candle.

"I don't let just anyone see this color," she whispered. "Not everyone can handle it." She tipped the candle so Louise could see it. "Look for yourself." Suzie breathed deeply, sucking the essence of the candle into her lungs. "Experience the redness."

Louise looked. This candle was no ordinary red. A person would never find this color hanging from an apple tree or painted on a child's wagon. No, this was a color to make the devil jealous. This red dazzled, bewitched, burned the cornea of anyone who dared steal a peek at it. And it smelled of passion. Rich, deep, a smoky, sinful Far Eastern scent that clung to the nose and swirled in the head. Louise gasped in awe. "It's perfect."

Suzie leaned in close and giggled. "And it works, believe me. I light one every year on New Year's Eve. Evan and I have never failed to ring in the holiday with a few fireworks of our own." She retied the cord and slipped the candle into Louise's purse.

"Suzie, you're making a candle convert out of me," Louise said.

"Not me, dear, the candles make their own magic. Have fun."

LOUISE CALLED VICKI on her cell phone when she passed by the causeway to Pintail Point. "I'm almost there," she said.

"On my way," Vicki responded. She met Louise at the front door of Buttercup Cottage ten minutes later.

"Where'd you park your car?" Vicki asked.

"I left it on the side of the road just around that curve," Louise explained. "Is Jamie ready?"

"Yep. He's going to call Wes in a little while to determine his true ETA. He took the letters from Wes's mailbox and is going to pretend he did it by mistake and Wes should stop by the houseboat and get the mail before coming home. Then, as soon as Wes leaves the *Bucket,* Jamie will call us, and I'll get outta here. The rest is up to you."

Louise found the rock, retrieved the key, and the two women went inside. Vicki looked around at the furnishings. "Boy, this guy *is* a neat freak."

For the next two hours Louise and Vicki turned Wes's compact, clean little world into a scene of romance. They hung nets from the ceiling and decorated them with crab trap buoys and colorful plastic sea creatures from the party store. They replaced Wes's hundred-watt bulbs with softer ones and hung wispy blue scarves over the lamp shades. They plugged in the iPod player and played an album of soothing ocean sounds. And last, they displayed Louise's snacks on silver trays.

At seven-thirty Louise took her costume from its plastic bag and laid it on the bed. She surveyed the room and smiled. "It looks good, Vic. I'm starting to believe I won't regret the two hundred bucks I spent for this outfit." She wiggled into the tight bottom and tied the halter top. She draped her throat with a shimmering mother-of-pearl shell necklace and attached silver seahorses to her ears. She was trying different positions on the couch when Vicki's cell phone rang.

"He's on his way," she said. "I'm gone." Vicki picked up her purse and rushed to the exit. Before she crossed the threshold, she turned to admire their efforts one last time. "It's perfect, Lulu, and you look like dynamite."

"Wait!" Louise hollered as Vicki started to leave. "The candle. We forgot it."

Vicki came back and lit the wick. "Now then, remember what I told you. Just be yourself."

They both stared at the sparkling scales that slithered down Louise's legs and the large, fan-shaped fins that covered her feet and draped across the foot of the bed. "Be myself?" Louise repeated, and they both burst into a fit of laughter.

After Vicki left, Louise decided that romance could indeed be fun—unless this woman totally misread her target.

WES TURNED OFF the causeway from Pintail Point and headed toward Buttercup Cottage. *That was the strangest meeting with Jamie just now,* he thought, glancing at the stack of envelopes beside him. *What was so important in this batch of ads and bills that couldn't wait until tomorrow?*

"People are just funny I guess," he said aloud, and rolled his shoulders to relieve the stress of driving for hours. He was halfway to the cottage when he noticed the headlights of another car. He glanced at the driver as they passed each other. Even in the darkness he recognized Vicki Malone. What was she doing driving on Sandy Ridge at this hour?

Of course, seeing Vicki reminded him of Louise. Not that he needed any outside stimulation to bring her to mind. He'd been thinking of her for weeks, and never more so than these last six days while he'd been out of town. He'd gone over the chance encounter with the EEOC rep in his mind dozens of times and always with an unsatisfactory conclusion. Louise and Christopher Tenant had had dinner together on Monday night. But was that all they'd done together? Had Tenant been successful in his attempts to hit on Louise?

Wes's hands tightened on the steering wheel. All right, so he had no claim on Louise, but surely she wouldn't, she *couldn't* succumb to the sleazy play of a guy like Tenant.

But what if she had?

Wes turned into the driveway of Buttercup Cottage, parked around back and lifted his suitcase from the rear seat. He hadn't bothered to change after leaving his class records with his commanding officer this morning, and after the long drive, his dress whites needed a good pressing. He'd drop them off at the cleaners on Monday. Even if he didn't need them again for a while, he liked knowing his uniform was ready to wear at all times.

"You can take the boy out of the military," he said as he opened the back door of the cottage, "but you can't take the military…"

He stopped just inside the door. What was that sound? It was lyrical, like muted chimes in a gentle breeze. And waves, swishing and receding in soothing repetition. But it wasn't coming from outside. It was coming from his... No. It couldn't be coming from his living room.

He dropped his suitcase on the kitchen floor. As he approached the living room, he noticed a soft aqua glow. And an unusual smell. It reminded him of the market in Marakesh. He hadn't thought of that exotic place in years.

"What the...?" he said aloud. Having no idea what to expect, he slowly walked forward. Part of him tingled with the prospect of getting to the bottom of the strange stimuli assaulting his senses. Another part shuddered with the thought that he should return to the kitchen for a knife in case he needed to defend himself against an intruder.

He stood on the threshold, his legs spread wide, his hands clenched at his sides, and stared into the darkened room lit only by a blue glow shimmering under silken scarves. His mind absorbed many details at once. Nets hanging from his ceiling. Starfish, glass balls, sea life dancing along his walls. And those chimes. Delicate, seductive. And that scent. Cloying, mysterious.

And that intruder!

The woman who had haunted him for the past six days leaned slightly forward from pillows piled against his couch. Her long black hair spilled over one shoulder and curled at the top of a bodice-type thing that was covered in seashells. And her legs…whatever she was wearing covered all of her gorgeous legs in glittering sequined splendor that hugged her hips and molded to her calves like a second skin.

He took a step closer, half expecting the strange, alluring image to fade. It didn't. In fact the very real vision moved again, gliding with grace and elegance.

"Louise?" he whispered hoarsely. The word was nearly lost in the elusive melody of tinkling chimes.

She smiled. "Welcome home, sailor."

She shifted, and the strangest sight stole his breath. Her feet—no, her *fins* lifted from the couch and fluttered in a brazen salute. "I'll bet you've never caught anything like me before," she said.

He was rooted to that spot. His eyes took in all of her while his feet refused to lead him closer. She was perfection. She was glorious. His mind careened in so many directions he didn't quite know what to do next. "Wow," he said. "You're a mermaid."

"And you're a commander in the U.S. Navy." Her lips curled in a smile.

She placed her fists on her waist, just above the hip-hugging band of her costume. Her eyes narrowed, became serious. "Wesley, this isn't that hard to figure out."

He nodded his head. "I get the idea."

"Well, good. For a minute I thought you were considering taking me to a laboratory for blood and organ testing."

He smiled. Finally. "No, ma'am, Miss Mermaid. I assure you. I don't have any interest in taking you from that spot right there to any other place on earth."

She patted the couch. "Then come on over and test the water."

He'd never in his wildest dreams expected to be this lucky. Other guys were lucky. Wesley Fletcher sometimes found himself in favorable situations. But never in his life had he been this out-and-out lucky to be in his skin at this place for this wild, wonderful moment of time.

He hardly recognized his own voice when he said, "Louise, how did you—"

"Don't ask for explanations, Wes," she said. "I learned today that sometimes you just have to accept the magic."

His arms came down and encircled her and he pulled her close. He held the back of her head and kissed her. It was magic.

LOUISE MUNCHED ON A CRACKER mounded with crab dip. Never in her life had she felt so utterly peaceful—both with the company and those kisses. Of course, she didn't know if Wes felt the same. He wasn't the type of man who'd talk about his grocery list, much less about kissing. But she knew he'd enjoyed himself.

She turned, offered him a bite of cracker, and decided to risk prying the truth out of him. "So, Commander, what are you thinking?"

He smiled down at her. "If you have to ask, Louise, then I guess everybody's been right all these years, and I truly need to work on expressing my emotions."

"No, no. You expressed them very well. But I was a little worried that you might have some regrets. Vicki called our plan a lesson in separating business and pleasure." When she noticed a strange twinkle in his eye, she added, "I guess you figured out that Vicki and Jamie were somewhat involved in what went on here tonight."

"Oh, yeah, I figured that out."

"Anyway, I have no problem in accepting the difference. I think it's entirely possible to have two independent lives, the public, business one and the private, pleasure one. But I'm not so sure you agree."

"I'll admit I had my doubts. Maybe I still do to a degree. It's hard to accept ethically that we can be on opposite sides of a legal debate and still…" He stopped, blew out a breath.

"Date?" she suggested, filling in for him.

"Yeah."

"Wes, I'm ninety-nine percent certain that this case will be settled by an impartial third party. If I thought that you and I would have to face each other across an actual courtroom, I'd be a bit cautious about our relationship myself."

She ran a fingertip down his chest. "Wesley, we're both lawyers. I'm a good one, and I assume you are as well. So when I speak for the women at the candle factory, I'm going to do the best job I can. And I expect you to do the same for the men you're representing." She picked up his hand and kissed his palm. "I'd be terribly disappointed if you didn't."

She nestled closer to him and felt his heart beat. "While this case is being settled, we're both going to do our jobs. But when we're together like this, I plan to be the best girlfriend I can. And I'll be terribly disappointed if you don't do the same."

He tightened his arm around her. "You present a convincing argument, Counselor. But I wonder how this scenario will play out in Bayberry Cove."

It was understandable that he would be

concerned about gossip and small-town attitudes. This was where he grew up. These people looked up to him, supported him, cared about him. She was beginning to understand how citizens of small towns felt. And it was nice.

"What we do in this room, Wesley, will be witnessed only by an audience of two," she said. "And I won't ever tell, though I may have a hard time explaining the glow that will be part of my aura from now on." She leaned up and kissed him.

"But where do we go from here, Louise?"

That was the question that had no answer... at least not yet. Louise still intended to return to her life in Florida, and she knew Wesley wouldn't give up his research for the NOAA's Fisheries Service. But in the last hour she had begun to wonder about the frequency of flights to North Carolina.

"No answer to that one?" he said.

"I should go."

He stood up. "Can I see you tomorrow?"

She smiled and said, "How soon?"

AT EIGHT O'CLOCK Sunday morning Louise let herself into Buttercup Cottage with two cups of coffee. Wes sniffed the air as he came to greet her. "You're early," he said, taking a steaming mug from her. "I didn't even hear the car."

She handed him a coffee. "It's a curse. It comes from being raised by two obstetricians who've never kept normal hours."

She reached for her purse and withdrew her cell phone. "I'd better check my messages. I just realized I forgot to turn on my phone on the way home last night." She turned on the power and recognized the persistent beep indicating someone had tried to reach her. She scrolled through the list of missed phone calls recorded on the small screen and frowned.

Wes leaned toward her. "Something wrong?"

"I don't know. Probably not, but I have four messages from women in town. Two are from Darlene. One is from Kate. And the other is from the Bayberry Cove Kettle, so I assume that's Bobbi Lee."

His eyes widened with amusement. "You have the Kettle's number programmed into your cell phone?"

She shrugged. "What can I say? A girl's got to eat."

She listened to the first message. Kate Malone's voice was urgent, almost desperate.

*"Louise, dear, I'm trying to find you. It's midnight on Saturday. I'm at County Hospital.*

*Pete Granger has taken a bad turn. They don't expect him to come out of this. Can you come?"*

The other three messages were similar in content. Louise jammed her phone into her purse. She saw the concern on Wes's face.

"Is there something I can do?" he asked.

"It's Bessie Granger's husband, Pete. He's..." She paused, as if time would alter the facts. "He's dying. I'm going to the hospital."

Wes set his cup down. "I'll drive you."

"No you won't. I appreciate the offer. Really I do. But this concerns our public lives, Wes. It's eight o'clock on Sunday morning. Why would you be driving me to the hospital?" To soften her tone, she padded to the bed and kissed him. "It's time to shut the curtains, Commander. Remember?"

He didn't argue. "I hope Bessie's okay."

"I'll call you," she said. "And all that mermaid stuff I left here last night..." She threw him a smile over her shoulder as she walked to the front door. "You can keep it here. I don't think I'll be wearing it anyplace else."

## CHAPTER FOURTEEN

LOUISE TOOK THE EXIT off the interstate that led to County Hospital. Despite the serious circumstances of this journey, she was experiencing a strange sense of satisfaction that had nothing to do with the evening she'd just spent with Wesley, although that had been truly fantastic. This odd contentment, or whatever it was, began right after she'd checked her messages, spoke to Kate and realized that these women thought enough of her to include her in the tragedy unfolding in one of their lives.

For well over a decade, Louise had had only one true friend in her life: Vicki Malone. She knew many other women, of course, ones in the South Florida business community, saleswomen who appreciated her patronage, female members of her health club. But she'd never been part of a family of women who cared for and looked out for each other. Since coming to Bayberry Cove, she felt as if she belonged to a kind of sisterhood.

She arrived at the hospital and found the intensive care waiting room. Kate and Darlene met her at the door. Their faces were drawn, their eyes tired, their clothes wrinkled. They embraced Louise.

"Is there any news?" she asked. "How's Bessie?"

"She's in with Pete," Kate explained. "The doctors can't do any more for him. They've just made him comfortable, but it's as if his system just shut down. They're calling it congestive heart failure, but I think Pete's just tired of trying."

"Can I do anything for the two of you? Get coffee?"

Kate smiled. "We've had enough of that to float a shrimp boat. Just sit with us awhile." She took Louise's arm to escort her to a chair, but stopped when Haywood Fletcher burst into the room.

Concern was etched on his features as he walked up to her. "Katie, what's wrong? I got up this morning to find a note that you'd gone to the hospital. I checked the names of every patient when I came in here to determine why you'd come. Thankfully your name wasn't among them." After finding her in good health, he scowled at her, but his eyes were still shadowed with worry and relief. "You could have been more explicit to keep me from blowing my cork, you know."

"I'm sorry, Haywood. I guess I wasn't thinking. When Bessie called, I just scribbled a few words and ran out. I didn't realize how the note would sound."

"You took about ten years off my life, woman," he said, and moved as if he might take her in his arms until he realized they weren't alone. "Miss Duncan, what are you doing here?"

"Same as you, Mr. Fletcher," Louise said, and then couldn't resist a little jibe. "When a member of the community, and its largest business, is in need, we all want to lend support."

"Well, you can go. I'm here now, and I'm capable of providing the support these people need in this time of trial—"

Kate administered a jab to his ribs. "Leave off, Haywood. Now's not the time for preaching. Now's the time for praying."

He clamped his lips shut, but seemed about to speak again when Bessie Granger came out of her husband's room. Everyone stood silently as she moved toward them. In answer to the unspoken question, she nodded her head once. "It was a peaceful passing."

Kate hugged her. "Pete's with the angels now, love."

Louise told her how sorry she was.

Haywood mumbled a message of sympathy.

And Darlene marched right up to him and spewed all the frustration and anger of a tense situation and a sleepless night right in his face. "You didn't even know him, did you?" she challenged.

Haywood blustered, cleared his throat. "I knew who he was. A fine man—"

"Stuff it, Mr. Fletcher," Darlene said. "*And* your thirty percent of the candle factory. Don't think you can march in here while poor Bessie's grieving and make a few empty comments about the man Pete was. He would still be alive if Bessie'd had health coverage. If she'd been home with him more. If Justin Beauclaire had allowed her more personal time…."

Louise reached for the young woman's hand. "Darlene, don't—"

Bessie waved Louise back and put her arm around Darlene's shoulder. "Shush, now, honey," she said. "None of that's true. Pete had the medical help he needed, and I was there for him during those times when he got real bad." She ran her hand over the girl's short blond hair. "Pete was just real sick. You know that. The factory's not to blame. Pete's time was up."

Darlene broke into tears. "But what are we fighting for? We're trying to make things better...."

"For the living, Darlene. For the future and women like you." She looked at Louise. "And we will, won't we, Louise?"

"We're sure going to try," she vowed.

Bessie grasped Darlene's shoulders and stared into her eyes. "You're exhausted. All of us are. I want you to go home and get some rest. Everything's going to be all right. We'll go ahead with our plans, just like we talked. And, honey, if you really want to do something for me, you stay away from Luke Plunkett, you hear?"

Darlene's sobs subsided and she nodded her head. "Okay. I am pretty tired." She turned around and glared at Haywood. "But don't expect me to apologize to that—"

"No, no, darlin'," Kate said. "Nobody's expecting you to do any apologizing." She kissed Darlene's cheek while gesturing behind her back for Haywood to leave.

He stalled a few seconds and looked as if he might actually try to say something. But to his credit, he backed toward the door, turned and left. A few minutes later, Darlene followed.

Kate, Bessie and Louise sat in the waiting room and discussed plans for Pete's funeral. When they'd come up with a preliminary schedule, Bessie thanked them and rose from her chair. "I'm going home myself," she said. "There's much to be done. And Louise, you might have heard what I said to Darlene. We've come up with a plan, and we need to talk to you about it." She sighed with fatigue. "But not today."

She left, and Louise studied Kate's closed expression. "Do you know what Bessie's talking about?" she asked.

"I might have an inkling," the Irishwoman answered smartly. "You probably should call a meeting of the candle factory workers again in a few days, but I'll tell you this much. The folks in Bayberry Cove, especially those boys down at the factory, are going to know that the women who make the candles are a strong and clever lot."

Louise studied the resolution in her features. "Tell me something, Kate," she said. "Why are you so involved in this? You've lived in Bayberry Cove for five years, most of it in the Fletcher mansion. It's no secret that Haywood and I are at swords' points most of the time, but you and he are apparently a good match.

Why would you risk your relationship with him to stand with the factory workers?"

Kate took a deep breath. "Don't get me wrong, Louise. I do love that ornery man. And you're right. My life here has been pretty good. But for all I mean to Haywood, I've always been just on the fringe of his life, as if I'm forever standing at a door he won't open all the way."

Louise understood. "The door to matrimony, you mean?"

Kate nodded. "I've been Haywood's girlfriend and housekeeper for years now, and I thought I had to accept that I'd probably never be his wife. Then you came along and opened my eyes to the possibility of women getting what they want and deserve. Now I'm not so sure I'm willing to settle for Haywood's terms."

Louise wasn't at all certain she wanted to take the credit, or the blame, for Kate's revelation.

"I see myself in the women at the factory," Kate continued. "We want what we've been denied. Our goals may differ, but our will is the same, and we mean to be heard." She smiled. "And you know? For the first time, I think Haywood may actually be ready to listen."

"I hope so, Kate. I hope you get what you want."

Kate patted her hand. "Now, then, let's you and I get out of this hospital. We can't do anything more for Pete, and like Bessie said, there's much to be done elsewhere. Oh, by the way, Wesley was supposed to be home yesterday. In all this sadness, I forgot to check if he made it back from Newport. Have you seen him?"

Louise looked for some sign of duplicity in Kate's expression, some evidence that she was fishing for information she already suspected. Finding none, she said, "Jamie's seen him, I believe."

"Fine. Wes is a grown man, but I still worry."

The two women walked out of the waiting room. When they reached the hospital exit, Louise stopped Kate. "Whatever the ladies are planning, Kate, is it legal?"

"I never heard of a law against it. And even if there were, I wouldn't want to be the sheriff who tried to arrest any of us."

THE TOWN TOOK SEVERAL days to grieve for Pete Granger. At Bessie's tidy little bungalow, the dining room table overflowed with casseroles and baked goods. The garage refrigerator was pressed into service to keep cold dishes from spoiling. Included was the pasta salad Louise prepared with her own two hands and a *Good Housekeeping* recipe.

The funeral was held on Wednesday, four days after Pete's death. More than one hundred people attended, an impressive number to show respect for a man whose life had been decent and good, if not remarkable. Haywood and Wesley came, the only representatives from the so-called upper echelon of the candle factory. Despite tensions between factory workers and executives, Bessie's friends accepted the Fletchers' presence with good grace.

"What did you expect, Wes, a public flogging?" Louise teased later that night when she was nestled in his arms on her sofa. "People tend to behave themselves in the presence of ministers, coffins and a couple dozen gigantic floral displays." She traced a nail down Wes's forearm. "Don't be lulled into a false sense of security, though. I don't think you or your father will be invited to any cookouts with my friends."

"No, I suppose not. By the way, on Monday Justin Beauclaire received notification of charges filed by the women workers concerning violations of EEOC laws. As I'm sure you know, the charges involve the Equal Pay Act and the Age Discrimination Act. I'm anticipating Christopher Tenant's next step in the filing process."

"You'd better warn Justin about what is to come," Louise said. "Chris already reviewed employee records, but he may request interviews with the head of Human Resources and Beauclaire himself. And he'll likely visit the factory and talk to people there."

"You should know, Louise, that I filed papers requesting that the charges be dismissed."

"I expected you would. It's what a competent lawyer should do." She shifted in his arms and looked into his eyes. "You don't think that's going to happen, do you?"

"No, I don't, but I've got to earn this big salary Dad and the guys are paying me."

She smiled. "I guess our salaries are about equal on this case." Then, more seriously, she said, "This will likely go to mediation, Wes. I hope you can convince your clients to consider that as a way of bringing the issues to a close. As we discussed before, neither one of us wants to see this go to court."

"I'm all for mediation, Counselor, but if you're expecting us to give in on every issue without a fight, I have to tell you a lot depends on what you ladies throw at us. Are there going to be any curve balls?"

"Truly I don't know what my clients have in mind, but they've asked me to call another meeting, so you can anticipate something in the near future. But either way, this will soon be over."

"I look forward to that." He kissed the top of her head. "But in the meantime, I left my Jeep parked behind the ice cream shop. Do you think anyone will notice it and wonder where I am?"

"They'll just think you've popped into town for a triple fudge sundae."

"Then they'll be wrong." He turned her to face him and captured her mouth with his. "I've popped in for something much sweeter than that."

THE SECOND MEETING of the Bayberry Cove Women's Movement for Employment Opportunities began at nine o'clock Saturday morning in Louise's apartment, with thirty-two women in attendance. She began the session by explaining the steps that had taken place so far. "The initial facts I presented to Mr. Tenant from the Equal Employment Opportunity Commission appear to support violations of the law," Louise said. "From this point on, the investigation will proceed according to the schedule of the EEOC rep."

One middle-aged woman who was attending for the first time stood up. "When do we go to court?"

"We don't really want to go to court," Louise replied. "And we shouldn't have to. But you should know that Wesley Fletcher has asked that the charges be dismissed—"

A hoot of indignation rose in a chorus of women's voices.

"Wait a minute," Louise urged. "That won't happen. His request is merely a matter of form. And he knows that the commission has already assigned an investigator to our cases."

The woman plopped her fists on her hips and scanned the crowd with a stern eye. "I want to go to court. Nothing can happen unless we get a judge on our side."

"Sit down, Goldie," Bessie said. "Let our attorney speak."

Louise continued. "The only way this will go to court is if conciliation efforts conducted by the EEOC are ignored by factory officials. That isn't likely to happen. When an EEOC representative becomes involved, mediation is almost always successful."

"So all we're going to do is talk?" the woman asked.

"What did you want to do, shoot everybody?" Bessie said.

Darlene raised her hand. "I have a question."

Grateful to be discontinuing the court discussion, Louise gave her the floor. "Okay, Darlene."

"I understand that we want the company to answer to the age discrimination and equal pay charges...."

"Right."

"But can we ask for more?"

Louise considered the question carefully. She hadn't intended to involve herself in other issues, although she did understand that health and child care concerns were important in this community of growing families. "Any employee can petition an employer for *anything*," she finally said. "You can ask the administration of the candle factory to consider any suggestions, but unless there is a specific statute governing the request, the company is not required to provide it."

Darlene reached down and withdrew some papers from a canvas sack on the floor. She stood up, thrust her shoulders back and began speaking again. "I went to the library last week and did some research on the computer."

"What did you find?" Louise asked.

"I looked up the top ten companies in this

country who treat their female employees with the most consideration."

Several ladies nodded in approval of Darlene's innovative step.

"Some companies offer child-care facilities right there where the mothers work. Some even offer in-home care when it's needed."

A few women chuckled. One said, "Can you imagine Justin comin' to the house to baby-sit?"

"Some offer paid leave to new mothers, and—" she looked at Miranda Lopez "—none of them make a pregnant woman give up her job when she's in her last trimester." She flipped through her pages of notes. "One company has programs for women so they can learn new skills and advance themselves. And another one gives college scholarships to employees' children."

The woman who was eager for a court battle spoke again. "We should get some of those things." A few backed her up with encouraging comments.

"Ladies, please," Louise said. "Darlene is telling you about the top ten companies in the nation with regard to women's employment opportunities. Naturally they are going to have stellar programs, but the fact is, most companies do not." She looked around the room, capturing each woman's attention. "You can't expect the executives at the candle company to give in to demands that only the top companies in the nation subscribe to.

"And remember, until a few weeks ago, you were working under conditions that clearly violated basic government standards. We will do well to correct the most blatant violations we picked as examples without trying to change the entire structure of company operations."

Darlene dropped her papers to her side. "You mean we can't get any of this stuff?"

Louise sighed. "As I said, you can ask for anything, but you won't…" She stopped. *Wait a minute. What is mediation for, anyway? It's a give-and-take process.* "I have an idea," she said. "Which of these issues do you think is most important to you?"

After considerable debate, it was decided that health coverage and child care were most vital to the majority of women at the candle factory.

"Okay, those aren't covered by the Equal Employment Opportunities Commission, but let's try for them," Louise said. "How do you plan to make your wishes known? Will one of you appoint yourself spokesperson and meet with Justin Beauclaire?"

The women exchanged puzzled glances around the room. It seemed no one wanted to take on the responsibility of arguing their case. "We thought you would, Louise," one lady suggested.

"I've agreed to follow the mediation process with regard to Bessie's and Darlene's age and pay discrimination charges. I can't represent you on issues not covered by the EEOC. So any requests for further benefits should first come from you all. You're the ones with small children and medical bills, and I don't see anything wrong with asking the company to consider these needs."

"She's right," Bessie said. "And we've got a plan that will catch their attention."

Louise looked to the corner of the room where Kate Malone sat with a cool smile on her face. She slowly nodded her head, warning Louise that she was finally about to discover what this mystery plan was all about.

"You're absolutely right, Louise," Darlene said. "It's up to us to get those boys down at the factory to listen to us, and we know the way to do it." She grinned. "We think Wednesday night just after dark ought to be a good time…."

HAYWOOD WALKED TO the sink and ran hot water into a steaming pot. Then he added a few drops of detergent, hoping to loosen the scalded milk stuck to the bottom. "Argh! I never knew a stove was so hard to operate. Medium ought to mean 'medium,' not 'boil over.'"

He took the glass of milk he'd salvaged and walked toward the den. Maybe he could find a good book that would take his mind off the fact that it was nearly midnight on Saturday night, and he had no idea where Kate was. He knew Louise Duncan had called a meeting of her ladies' brigade this morning, and he figured Kate had probably attended. He'd been waiting all day to give her a piece of his mind. A man could take only so much, and Kate had driven him over the edge. He was going to lay down some ground rules and get his life back in order, or else…if only she'd come home.

He entered the dark den and turned on the lamp sitting on the desk Kate used to pay bills and write letters. How many nights he'd sat close to her in this room while she composed page after page to her two boys, who'd been in prison in Ireland for more than a decade. She never gave up on those two, always planning for the time they'd get paroled and come to America. He didn't have the heart to tell her that any militant Irishman who'd been imprisoned for setting bombs and blowing up businesses loyal to British rule wasn't ever going to be given a visa to enter the United States.

He smiled now as he perused the books lining the den walls. "Never underestimate Katie," he chuckled to himself. "She's got enough old-fashioned grit to take on the entire immigration service and get those boys over here, after all."

He turned away from the bookshelf to settle into his favorite chair with a copy of *Ivanhoe* in his hands. Instead he found himself staring into soft hazel eyes that looked up at him from a face sad with weeping. "Kate! I didn't know you were home," he said.

She wiped a tissue under her eyes. "I've been here awhile," she said. "I was thinking about my lads, just as you were now, about the way their paths ended up. Thankfully Jamie never got caught up in their rebellion. They never hurt anyone, you know that, don't you, Haywood?"

"You've told me, Kate."

"They destroyed property, and that was wrong. They were angry boys with fire in their hearts. But everything they did was for a cause they believed in." She shook her head.

"Believing in causes can sometimes break a heart."

Haywood set his milk and book on an end table and sat in an uncomfortable straight-backed chair close to the one she occupied by the cold fireplace. "What is it you want, Katie?"

"I want to see my sons again."

"I'll send you to Ireland then. Whenever you want to go."

"That's not all, Haywood. I want you to ask me to marry you and go with me as my husband."

He squeezed his eyes shut, not daring to look at her. "Ah, Kate, you know how I feel...."

"Yes, and you know how I feel."

"You've told me before, woman. And we've always disagreed. I'm not going to marry again without a prenuptial agreement. Four mistakes is enough for any man...."

She sat straight and faced him squarely. "So, that's how you see me, Haywood? As another mistake?"

"I don't know, Kate. It wasn't how I saw the others until it was too late. Until I'd lost—"

"Back to your money again, is it?"

"Kate, be reasonable. We've both been down the rocky road of marriage."

"If you're referring to what I had with Frank Malone, you're wrong. It wasn't marriage. It was bondage. I never had the real thing with Frank—the trust, the pledge of faith, the true meaning of words spoken at an altar."

Her eyes pleaded with him so much he could barely look at her. "I want it now, Haywood, without your fancy legal document meant to destroy the union of a man and wife. I want your pledge to me, and mine to you, in the eyes of God, to be all we ever need. And I want it before I'm too old and gray... and bitter."

He reached for her hand. She let him hold it, but her fingers were limp, unresponsive. He couldn't really blame her, but he'd had four wives, and all of them had stripped him of his pride and half his bank account. He thought he'd done it right with Kate. He'd kept his assets while being generous to her. "I never meant to hurt you, Kate," he said. "But you know I won't marry you unless it's on my terms. Ask me anything else." He smiled at her, squeezed her hand. "Ask me for the moon, Katie, and I'll deliver it on a sterling platter at your feet."

"I have no use for the moon, Haywood." She stared into his eyes with an intensity he found almost too much to bear. "I don't want your money. You can keep every cent of it. And I won't sign a paper saying our marriage is based on mistrust. I only want your name and your word, spoken in front of our friends and family, that you believe my pledge to you is true."

"But you have my love, Kate. It has to be enough."

"Not anymore, dear." Her gaze wandered to the window, which looked out over the front drive and from there to Bayberry Cove. "I want what they have out there."

"Who, Kate? What who has?"

"The people who live in Bayberry Cove, in little houses with platters made of crockery, not sterling. They're women with husbands who've not signed a thing but a marriage license." She turned to look at him again. "I want to be like them."

His world had been so perfect. He'd been in charge of it, and Kate had let him rule. If she'd been unhappy—and he supposed she had been sometimes—she'd mostly kept it to herself. She'd brought up the marriage issue a time or two, and he'd thought they'd discussed it logically. She'd always dropped the subject when he wouldn't budge. Until now. Until this lady attorney had come to town and upset his perfect world. He supposed that Louise

Duncan was going to have her way about some things. But not this.

He stood up. "I'm sorry, Kate. I want you to stay here with me, but on my terms. They're the same terms you've lived with for five years. And I'm the same man."

Her lips trembled, then curved upward. It was a sad, accepting kind of smile. "Yes, Haywood, you are. I'm going to bed now."

He didn't find out until the next morning that she'd moved in with Bessie Granger.

## CHAPTER FIFTEEN

WES SAT AT A TABLE by a window in the Bayberry Cove Kettle and scowled down at his plate of cottage cheese, pineapple, and green salad. He should have ordered the Philly cheesesteak. That's what he really wanted, not this rabbit food. And then he thought of his expanding waistline and resigned himself to doing the right thing.

He scooped a mound of lumpy cheese onto a fork, looked out the window and spied a familiar face. At least he wouldn't have to consume this miserable lunch alone. He rapped on the glass, catching Jamie Malone's attention. Jamie smiled and headed for the restaurant entrance.

"What's up?" he said as he plunked himself down in the chair on the other side of Wes's table. "What are you eating?"

"No comment. Have you had lunch?"

"Nope."

"Then order something wonderful that I can at least smell," Wes insisted.

Jamie called Bobbi Lee over. "What's good today, Bobbi?" he asked.

"Same as every Wednesday, Jamie, as if you didn't have the menu memorized. Corned beef hash, and Max is piling it on pretty thick today."

"Okay, I'll have that. And a Mountain Dew."

Bobbi wrote the order on her pad and then curled her hand over one well-rounded hip. "So, you boys gonna be around tonight right about dark?"

"Hadn't planned to be," Jamie said. "But you're not the first female who's hinted that there's something going on in town tonight. You want to provide more details?"

Bobbi arched her penciled brows. "Nope. Don't care to at all. But I think you should be here, and spread the word, too." She gave a pointed look at Wes. "And since I've gotten over being mad at you, I'll advise you specifically to be here."

Wes waited until she had left before he said, "You know what's going on?"

"Haven't a clue."

"Where did the girls go this morning?"

"I don't know that, either." Jamie set his chin on his fist and glanced out the window. "Wherever two women go to spend money when one of them is pregnant and the other one is chasing a man." He dropped his hand and gave Wes a guilty half grin. "About that chasing thing, I hope you're not steamed over the part I played in that little stunt a week ago Saturday."

Wes laughed. "I have to admit you confused me when you pilfered my mail, and I was a little concerned when I walked into the cottage and realized I wasn't the only one there."

Jamie chuckled. "I'll bet you weren't half as scared as when you recognized exactly *who* had broken in. A burglar is easier to handle than Louise when she's on a mission."

Wes purposely picked at his food and pretended nonchalance. "I handled her just fine," he said. "I've even left the net and all those plastic starfish hanging on the bedroom wall to remind me of Lulu's Big Adventure."

Bobbi brought a platter of corned beef and set it in front of Jamie. He dug in with all the gusto Wes lacked.

"So where do you and Louise go from here?" Jamie asked between bites. "It must be hard to meet in secret so folks in town won't know what's going on."

"It's tough, but I've come to terms with it. We're taking it day by day right now. In a few weeks Louise is going back to Florida, and I'll have collected enough data to start preparing my reports to a congressional committee."

Jamie's jaw dropped. "Whoa! So it's going to be back to square one with the two of you? Like this whole thing has just been a spring fling?"

"I guess so." Wes took a swig of coffee and found it bitter. "I don't have to like it, but all along I've known that Louise and I are about as different as two people can be. And she's been forthright in telling everyone her future doesn't include a life in Bayberry Cove. She would never be happy here, and since I've been back, I've come to accept that I'd never be happy anywhere else."

"Have you asked her?"

"Asked her what?"

"If she could be happy here? She might surprise you."

"I don't have to ask. She's told me a lot about her practice in Fort Lauderdale. She's a very successful attorney with a long list of corporate clients. She came up here to see Vicki and to mellow out, as she puts it, but she fully expects to go back to her job. And she should. She's invested a lot of time and skill in that position."

Wes pushed his plate aside. "Even if she

flat-out said she loved me, which she won't because I don't think she does, I couldn't ask her to stay here. It wouldn't be fair. There's only enough work for one attorney in this town, and Dad's got it covered. And we all know how Dad feels about Louise. He's not about to share the town's legal dilemmas with her. He blames her for everything from the split between him and Kate to the crabgrass in his backyard."

Jamie shook his head. "That's another mess, isn't it? Your father and my ma going their separate ways."

Wes nodded. It definitely was a mess. Kate Malone was the best thing that had ever happened to Haywood, and in Wes's opinion, his father was a fool not to do whatever it took to keep her in his life.

"My faith in the course of true love is being tested in this town lately," Jamie said. "I almost regret helping to set you up with Louise. Maybe it wasn't such a good idea."

Wes had pondered that very thing several times. And he'd always come to the same conclusion. He wouldn't have missed a minute of Louise's amazing company for anything. She'd revitalized him, challenged him, made him laugh and made him happy. She wasn't at all the kind of woman he'd pictured for himself when he came back to Bayberry Cove with semi-serious thoughts of settling down and starting a family. Now, though, he had no problem envisioning lazy summer days and long winter nights with her nestled in his arms at Buttercup Cottage.

But that wasn't her dream. She would never be a stay-at-home wife. She was big-city excitement and sophistication.

He leaned over and squeezed Jamie's shoulder. "It was a great idea, my friend. The best one you've ever had—next to going after Vicki." He motioned for Bobbi Lee to bring the check. "In fact, I'm going to buy your lunch, even though I'm jealous of every bite you took."

Wes left several bills on the table and walked to the door with Jamie. "So what about tonight? You going to be here?"

"I wouldn't miss it," Jamie said. "Something tells me this is going to be a night for us lads to stick together."

IT WAS JUST AFTER DARK when Wes noticed a glow coming from the square. He found the last parking space down the street from the shops, got out and started walking. Not only were all the parking places taken, but cars lined the entire perimeter of the square and filled the side streets. The light from the square grew brighter as he came closer. When he reached the furniture store, he looked up at Louise's windows. Dark. She was out here someplace.

He crossed over, captivated by a flickering glow that permeated the entire two acres of the park. The dusky saffron hue was produced by hundreds of candles! Candlelight was everywhere. On the benches, in the bandstand, hanging from tree limbs. And scattered across the green lawn as if the clover had caught fire.

He stopped at his grandfather's bench and regarded the old man. Mason had a huge grin on his face. His foot was beating time to the strains from a trio of guitars and women singing an old Bob Dylan song, "The Times They Are A-Changin'."

"Good evening, Wesley," Mason said. "Looks like we're having a good old-fashioned country jamboree."

"It does at that, Grandpa." If he didn't know that trouble was brewing in Bayberry Cove, Wes might have tapped his foot along with his grandfather. He might have strolled down the row of concession wagons and tasted a candy apple, or bought himself a hot dog and a soda. That's what the kids were doing. But all this laid-back charm was masking the very real purpose of this night's events. The true meaning could be read in banners stretched between trees and flags waving from women's hands.

We Love Our Children. Keep Our Babies Close. We Support a Child Care Center. Justin Beauclaire, Open Your Eyes. A few signs advocated universal health care as well. Wes read one message after another as a steady procession of women passed by in an organized demonstration.

"Don't this beat all?" Mason said. "I wish Buttercup was here to see it."

The reference to his grandmother made Wes smile. From what he remembered of the outspoken lady, he believed if she were still alive, she might be carrying a sign of her own.

"Hope they don't burn down the town, though," Mason added.

It didn't seem a credible threat. The women had thought of everything. The candles Wes could see were elevated on metal platforms or tucked into punched tin boxes, keeping the flames out of the wind. And for extra precaution, the town fire truck was positioned just off the square.

Though he feared the answer, Wes leaned down to speak into his grandfather's good ear. "Gramps, where did they get the candles?"

The old man cackled with genuine good humor. "Been stealin' 'em for weeks, from what I heard. Right out from under Beauclaire's nose."

"I was afraid of that," Wes said.

"Wes! Wesley Fletcher! Don't you move!"

Wes heard the voice and flinched at the commanding tone that could only belong to his father. He turned around and saw the powerful figure of Haywood Fletcher bearing down on him. He wanted to ignore his father's warning and move as fast as he could, but naval commanders stood their ground, even if it was littered with miniature fires and flowery scents.

"Hi, Dad. How you doing?" he said when Haywood practically barreled into him.

"How am I doing? What kind of a question is that? How do you think I'm doing? These crazy women are burning up profits left and right."

"Excuse me, Mr. Fletcher, but that's not exactly true."

All three men gawked at Bessie Granger, who'd silently come up behind them.

"You didn't steal these candles from the factory?" Haywood challenged.

"Well, yes, we did, but they're mistake candles."

Haywood's face turned crimson, a fitting color for a night consumed with fire, even harmless twinkling little blazes. "What are you talking about?"

"Surely you know about the factory's policy with regard to mistakes, Mr. Fletcher," Bessie said.

"Of course I know it. We do, don't we, Wesley?"

Wes shrugged. "I don't know it."

Bessie smiled patiently. "Bayberry Candles are known across the nation for their quality and reliability. If anything goes wrong in production, if a dye is slightly off, if the wicks aren't completely straight, if the pillars are slightly tipped, if the scents—"

"Go on," Haywood said irritably.

"Well, those candles that don't meet the rigorous standards of our executive inspectors are thrown into giant bins and are either recycled into wax slabs that must be removed of color and scent, or, if they're not reusable in any form, are tossed into the Dumpsters. I've always thought it quite a wasteful practice, really."

Haywood snorted. "So you're saying you ladies have been filching the mistake candles?"

"Exactly. Every day for weeks, a few at

a time in our lunch buckets or purses." She smiled sweetly. "Your profits are safe, Mr. Fletcher."

"Hardly safe, Mrs. Granger," he bellowed back. "You women are causing enough of a ruckus to upset candle factory operations in a much larger way than the loss of a few mistake candles. You've got the whole town buzzing about what's going on at the factory."

"In all honesty, Mr. Fletcher," Bessie said, "that is exactly what we intended. We felt this was an appropriate way to draw attention to our cause, in an orderly, law-abiding way. Mr. Beauclaire has never listened before…." She gazed off across the square to where Justin was standing close to a van with an antenna reaching high into the night sky. "I think he's being forced to consider our wishes tonight."

Haywood squawked in mortification. "That's a Channel Six News truck next to Beauclaire!"

"Oh, no," Wesley said. "And that's Louise with him."

Haywood cupped his hand over his eyes and squinted hard. "That woman in the pink suit is a reporter for the eleven o'clock news. Wesley, you get over there and do damage control. We don't know what Beauclaire is saying. And I don't even want to think about what that attorney friend of yours is spouting off about."

Wes took off at a jog. "I'll do what I can, Dad." As he closed in on the group at the van, he was caught in the glow of a spotlight running off the van's generator. The reporter, Justin Beauclaire and Louise were in the center of the beam. The reporter held a microphone.

"So it's your contention, Miss Duncan," the woman said, "that the Bayberry Cove Candle Company has been guilty of Title VII labor and employment violations for a number of years?"

"Exactly," Louise answered. "We intend to prove that female employees at the factory have been consistently overlooked for pay raises and promotions."

Justin was growing red in the face, and he actually grabbed for the microphone. Wes stepped up in time to stop him, but was unsuccessful in silencing his verbal outburst.

"Wrong!" Justin said. "There's just not a word of truth to what this lawyer is telling you. We're all a happy family at the Bayberry Cove Candle Company. There's never been a day when our employees weren't treated with respect and dignity."

"So there have been no pay raise violations,

and women have advanced according to their merit?" the reporter asked.

"Absolutely—"

Wes cleared his throat. "Excuse me, Justin, if I may…"

"And you are?" The reporter shoved the microphone at Wes's jaw.

The light swerved to his face, and he blinked at its intensity. "I'm Wesley Fletcher, legal advisor to the candle factory."

"And what is your take on these proceedings tonight, Mr. Fletcher? Did you know the women had organized a public demonstration?"

He darted a glance at Louise, who responded with a slight nod and an almost imperceptible rise in one shoulder, as cocky a shrug as he'd ever seen. Was she enjoying this or regretting the fact that she hadn't warned him?

"No, I wasn't aware of the activities in the square tonight, but I certainly have no objection to the women expressing their opinions in an open forum such as this one."

"And do you agree with Mr. Beauclaire, that no violations have occurred?"

"Of course he agrees with me," Justin interrupted. The reporter quickly switched the microphone to pick up Justin's comments.

"Wes here is a hometown boy." He jabbed a thumb in Louise's direction. "This lady attorney's come from Miami or someplace. What she knows about Bayberry Cove wouldn't fill a thimble."

Wes discreetly stepped in front of Justin. "Whether or not violations have occurred is not for me to say. This matter will undoubtedly progress to the mediation stage, at which time I'm sure a conciliatory agreement will be reached between both parties."

"And what about the women's desires to have a day care center at the factory and health care provided by the company?"

"Those are not issues regulated by the Equal Employment Opportunity Commission," Wes said. "The women are of course within their rights to voice any of their suggestions to the owners of the candle factory. But the owners are under no obligation to comply with demands not covered by Title VII and the EEOC."

The reporter turned away from the group and commanded the attention of her cameraman. "There you have it, folks. It's almost a festive atmosphere in little Bayberry Cove tonight. But aside from all the candlelight, music and refreshments, issues of extreme importance to this community are taking center stage. Is this a case of some good old boys ignoring federal labor statutes for years? Or are we looking at an example of the age-old animosity between the sexes? Either way, I'd say the ladies have the advantage tonight. We'll keep you posted. This is Rochelle Vassar, 'Channel Six Nightly News.'"

Ms. Vassar flashed a dazzling smile at each of the people she'd interviewed. "Thanks, folks. You can catch this story tonight at eleven."

Louise walked off to join a group of women who'd been watching events unfold. She was soon swallowed up by the enthusiastic females, whose expressions clearly indicated that they thought they'd scored a victory in the interview.

Wes escorted Justin away from the news van. "I think we did pretty good, Wes," Justin said. "Came across like real men who aren't going to lay down and roll over just because a few women are trying to scare us." He grasped the lapels of his jacket and practically strutted to the bench where Mason and Haywood Fletcher—and about a dozen other men with worried expressions—waited.

"It'll be on at eleven," Justin announced. "Can't wait to see what I look like on TV. Wes sounded real good using all that legal lingo. And I managed to say a few choice words about that lady attorney from Florida."

Haywood looked as if his last meal was about to stage a revolution. He stared at Wes, obviously searching for some sign that Justin hadn't single-handedly inspired the citizens of Bayberry Cove to come after the factory executives with tar and feathers.

Wes rolled his eyes. It was the best he could do.

WES TUCKED THE BAG he was carrying under his arm and left the town square. It was eleven o'clock, and the banners and flags had been taken down. The concession trucks were gone. The determined demonstrators, curious onlookers and baffled men had gone to their homes. And as Wes walked down the dark, deserted street he knew that in the next few minutes Bayberry Cove was going to be in the spotlight, at least for the area serviced by Channel Six News in Raleigh.

He smiled, something he'd managed to do quite often this evening as he'd encountered the people he'd grown up with, and tried to explain that the events at the factory weren't signaling the downfall of civilization as they knew it.

He glanced up at Louise's windows again as he passed by McCorkle's. Still dark. She was probably watching the news with her clients. He felt a stab of disappointment that he wouldn't see her tonight. In spite of everything that had happened, he'd come away with one significant conclusion. Louise looked really good in candlelight.

His Jeep seemed lonely and forlorn in the last parking spot at the end of the street without even the glimmer of one streetlamp shining upon it. He opened the driver's door, slipped inside and immediately encountered two long, slim legs encased in denim stretched out along the passenger-side floor. He jerked back, nearly falling out of the vehicle, and dropped his sack between the seats.

"'Bout time you got here," Louise said.

"Louise, are you trying to give me a heart attack?"

"Sort of. But not in the way you're thinking."

She pulled the lever at the side of the passenger seat, raised herself from a reclining position and rotated her neck. "I'm glad you're here finally. I'm in pain from crouching down to avoid public detection." She scanned the deserted neighborhood. "It looks okay now, but you might want to start driving just in case."

He glared at her, but couldn't begin to come across as angry. He was simply too delighted to see her. "You beat everything, you know that?"

"I'm trying, but I'm not all that familiar with my competition. And speaking of competition, you pulled off the Channel Six interview quite well. I'm impressed."

"Thanks. Need I tell you that it was totally impromptu? I didn't have a chance to prepare any comments."

"Yeah, I know. I couldn't give you a heads-up on this one, Wes. Lawyer-client privilege. The girls wanted to catch Beauclaire off guard."

"And they did."

She smiled. "He sounded as pompous as I'd hoped he would."

"As pompous as I'd hoped he *wouldn't,*" Wes countered. He started the engine. "Where do you want to go?"

"I don't care. You'll think of someplace."

He already had a destination in mind and headed west out of town.

"Have you checked your mail today?" she asked.

"Yes, a lot of good it did me. The regular

mail person was off, so naturally I didn't get delivery."

"Oh. I'm sure you'll get a letter tomorrow."

"From whom?"

"Christopher Tenant. Remember, he's the rep from—"

"I know who he is." Wes scowled out the side window.

"Anyway, he's coming on Monday with a federal mediator. We're meeting in the council room at city hall at one o'clock. You're supposed to bring Beauclaire, Winslow and McGovern."

Tenant was efficient, Wes decided, along with other, less admirable qualities. He'd interviewed the factory executives by phone this week after requesting more company records, and now had already arranged the mediation. Wes wasn't kidding himself. He knew the men were going to have to give in on a number of issues. They were guilty of good ol' boy management. But if he could keep them quiet, at least he might preserve the company's dignity and end the proceedings on a cooperative note. And keep the women from running away with benefits that would seriously threaten the company's finances.

As if reading his mind, Louise said, "So

what did you think of the demonstration tonight?"

"The music was good."

She laughed. "I saw you talking to some of the men when it was over. Are they giving you a hard time?"

"Some of them. Guys like Evan McCorkle and a few of the older husbands of factory workers. They aren't too happy about Saturday meetings and Wednesday night carnivals." He smiled at her. "But they'll get over it. Pay raises will go a long way to smooth ruffled feathers. But Beauclaire and the boys—that's another story. Frankly, Louise, I'll just be glad when this is over and things can return to the way they were before this mess started. I need to forget about law and all the entanglements this case has brought to my life, and get back to my NOAA studies full time."

Aware of her sudden intense stare, Wes turned to face her. "What's wrong?"

"I was just thinking about something," she murmured. "It doesn't matter." She focused on the bag he'd dropped earlier. "What's in there?"

Feeling a little foolish because he hadn't expected her to discover his contraband, he smiled sheepishly. "What do you think? Candles."

"Really?" She reached for the sack. "May I?"

"Help yourself."

She opened the bag and dumped a half-dozen candles on her lap. "You took these?"

"Hey, they're only mistake candles, anyway."

"What are you going to do with them?"

"I'd planned to take them home." He watched her face for a reaction. "They're good to use when someone unexpectedly drops by. Someone who looks especially great in candlelight."

Whatever was bothering her seemed to fade from her features, replaced with a grin. "Why, Wes Fletcher, you *are* a romantic."

"That's me. But now I've changed my mind."

"You have?"

Was that confusion on her face? Disappointment? Whatever, he had her wondering what was on *his* mind for once. "There's this place about ten miles from town. It's something you should see."

"Oh?"

"It's our very own waterfall, in Bayberry Park. Quite an attraction for an area that's at sea level. It's a real waterfall with rocks and a babbling brook at the bottom. A result of some prehistoric earth burp, I imagine."

She looked out the window, seemingly aware for the first time that they'd been driving for a while. "Is that where we're going?"

"Yep. It's after eleven o'clock on a school night, so I figure the teenagers who usually hang out there have gone home. I've got a blanket in back. I thought we'd sit awhile, watch the moon on the falls, light some candles and have a little demonstration of our own."

She pretended to be stunned at his announcement, a good acting job, since he doubted Louise was ever truly shocked about anything. "Ohh… Are you saying that you're taking me to Bayberry Cove's version of Lover's Lane?"

"That's what I'm saying. Unless, of course, you want to go home and see yourself on TV."

She carefully replaced the candles in the bag. "Would I have been in this Jeep if I wanted to do that?"

## CHAPTER SIXTEEN

JUST BEFORE ONE O'CLOCK on Monday, Louise stood in front of her dresser mirror and adjusted her silver medallion so it lay against her skin in the exact center of the open placket of her blouse.

"I've always admired that piece," Vicki said from the sofa. "Didn't you tell me it was an old family crest?"

"That's right. My mother inherited it from her grandmother, who originally brought it from Scotland. I've always thought of it as sort of a good luck charm. Anymore, I don't think that's so true."

"Why not?" Vicki asked. "Don't you think the mediation will go your way today?"

"Yes, I think it will. I was referring to a matter that is more personal. And frankly, I believe my luck has run out in that regard."

Vicki was thoughtful for a moment before she said, "So this has nothing to do with the career side of your life. I can only assume, then, that you think your luck has run out with regard to Wes Fletcher."

"How'd you guess?" Louise asked sardonically. "By the end of the day, the women at the candle factory will have opened some very significant doors. Unfortunately, Wes and I will have closed some."

"What are you talking about? You and Wes see each other nearly every night, don't you?"

"Yeah. I guess I like long goodbyes."

"Goodbye? This is June fourteenth. You're not leaving till the end of the month."

"That was my original plan, but things have changed. I've decided to return to Fort Lauderdale by the end of the week. I called my cleaning lady this morning and told her to give my condo a good going-over, that I would be sleeping in it on Thursday night."

"No!" Vicki sat forward on the sofa and gaped in shock at her best friend. "You're telling me that we've only got a couple more days together? Has Roger Oppenheimer called you to come back?"

Louise sighed. "No, he hasn't, and that is something of a problem. But he did suggest I take a couple of months off, and it's only been six weeks." She picked up the navy-blue jacket of her business suit she'd brought from home, and slipped her arms into it. "I have to believe that I'm going to hear from him soon, and that I still have a place at the firm."

Vicki's expression turned angry. "You have a place here, Lulu. Don't you know that?"

Vicki's words stung. "As what, Vic?" she snapped back. "An attorney without a license to practice in North Carolina? A sometimes-companion of Wes Fletcher's, someone to keep him occupied while he searches for a proper wife who cooks and cleans and waits for his boat to return from Currituck Sound every day?"

"He doesn't want that in a woman."

Louise stared hard at her friend, trying to make her see what she herself already knew. "Yes, he does, Vicki. And he should. He has a right to settle down with the woman of his dreams and accept nothing less."

"But you're that woman."

"I'm the woman of his fantasies, honey— not his dreams. And I've been happy to play that role while I've been here, but now it's time to accept reality and go home."

"What makes you so certain that Wes wants this classic homemaker you're describing? You could be wrong."

"We talked last night, a lot. Mostly he told me about Donna, his first wife." Louise picked up her purse, rummaged through it to determine she had her wallet, cell phone, the essentials. Doing something so mundane kept her from thinking too seriously about last evening's conversation. "And now I understand what he didn't come right out and say. I am a lot like Donna. I'm driven, competitive, independent." She smiled when she remembered Roger Oppenheimer's assessment of her character. "But I am nicer now," she admitted. "Bayberry Cove has brought out the compassion in me, I think. But I'm still not Suzie Homemaker." She laughed, though it sounded cold, like breaking ice. "Vic, I'm not even as domestic as you are, and you're the busiest woman I know. You keep tabs on a business in Fort Lauderdale while you light up the life of a doting husband, and build a house and a baby at the same time."

Vicki blushed, something she did more charmingly than anyone Louise had ever known. "Of course you're not me. You're uniquely you. There's no one else like you, though many women would like to be. And I don't care what you say. You're the woman Wes Fletcher wants."

"I think you're wrong," Louise admitted.

"Have you asked him about this, Lulu? You're very analytical and usually right about your instincts. But in this case I think you're trying to get into Wes's head, and coming up with the entirely wrong conclusions."

Louise snapped her purse closed and picked up her briefcase. "That's where you're wrong again, Vic. Wes told me he couldn't wait for this whole candle factory situation to be over. That all he wants is to get back to his old life with his fish and his aquariums and his one-man show to save Currituck Sound. He wants the peace and quiet he came back here for."

"He said that?"

"Yes, indeed. And it's okay. He had a satisfying life before he met me, and I don't blame him for wanting to go back to it now. And I had a satisfying life, as well. And I'm going back to it. Square one, Vicki." Louise forced a smile. "There's nothing wrong with solidly planting your feet on square one. For many people it's where they belong."

"Have you told him you're leaving?"

"No. I just decided a couple of days ago. I'll tell him today." She smoothed her jacket over her skirt. "How do I look?"

"Like you're going to win, at least at the mediation," Vicki said. "But then, you always do."

"Nobody wins all the time, honey." She patted Vicki's tummy. "Except maybe you. So don't mess up now."

The women went downstairs. Vicki got in her car and headed toward the *Bucket O' Luck*. Louise looked down Main Street toward city hall. It was a short walk. She didn't need her car. As she passed the BMW, she couldn't help noticing that Bayberry Cove dust had settled on the normally pristine black exterior. She smiled, thinking how the small town had worked its way into her life in the strangest of ways.

She'd only gone a few feet when she heard Mason Fletcher call out to her from his bench in the square. "Today's the day, isn't it, Louise?"

Having a few minutes to spare, she crossed over. "This is it, Mason."

He chuckled. "Don't make my grandson look too bad."

"Nobody could. Least of all me."

He smiled a bit, crinkling his eyes. "What'd you think of the demonstration last Wednesday night? Imagine those gals from the factory takin' all those mistake candles and lighting them all over the town square. Very clever if you ask me. Put them to good use, too."

Louise consulted her watch. "That they did," she said. "Well, I'd better go." She started to walk away, Mason's words replaying in her mind. *Put them to good use...* She stopped suddenly. An idea had popped into her head, as if some serendipitous fate had struck a deal with her common sense. She turned, hurried back to the bench. "Mason, will you still be here in a couple of hours?"

"Can be." He slipped his cell phone out of his pocket. "That fussy nurse of mine doesn't come for me till I call her on this gadget."

"Great. I have a business proposition to discuss with you."

That settled, Louise strode purposefully to city hall.

KATE MALONE TOOK her powder-blue sweater out of the bureau in Bessie Granger's guest bedroom and folded it over her elbow. It would look fine with her white blouse and gray skirt in case the temperature was a bit chilly in city hall. Besides, her gray jacket, which would have been preferable in this instance, was still at the Fletcher estate, so she had to make do without it.

She walked down the short hallway of Bessie's bungalow and stepped into the living room.

Bessie came out of the kitchen looking confident and very un-Bessielike in black slacks and a red blouse. "Too much for an old denim gal?" she asked, plucking at the satiny fabric of the shirt.

"Absolutely not," Kate assured her. "Red is a power color. That's what you need today." She glanced with some embarrassment around the parlor, which was brilliant with flower arrangements, none of which had anything to do with Pete's funeral now twelve days past. Those bouquets were on his grave site.

"How long are you going to make him suffer?" Bessie said, leaning over to smell a particularly resplendent arrangement of pink roses.

Kate had moved out of Haywood's house nine days ago, and now, an equal number of floral arrangements occupied every flat surface of Bessie's living room. The first to arrive—a modest little bouquet of white carnations and baby's breath—was currently turning brown in the sunlight coming through the bay window. The card, a simple white vellum, had succinctly stated Haywood's demands. "Kate, come home." Since then, the arrangements had become more elaborate and so had the flowery sentiments expressed on the cards.

"I don't know," Kate answered honestly. "Until Haywood stops letting flowers speak for him and says the words I want to hear himself." She gave Bessie a sympathetic look. "But I will start clearing out some of the older bouquets tonight. It really is an excessive display."

"He has apologized on many of these cards, you know," Bessie pointed out.

"Oh, yes, I know." Kate picked up her purse and marched to the door. "I'm just not convinced he knows what he's apologized for."

Bessie followed her outside. "I appreciate you going with me today, Kate, but I doubt they'll let you into the mediation room."

"That's all right. I'm content to be your moral support in the hallway." Kate squeezed Bessie's hand. "You'll know I'm there."

Once they were in Kate's car, Bessie presented an interesting challenge. "What if Haywood is there in the hallway providing moral support to Justin Beauclaire?"

Kate carefully backed out of the driveway, put the car in drive and shot down the narrow street. "That's his right, of course, but it won't make a bit of difference to me. Besides, he won't be. Wesley told me that Haywood has more or less washed his hands of the whole affair." She grinned with a small show of victory. "It seems he wasn't too pleased with Justin's performance on the news the other night, and has decided to remain in the shadows for once and let Wes handle everything."

"That doesn't sound like Haywood Fletcher," Bessie observed.

Kate nodded. "And that, my dear friend, is a good sign."

LOUISE MET BESSIE and Darlene in the hallway outside the meeting room in city hall. "How are you both feeling?" she asked.

"Ready to go," Bessie said. "Good or bad, I'm not afraid of the outcome."

"Me neither," Darlene said. "I'm ready to kick some corporate butt."

Louise laughed. "That's good, Darlene, but let me do the butt-kicking in there, okay?"

"You're the boss." She took Louise's elbow and leaned close to her. "We are going to win, aren't we? And if not, you're going to help me get another job?"

Louise patted her hand. "We're going to win, Darlene. Not everything, but enough. And if this turns out the way I think it will, you are going to like your new job at Bayberry Cove Candle Company."

After an encouraging word from Kate, the three women entered the meeting room. Wes was already there, seated between

Justin Beauclaire and Hatch Winslow. Along with Warren McGovern, head of sales and marketing, they occupied one side of a conference table. The ladies walked to the opposite side.

"Hello again, Mr. Tenant," Louise said to Chris, who sat at one end of the table. In this formal situation she would never have considered using his first name. And from the scowl on his face, she doubted she'd ever use it again.

"Ms. Duncan." He gestured to a man at the other end of the table. "This is Harold Freeman, a federal mediator who works for the Equal Employment Opportunity Commission."

Louise shook the man's hand and introduced her companions. After the ladies were seated, she spoke to the three executives from the candle factory. "Nice to see you again, Mr. Beauclaire," she said. He mumbled a guttural response.

And then she allowed herself a good long look at Wesley. Despite her years of experience and normally cool demeanor, Louise was thankful she was sitting. Otherwise her knees might have buckled with the flush of heat making her body feel limp and tingly at the same time.

In a charcoal suit, white-and-gray pin-striped shirt and a tie with a dash of royal blue, his sandy-colored hair neatly parted and spiked onto his forehead, this ex-navy man was a model of civilian sophistication. She arched her brows in a silent message she was certain Wes would understand and said, "It's good to see you looking so well, Mr. Fletcher."

He gave her a little grin. "Ditto, Ms. Duncan."

The mediator took over. "All right then. All participants are present, so let's begin." He tapped a pen on a fan of papers spread out in front of him. "I've had a chance to look over the charges by Mrs. Granger and Miss Jackson as they've been presented by Mr. Tenant, our investigator. So let me start by giving you my conclusions."

Mr. Freeman's conclusions coincided with Louise's expectations. Personnel records supported Bessie's claims that she had been passed over for promotions a number of times, the most recent being when a relative of Hatch Winslow's had been hired as supervisor of candle-making operations. Also, pay raises had been denied her without substantiation.

Wesley argued that Bessie had never made her expectations known through proper channels, and the company had perhaps acted negligently but without malice. Therefore the board should not be expected to award any back pay for punitive damages. In accordance with Freeman's suggestions, Wes agreed that company executives would appoint Bessie to the next supervisory position. Mr. Freeman then established a time frame of six months for the promotion to occur and further stated that Bessie's salary should double effective immediately.

Louise agreed to those terms when she looked at Bessie and realized the woman was beaming with satisfaction.

They moved on to Darlene's complaint. Louise pointed out the characteristics demanded of a marketing/sales associate according to the candle company's own specifications. And she proved with results of personality and employable skills tests that Darlene met nearly all of the criteria the factory required to hire someone on this level. Darlene's personnel records supported her claim that she had been passed over for a sales position repeatedly without ever being given follow-up interviews with regard to her application.

"In direct violation of Title VII's job description policies," Louise said.

The mediator strongly suggested that

Darlene's application be considered at once, and that she should be awarded a sales position or be placed in an apprenticeship program to acquire skills needed for the job. Since Hatch Winslow had nothing to say in his defense on this issue, the matter was settled.

Freeman referred to a last charge in his stack of papers, the one that concerned an anonymous Hispanic worker and her claim that she had been forced to miss work during the latter stage of her pregnancy for unspecified safety reasons. The mediator regarded both attorneys. "Would either of you care to address this issue?"

Hoping to avoid using Miranda Lopez's name, as she'd promised, Louise said, "I would, sir. My client isn't here today. But she is willing to drop her case against the candle factory if the executives would consider providing licensed day care at the facility."

Justin Beauclaire pounded a fist on the table. "Babies at the candle factory! We won't have that. We can't!" He looked to Wes, who had laid a placating hand on the older man's arm. "I told you all hell would break loose after that demonstration the other night."

"In all fairness, Mr. Freeman," Wes began, "this isn't an employment issue, and the candle factory is under no obligation to provide child care. Besides, the current facilities are not conducive to such a program."

Louise held up her hand. "Actually, Counselor, they are. In the office structure in front of the warehouse, there is a large sunny room that, according to my studies, is hardly ever used."

"The executive lunchroom!" Justin bellowed. "She's talking about turning the executive lunchroom into a playground."

"The executives rarely use that room, Mr. Freeman," Louise said. "I've kept a record of the noon eating habits of the office staff at the candle company. Almost without exception, the executives go out to lunch." She handed the mediator a sheet of paper. "This is a list of the restaurants the men choose, a different one for each day of the week. As for the administrative help in the office, the women I spoke to said they are not permitted to use the lunchroom facilities, anyway, and they will continue eating their lunches at their desks."

Freeman looked at the list. "These are all fine eating establishments I noticed myself on the way into town," he said to the men. "I wouldn't mind an extended lunch hour at any one of them." Then he leveled a serious stare on Louise. "However, as Mr. Fletcher pointed out, this is not an employment issue, Ms. Duncan, and therefore—"

"Don't you think it's just a matter of time before child care will be mandated for female employees?" she said. "Many companies with large numbers of women workers are providing some type of care for their staff's children now. I don't think it's out of line to discuss it today in preparation for the time it becomes an employment issue. And I would very much like these men to consider it."

Wes cupped a hand over his mouth, but she detected a smile of respect for her argument. "Mr. Freeman," he said, "since none of us in this room has a crystal ball, I suggest we table this discussion for now until we see where future legislation leads us."

The mediator looked at Louise.

"Fine," she said. Louise had known she would lose the argument. However, she had one more card to play.

"Mr. Fletcher, would your clients consider health care symposiums at the factory? Scheduled times when professionals in the field of providing coverage could come in and speak to the employees about their options? Perhaps if my clients knew about modestly priced individual policies, or about state-funded coverage for children under the age of eighteen, this issue could be tabled for now with no hard feelings."

Wes switched his attention to Beauclaire. "Justin? Any objections?"

The older man ran his hand down his jaw and looked very much as if he wanted to come up with a powerful objection, but Louise knew he couldn't. She wasn't asking for more than a little company time. To deny that would put him in a bad light with Freeman.

"No, I suppose not. I'll have someone look into it."

"Thank you," Louise said. "Now if I can just reopen the topic of day care…"

Mr. Freeman gave her a stern look. "Ms. Duncan, we have settled this matter, and I must warn you—"

She opened her briefcase and pulled out a number of folders. "Sir, what I have here are additional cases of Title VII EEOC violations perpetrated on factory workers by the Bayberry Cove Candle Company. I could file charges on each of them, but the women represented by these claims are willing to forgo personal gain and almost certain punitive damages for mental anguish and inconvenience *for the time being…*" she switched her best no-nonsense courtroom stare on Beauclaire "…if the gentlemen over there agree to abide by EEOC regulations from now on."

She paused for emphasis, letting her implied threat sink in. "And if the executives will consider establishing a day care center, which will ultimately benefit everyone in the community."

She selected another folder from her briefcase and slid it across to Wes. "These are statistics showing how child care centers across the country have decreased absenteeism while increasing employee performance. And exact figures on the cost of turning the executive lunchroom into such a facility, which will positively impact the future of candle-making specifically and Bayberry Cove in general. A modern, well-equipped center will cost less than one golf weekend at Hilton Head. Surely you gentlemen can give up one weekend?"

The company executives bristled at the implied condemnation of the long-standing company benefit. Out of the corner of her eye, Louise saw a look of surprise on Freeman's face. "Do this for the children," she added. "You won't be sorry. And your community will thank you."

Freeman stared at Wes's team. "While this issue is not within my jurisdiction, gentlemen, I will go out on a limb and strongly suggest you think about the ladies' request. Considering that stack of complaints Ms. Duncan has, I guarantee it will save you a lot of headaches in the future." He removed his glasses and set them on the table, making his gaze that much more penetrating. "And besides, it's the right thing to do."

Wes regarded his three associates. Each remained stone-faced. Obviously interpreting their reluctance to comment as capitulation, he stood up and extended his hand to Louise. "I believe we've reached an agreement, Counselor." He smiled at her. "The lunchroom will undergo the modifications to make it a suitable child care center."

Bessie and Darlene hooted in victory and grabbed Louise for breath-stealing hugs. And if Louise had just won a case before the Supreme Court, she wouldn't have felt more pride.

"I guess this concludes our work here today," Mr. Freeman said. "And I can make it back to Raleigh in time for dinner." He stuffed his papers in his case, stood up and headed for the exit. "Good luck to all of you. And you gentlemen…" He stared pointedly at Beauclaire, Winslow and McGovern. "Your attorney, Mr. Fletcher, has kept you from facing more serious consequences. But I want you to remember that your employees are your most valuable assets. I urge you to abide by all legislation in the future. This is a nice little town you have here, but I don't want to come back." He smiled. "Unless it's to buy a candle."

Louise barely heard his words. As the mediator walked out the door, her focus was on Wes. He tried to console his clients by restating the small victories they'd won. While the mediator's warning had been serious, the company hadn't been fined. The dignity of the corporation was intact, so long, Wes added, as no one else appeared before a television camera. As his clients grumbled, Wes flashed Louise a grin and a thumbs-up, making it blatantly clear he admired and respected her.

She knew that leaving Bayberry Cove was going to be the hardest thing she'd ever done. While she accepted the congratulations of Bessie and Darlene, she could only think that she would be saying goodbye to them very soon. For that reason the smile she gave was forced. And she was going to miss Wes... more desperately than she'd ever imagined. In two days she would head to Fort Lauderdale and get her life back in order as the more compassionate, people-friendly attorney her weeks in Bayberry Cove had made her. But she wouldn't have Wes, because admiration, and even mind-numbing kisses, weren't enough.

WES WATCHED LOUISE FOLLOW Bessie and Darlene from the room. Thankfully this business was over. Louise had been spectacular. Stunning. She belonged in a big city courtroom where other competent legal minds could be blown away by such superior ability coming from such a captivating package. What right did he have to ask her to stay in little Bayberry Cove? How could she give up what she'd worked years to achieve? What did this little town, and for that matter, this ex-navy biologist, have to offer her that could compare with what she would give up? Nothing.

But he still had two weeks to try, and for the next fourteen days he was going to mount an all-out offensive to get her to stay. Because how could he let her go?

# CHAPTER SEVENTEEN

OUTSIDE CITY HALL, Wes stood to the side while Louise, Kate, Bessie and Darlene celebrated. Their victory was well deserved. Wes was satisfied with the case he'd presented, but he'd known all along the ladies would come out ahead. The factory administrators had gotten away with a flagrant disregard for the law for a lot of years, and no lawyer could have spared them the embarrassment of the dressing-down they got today.

Louise shot him a glance over her shoulder and then spoke to the women. "Thanks anyway, but I'll catch up with you later. You guys go on."

"Thank you for everything," Darlene said. "I'm sorry I had an attitude about all this at first."

"Forget it," Louise said. "A little attitude can be a good thing." She gave each woman a hug and watched them walk off together.

When she was alone, Wes came up behind

her and whispered in her ear. "You were magnificent."

She leaned against him. "So were you. I only won because the case was so indisputable. I'd hate to face you in a courtroom when the scales were balanced."

He put his hands on her elbows. "Flattery like that will get you a slice of pie down at the Kettle. What do you say? It's two forty-five, perfect pie-eating time in this part of the country, and we don't have to play hide-and-seek any longer. Besides, it's only fair that we give Bobbi Lee a chance to gloat."

Louise laughed. "You've got a deal."

They were approaching his Jeep in the city hall parking lot when a mud-caked pickup roared by them. Instinctively, Wes sheltered Louise with his own body. When he recognized the driver, he said, "That's Luke Plunkett. And it looks as if his truck's not the only thing gassed up this afternoon."

Louise quickened her pace. "And that's Darlene just ahead of us, going to her car."

The truck careened to a stop a few feet from Darlene. Luke got out and slammed the door. He stood in front of her, his hands on his hips, his legs spread wide.

"I just saw Beauclaire," he said. "You women got your way, didn't you?"

"Yes, we did," she answered. "And you might at least congratulate me."

"There's no way I'd congratulate you for turning your back on me and pretending to be something you're not."

"I'm not pretending anything. We deserved everything we got." She jabbed a finger at his chest. "It might interest you to know, Luke Plunkett, that it took a lot of courage for me to be one of the test cases today."

He let out a bark of laughter. "Courage? Stupidity is more like it."

"Don't call me stupid!"

He leaned over her. "I'll call you whatever I want. Stupid. Ignorant. A lying witch. You've treated me like garbage the last few weeks, and it's going to stop." He grabbed her. "We're getting out of here so I can straighten this mess out once and for all."

Wes lunged forward. "I've heard enough."

He'd gone a couple of feet before Louise reached for his arm. "Wait a minute, Wes. Let's see what happens."

In disbelief he turned to stare at her. "I know what's going to happen, Louise. I've seen Luke in action before."

"But not against this adversary," she said.

Against every instinct urging him to Darlene's rescue, Wes halted. He watched for any twitch of Luke's body that would indicate a renewed threat. But none came.

In fact, Darlene shoved him away from her with enough force to send him stumbling into the side of his truck.

He pushed himself up and dusted off the seat of his jeans. "What are you doing, woman?" he shouted at her.

"Something I should have done a long time ago. You're not going to bully me any longer, Luke. I've got a future now. I'm going to be traveling around the country to shows and selling our candles."

He approached her, drawing dangerously near once more. "No you're not. You're my woman, and that's not gonna change just because you won a stupid contest with Justin Beauclaire. You're staying right here where I can watch you." His arm shot out to snatch her again.

Wes flinched.

And Darlene stood her ground. "You come one step closer, Luke, and I'll scream at the top of my lungs." She stuck her arm out with a determined finger pointed at city hall. "Deputy Blackwell is just inside. He'll come running out and slap handcuffs on you so fast you won't know what hit you. I'll press charges this time, Luke, and I'll watch you go to jail."

He stared openmouthed at her. "What kind of talk is that?"

"It's truth talking, Luke. I'm through with you. I've got a chance now, away from you and that miserable hopeless farm. I'm leaving here and you're not going to stop me."

He narrowed his eyes as if seeing her for the first time. "Now come on, honey…"

"Don't 'honey' me, Luke. Climb in your truck and get out of here. Now."

He turned, started to walk away, but whirled back around to face her again. She waited, unmoving, unyielding, unrelenting.

Luke paused for several seconds, then stomped around his truck, got inside and peeled out of the parking lot.

Wes shook his head. "Do I believe what I just saw?"

"I believe it enough for both of us," Louise said. She wrapped her hand around his elbow and tugged him toward the Jeep. "It's a day of victories. Let's eat pie until we bust."

As soon as Louise and Wes entered the Kettle, Bobbi Lee raced over to seat them. "Well, how'd it go?"

Wes affected an injured look, nodded

toward Louise and said, "Ask the lady who schooled me in the art of argument."

"Whoopee! That's the best news I've had all day."

Wes smiled. "Can you tone it down a little, Bobbi? There's a person here who's trying to heal an injured ego."

Bobbi nudged him between tables to a prime spot by a window. "You're a big boy, Wesley. You'll get over it. Now, Louise, tell me everything. What happened with Bessie and Darlene?"

"I'm so proud of them," Louise said. "They stood up to the executive board and achieved what they've worked for. Bessie's getting a big pay raise and a promotion. Darlene will soon be selling Bayberry Cove Candles at trade shows across the U.S."

"Go ahead, tell her the rest," Wes said, pretending the news really hurt. "You might as well give her all the humiliating details."

"Oh, yeah," Louise added. "As an added bonus, there's going to be a child care center occupying the executive lunchroom."

Bobbi Lee flashed her brightest smile. "You go, girl."

"Thanks," Louise said, "but the women of this town should be given most of the credit.

I was just the key that started their engines running."

Bobbi Lee leaned close, as if she were hiding her next comment from Wes. "Order everything on the menu, honey. I'll make sure Wesley gets the bill."

"We want pie, Bobbi Lee," Wes said. "Bring us huge slices of apple pie loaded with mounds of ice cream. And keep 'em coming until I'm drunk with sugar and my wounds are sufficiently licked."

Bobbi Lee chuckled and sauntered off. Wes stared intently across the table at Louise. "You are the star today. Especially in my eyes, and I'm the loser."

She felt her cheeks flush, a purely feminine reaction that warmed her all the way to her toes. "In that case, Wes, can I ask a favor of you before those fifteen hundred calories arrive and you forget what you just said?"

"Anything at all."

"Your grandfather is in the square. I need to speak to him. Would you mind going to get him and bringing him here?"

Wes stood up. "You and Gramps? That's an alliance I hadn't expected."

She grinned up at him. "Next to you, he's my favorite Fletcher." She watched him cross the street, speak to Mason and point toward the Kettle. A few moments later, both men came inside and sat down.

Wasting no time, Mason increased the pie order and said, "A business proposition, you told me earlier. Let's hear it."

Wes, clearly curious, looked from one to the other.

"That's right," Louise began. "Did Wes tell you that the role of women at the candle factory will be expanding very soon?"

"He did. Congratulations, young lady. I'm not surprised by your success. The more I've gotten to know you, the more I've come to realize that you have the tools to get what you want. But I'm still amazed you couldn't talk Wesley out of Buttercup Cottage when you had the chance weeks ago."

Louise put on a crestfallen expression. "Some battles simply can't be won, Mason. Your grandson taught me that."

"Well, what can I do for you?"

Louise waited while Bobbi Lee set down plates heaped with the Kettle's trademark apple pie à la mode. She took a bite, savored its cool sweetness and continued. "Earlier you mentioned the mistake candles the ladies had at the demonstration. You said it was a clever idea to use them."

Mason wiped his mouth. "I did."

"It made me think."

Wes concentrated on his pie, but Louise knew he was listening intently to every word.

"What if the company could sell those candles?" she said.

"Who'd buy them?" Mason asked. "As I understand it, the company won't ship candles that don't meet specific requirements. A business has to be mindful of the quality of its product or risk losing its reputation."

"I agree," Louise said. "But what if the candles weren't shipped anywhere? What if they were sold as seconds right here in an outlet store?"

"An outlet store? Like the ones in that big shopping center off the interstate?"

"Yes. But it would be located in downtown Bayberry Cove. With a minimum amount of setup, a few shelves and supplies, plus a bit of advertising, a nice little outlet shop could be established on Main Street."

"And it'd sell only mistake candles?"

"Right. The ones with the imperfect colors or shapes, funky candles that came out of molds a little lopsided. Or close-out candles that were overproduced." Once she'd started, Louise's mind mushroomed with ideas. "Or out-of-season stock, like Christmas candles in June, or styles that for some reason never caught on and were returned." She leaned her elbows on the table and riveted Mason with a look she hoped would mirror her enthusiasm. "Even at half price, the candles would bring in a profit. Much better than throwing them out or remelting them into slabs."

"Could be," Mason said thoughtfully. "But what about operating costs? And where exactly do you have in mind for this shop?"

She leaned back, anticipating the first real resistance to her plan. "That's where you come in, Mason."

He sent her a skeptical glance and then focused on his pie.

She continued. "As you know, there's a vacancy coming up in two weeks right next to the furniture store. Mr. Adams is moving his realty company to Morgan City. It would be the perfect spot for the outlet store. And I have the perfect person in mind to run it."

He nodded, tuned in to her idea. "Suzie McCorkle."

"She's a natural," Louise said. "She loves candles. Who better to sell them in Bayberry Cove?"

Wesley had been silent during this exchange, but now he chuckled out loud. "I told you she's amazing, Gramps."

Louise gave him a smug look. "And that's not all."

"I didn't think it was," Wes said.

"But why involve me?" Mason asked. "I don't care if you gals rent the shop and set up your candles. Go see my accountant and have a lease drawn up, and—"

"Well, there might be a problem, at first...."

Wes sat back, leaned his arm on the table. "Ahh, here we go."

She shot him a warning look to which he responded with a grin. "It would be a while before the operation could show a profit," she explained to Mason. "There aren't any funds to start with, and even though I'm sure volunteers would get things rolling, it would be a few weeks, maybe months, before the rent could be met."

Mason's eyebrows knitted over clear blue eyes. "So you're asking me to float the rent indefinitely?"

"*Indefinitely* is such a vague word," she said. "And I haven't even brought this up to the executives at the factory or the women who would contribute to the success of the shop, so nothing is decided yet. But my plan would have more appeal if you would agree to postpone the rent for a time."

Mason threaded his gnarled fingers

together and sat still as a stone. Finally, when Louise thought she couldn't stand his silence another minute, he said, "It's a mighty poor businessman who sells, or rents, his product for nothing."

"Or a truly generous benefactor," she countered.

He tapped his fork against the empty plate for what seemed an eternity. Then he looked at Louise and said, "Three months. That's it. And you pay for my pie."

Louise closed her eyes for a second and said a prayerful but silent "yes!" Then she thanked Mason for his generosity and assured him that if her plan met with approval, everyone involved would know the project was only going ahead because of Mason's help.

"But," she said, "Wes has already agreed to pay for the pie."

Mason swung his index finger in front of her face like a pendulum. "No welshing," he said. "You pay for mine." He turned to his grandson.

"We're done here, Wesley. Cooked like a Thanksgiving turkey. Walk me back to the park and I'll call Cora May to come pick me up." He stood and supported himself against the back of the chair.

"One more thing, Mason," Louise said. "I

believe this will please you. I'm anticipating that profits from the mistake candles could be applied to the company's sponsorship of a health care program for employees. If the firm covers even a percentage of the cost, that will give the workers another option for medical care. Your contribution today could have far-reaching effects."

Wes slowly nodded his head while he took his grandfather's arm. "You never give up, do you, Louise?"

She returned his gaze and suddenly was overcome with an intense sadness. The future of Bayberry Cove would take shape over the next few months. Hers would be determined in the next two days. "Almost never," she said, and watched the two men walk away.

While Wes escorted his grandfather back to the square, she contemplated the best way to tell him about her plans to return to Fort Lauderdale. She decided to suggest a late-night dinner at her place, something simple that she could prepare herself. She was formulating a plan when her cell phone rang. She pulled it out of her briefcase, recognized the number and depressed the connect key.

"Hello, Roger," she said calmly, trying to mask her surprise.

"Louise. How are you? Enjoying your

vacation?" His voice positively chirped with good humor.

"Yes, very much. I'm so glad you advised me to take it," she added, with just the right amount of sarcasm.

"I knew it would do you a world of good, and that's why I've called."

"Oh?"

"I know I suggested you take a couple of months, but knowing you, I figured you must be itching to get back behind your desk here at the firm a few days early. Am I right?"

"I don't know that *itching* is exactly the right word, and frankly, Roger, I would think you'd be more interested in my mental state than a skin condition."

He laughed. "Always the kidder, Louise. That's what I miss about you." He cleared his throat in preparation for a more serious topic. "But tell me, how *are* you doing with regard to those little problems we spoke of before you left?"

"It must be the country air in North Carolina. It's made a pussycat out of me." As soon as she said the words, Louise knew her explanation to Roger was a gross oversimplification. True, she had changed while staying in Bayberry Cove, but not because of the country air. She'd encountered honest, hardworking people who cared about each other and who'd trusted a stranger enough to put their futures in her hands. And because of that, she now understood the deep-down gratification that comes from helping others.

"In fact, Roger," she added with a regretful sigh and a wish that it were so, "everybody here loves me."

"I knew you just needed some time away from the rat race," Roger said, his words sounding like a verbal pat on his own back. "But it's time you came home."

She'd already come to that conclusion, but hearing her boss say it with such conviction made the realization that she didn't belong here all too evident. "Are you saying you need me at the firm, Roger?"

He paused, prompting her to think he was trying to decide on the right amount of enthusiasm to inject into his response. Should he admit honestly that she was essential to the firm or hedge a bit?

"Well, sure we do, Louise. I only meant for you to get away for a while. You know the intent was always for you to return here. As a matter of fact, some of your old clients have been asking for you."

So, the clients who'd found her too

aggressive six weeks ago now wanted her back. There was some satisfaction in hearing that.

"It seems they miss that certain quality you brought to the settlement of cases," Roger added.

"You mean that quality that often won?"

He snickered. "Well, yes. So when can we expect you, Louise? I want to have your desk polished and your name entered in the race for the next promotion."

He was tempting her with the biggest carrot he had. The only problem was, Louise knew the next promotion might not come for years. Oppenheimer Straus and Baker was a firm with very little turnover.

She rested her forehead in her hand and closed her eyes, wondering why she found it so hard to answer his direct question. After all, she'd made this decision. She took a deep breath and said, "Coincidentally, I've already made up my mind, Roger. I'll be in Fort Lauderdale Thursday, and I'll see you in the office the next morning."

The sound of footsteps made her jerk back in her chair. She raised her head, opened her eyes and stared into the glittering ice-blue gaze of Wes Fletcher.

He'd heard. Roger continued talking.

Louise didn't listen. "I've got to go, Roger," she interrupted. "I'll call you later."

She pressed the disconnect button on her phone and set it on the table. "Wes, sit down, please."

He gripped the back of a chair, leaned slightly forward. "Is it true? You're leaving Bayberry Cove soon?"

His voice was devoid of emotion. Cold.

She nodded once. "I'm leaving Wednesday. I was going to tell you tonight."

"Well, now you don't have to."

"Wes, you always knew... I always knew..." His granite features didn't change. "I have a good job in Florida. I've worked hard for it." This wasn't going at all as she'd hoped it would. Her words sounded shallow, meaningless. "We can talk about this, Wes. Tonight. I was thinking—"

He threw the same words she'd spoken to Roger back at her. "I've got to go, Louise. I'll call you later."

He turned away and strode from the restaurant.

ALL RIGHT, he'd been childish when he'd walked out of the Kettle, but thinking back now, a half hour later, it seemed more sensible to have left than to have started breaking plates. Trying to reason with himself, Wes paced back and forth inside the kitchen of Buttercup Cottage. What did he expect? He knew she was going to go back to her old life. She'd never once indicated that her plans would change.

But so soon? He'd planned on two more weeks, two weeks when he could... What? Charm her? He'd tried that with what he'd thought had been some success. But it obviously wasn't enough. Cajole her into staying? No way. Louise was stubborn and determined. Promises? What could he possibly offer her that she didn't already have in Fort Lauderdale—except himself, a poor second to a lucrative law career?

He strode to his back door, looked out at Currituck Sound, which was glass-calm in the fading glimmer of dusk.

He loved her. That was the only explanation for the way he felt now—hopeless, helpless, panicked. This was a fine time to have that bolt of realization slice into his consciousness and blow his theory about Louise being too much like Donna. The truth was, Louise was like no other woman in the world. And she was the woman he wanted. He would have realized it in time. What he was feeling was too strong to be denied, and was worth fighting for. But he'd thought he had two more weeks!

And then an idea came to him that was so bold, so intriguing, that he was momentarily convinced it might actually work. A military man was never without strategic tactics. And Wes had thought of a good one. All he needed was a small army.

IT WAS NEARLY DARK when Wes knocked on Bessie's front door. She opened it, stepped back in shock and then peered intently. "Wes, what's wrong? Does this have anything to do with the proceedings today?"

"Who is it?" Kate called from the living room.

"Believe it or not, it's Wesley," Bessie said.

Kate came to the door.

"No, this has nothing to do with the mediation," Wes assured the women.

Kate grasped his arm. "Is it Haywood? Has something happened?"

"No. Dad's okay. I need to talk to both of you."

Bessie stepped aside. "Come in. Sit down."

He entered what looked like the showroom of a florist's shop and drew the correct conclusion. "I hope this means Dad's been courting you, Kate."

"In his way," she answered.

"Now, tell us what's wrong," Bessie said when they were all seated.

After Wes explained that Louise was leaving town in a couple of days, Kate made an assumption of her own. "You love her! I knew it. You and Louise are perfect for each other!"

He blew out a long breath. "Actually, everybody seems to have noticed except us. And that's been the problem. But I want her to stay right here. With me."

Bessie looked at Kate. They both nodded. "Well, so do we," Bessie said. "All the women down at the factory are grateful for everything she's done. Why, it's like Louise has lived here for years."

"That's what I wanted to hear," Wes said. "Now, here's what I think we should do…."

He explained his plan, and with each approving murmur and exclamation from Bessie and Kate, he grew more confident. When all the details were in order, he stood up and went to the front door. When he opened it, he saw his father striding up the sidewalk.

Haywood stopped at the bottom porch step. "Wesley, what are you doing here?"

Wes was able to smile for the first time in hours. "If I'm not mistaken, Dad, I think we're both here for the same reason. Because we're miserable failures in the romance department." He walked by his father and patted him on the shoulder. "I'm trying to do something about my blind side. I hope you can, too."

Believing he was on the right track, and with more people to see, Wes left.

"KATE, HAYWOOD'S HERE!" Bessie called.

Kate had already changed into one of Haywood's favorite dresses. She twisted a few springy red curls onto her forehead for a youthful look, dabbed cologne behind her ears, and walked into the living room.

"What can I do for you, Haywood?" she said, sitting herself in a Victorian mahogany chair flanked by two of Haywood's bouquets.

Bessie excused herself with a story about a cake baking in the kitchen.

"I heard everything went well for the ladies today," Haywood said when he was alone with Kate.

"Quite well, yes."

He brought a chair to within touching distance of her and sat. "I'm glad."

"You are?"

"Yes. I can't deny any longer that there

were cases of injustice at the factory. And I've come to see Justin Beauclaire in a new light."

"It's about time."

He raised his eyebrows and stared at her. A smile lurked at the corners of his mouth. "You're a corker, Katie," he said. "Those lips of yours can speak a sharp word, but I've come to know I can't live without them."

She sat primly, waiting.

"So…" He reached into the inside pocket of his jacket. "I've brought you a peace offering." Scanning the floral extravagance around him, he added, "Aside from the fortune I've already invested in posies." He handed her an envelope. "Open it."

She lifted the flap and withdrew two airline tickets to Ireland. All pretense of coyness fled from her body. She pressed her hand against her chest and squealed, "Ireland! I'm going to see my boys!"

"Yes, Katie. In two weeks."

With a great deal of effort, she managed to rein in her excitement when she realized the tickets might be nothing more than what he'd called them—a peace offering. "There are two tickets, here. Is one of them for Bessie?"

Haywood grinned like a boy. "No, but I'll buy her one if you want her to come with us on our honeymoon."

Kate pretended to search the envelope again, though her hands were trembling so she could hardly keep up the ruse.

"What are you looking for?" Haywood asked.

"Just checking that you didn't slip in a prenuptial agreement for me to sign."

"Yes, indeed, a corker," he said again. "There's no agreement of any kind in there, Kate. It'll be you, me and a marriage license to seal the deal. If you say yes."

He took a black box out of his pocket, lifted the lid and showed her a brilliant diamond ring. "Will you be my wife, Kate, in every way, for every day of the rest of our lives?" He took the ring out of the box and slipped it on her finger.

"Oh, Haywood, are you sure?" Kate kept her eyes on his face.

"I'm sure as I've ever been about anything. I don't want to spend another day without you." A teasing grin curled the ends of his thick mustache as he looked at the ring on her finger. "Besides, we no longer have to worry about money problems. I spent every last cent on that bauble."

Kate bounded onto his lap with the joy of

a young girl. She let her gratitude flow from her lips to his in one long, satisfying, coming-home kiss.

## CHAPTER EIGHTEEN

VICKI MALONE PACKED the last of Louise's dishes in a plastic carton and closed the door of the empty cupboard. "I really feel bad about taking these dishes home with me, Lulu," she said. "You just bought them six weeks ago, and now you're giving the set to me."

Louise secured the zipper on her largest suitcase and sat on the bed. "Easy Come, Easy Go, Vic. And Pack Light. Those are my mottoes."

"But you can easily fit this carton in your car. Why don't you take the dishes back with you?"

"Why? So I'll have three sets in my two-bedroom condo? Don't be silly. Besides, when I bought them, I thought of giving them to you when I left. You can see they're not my taste. I'm hardly the cherry blossom type."

Vicki looked toward the rear entrance of the apartment, where two other filled boxes sat by the door. "But those linens you're giving me. Surely you can use those in your condo."

"But I don't need them. And you do. You're the one building the new house." Louise rose, went to Vicki and put her arm around her friend's shoulder. "Quit trying to find reasons not to take this stuff. They're gifts. Accept them with good grace." She swept her arm to encompass all the cartons. "Besides, I told you at the time I didn't pay more than two hundred bucks for these things."

Vicki capitulated with a sigh. "What are you going to do with the furniture?"

"It's all taken care of. Have Jamie come by for the oak dresser he sanded. It'll look adorable in the baby's room. The rest will go into Suzie McCorkle's shop. She promised to buy everything back from me at half what I paid for it, which wasn't much in the first place considering it's all used." Thinking fondly of Suzie and her candles, Louise smiled. "I'm not going to ask her for the money, though. Suzie's been a good friend, and all her candle prophecies have come true."

"Not the one about you and Wesley," Vicki said. "You're leaving and Wes hasn't done a thing to make you stay."

Louise gave her a fond smile. "In all fairness, Vic, Suzie never gave me a candle that promised a long-lasting love. She gave me one for romance, and Wes and I definitely made that candle burn bright. And, in his own awkward way, Wes did suggest that I stay."

Vicki's expression brightened. "He did? You mean you've seen him since yesterday when he overheard you on the phone to Roger?"

Louise wished she could say what Vicki wanted to hear. Vicki had found her own happiness in Bayberry Cove, and wanted the same for her best friend. But there wasn't going to be that happy ending for Louise.

"Yes, I saw him today," she said. "He called this morning and offered to take me to lunch. We went to a nice place by the river in Morgan City."

"Well, what happened?"

"He apologized for walking out of the Kettle yesterday without giving me a chance to explain."

"Okay, that's a start. Did he ask you to stay?"

Louise tried to smile, but her lips trembled. "He said he wished I wasn't going. Is that the same thing?"

Vicki tried to look hopeful. "Maybe. It depends how he said it."

"He said it gallantly and politely, and even with meaning, but, honey, it wasn't enough." Louise busied herself by packing shoes into the last of the cartons. She couldn't stop to think now about Wes's hand over hers on the linen tablecloth, about his blue eyes reflecting the sun through the restaurant window, about his commander-perfect deportment slipping just a little when he asked for two more weeks.

She couldn't give him two more weeks because she knew that all the time in the world wouldn't change what they both knew to be true. They were two different people living two completely different lives. Yes, she had changed, but not enough. She'd never be the woman Wes wanted. In two days, or two weeks, or soon after, Wes would come to accept that. In the end, he would never be able to overlook the differences and love her for who she was.

Unfortunately, Louise had come to an entirely opposite conclusion. What she'd realized in the last two days was that they could have made it work. And if Wes had believed that too, she would have offered him more than two weeks. She would have given him the rest of her life.

She brushed a tear away and tried to ignore the burning in the back of her throat. Stupid Bayberry Cove and all the people who'd let her sample their joys and sorrows, victories and defeats while spinning a web of honesty and compassion around her heart. She wasn't the same woman who'd showed up here six weeks ago. Roger Oppenheimer would be pleased.

She drew a deep breath and blew it out slowly. "I guess that's everything," she said.

"I can't believe you're leaving tomorrow morning," Vicki murmured. "I'd really hoped… I thought that Wes…"

"Don't," Louise warned as she fought the urge to release a flood of emotion in her friend's arms.

*You're made of sterner stuff, Lulu,* she said to herself, and straightened her shoulders with the semblance of a smile.

"Hey, Vic, come on now. It's only a two-hour flight, a two-day drive. It's not like we're on opposite sides of the world. I'll be back when your baby's born, to make sure that if it's a girl, you don't stick it with a name like Lulu." Louise felt tears threaten and she turned away so Vicki wouldn't notice.

Much as she loved Vicki, she knew she wouldn't be coming back for the birth of the baby. Her broken heart was going to take much longer to heal.

THE NEXT MORNING at seven o'clock, Louise went into the Kettle for a cup of coffee, a

Danish and a last goodbye to Bobbi Lee. The restaurant was empty except for the owner and the cook, who were both lounging on bar stools at the counter. And Bobbi Lee was nowhere to be seen. Louise swallowed her disappointment with a few gulps of coffee and nibbled at the sweet bun.

After ten minutes she left money on the table and walked back toward her apartment. She passed by the door to McCorkle's New and Used Furniture Store and knew she would miss its quirky, warmhearted owner. She climbed the steps to her apartment, thinking about her dealings with Mason and Wes before she'd rented it, and accepted that this would be the last time she would climb these stairs.

She opened the door and realized that she'd neglected to lock it. This was the first time she could remember ever leaving a door unlocked. But then, this was Bayberry Cove. She felt the tears threaten to overflow onto her cheeks.

"Get a grip, Lulu," she said to herself as she looked around the room that had been her home for six weeks. It was still furnished nicely, but lacked the little details that had made it her own, the cherry blossom dishes, which she truly did like, the flowery bed linens, the candles. All gone now.

She picked up her canvas bag, the one piece of luggage she hadn't packed in the car last night, crossed the hardwood floor and turned around for one last look. The three windows that faced Main Street still shone with the scrubbing she'd given them when she'd first arrived. She remembered watching Wes jogging around the square, so fit, so strong, and now when he'd become vital to her existence, so lost.

Shaking off the malaise, she opened the back door, stepped onto the platform of the stairs and froze in disbelief.

There, eighteen feet below her in the parking lot, were dozens of Bayberry Cove citizens all looking up at her as if she'd just stepped from behind a curtain, center stage.

Standing at the bottom of the stairs were Vicki and Jamie, Bessie and Darlene, and many others from the factory. There was Mason Fletcher, and Kate and Haywood, holding hands like a couple of young lovers. And Suzie and Evan. And Bobbi Lee.

And in front of them all, with his foot on the bottom step, was Wes Fletcher, staring up at her with a devilish expression on his face and one hand hidden mysteriously behind his back.

Louise dropped her bag, let her purse slide

from her shoulder to the porch and gripped the rough lumber of the railing. She swallowed and reminded herself to breathe.

Wes looked up at her and spoke in a clear, strong voice. "Louise Duncan, this is an intervention."

She blinked, pursed her lips for a second and said, "Wh…what?"

"An intervention," he repeated. "It's what concerned citizens do for one of their own when that person doesn't have the good sense to know what's best for her."

Her hand clutched the soft fabric of her T-shirt. *One of their own?* "What are you talking about, Wes?"

"We're here to persuade you to stay, Louise." He looked behind and to the side, where his friends were nodding their heads. "Forever, if our demonstration goes as planned. But at least for two weeks if that's the most you'll give us." He sent her a stern look. "It is, after all, what you promised, and you've convinced us you're a woman of your word."

Suzie McCorkle stepped up and nudged him from behind. "Go on, Wesley, show her."

He cleared his throat. "There are some among us this morning who believe that the responsibility of getting you to stay falls squarely on my shoulders."

The crowd nodded again. Several individuals shouted words of agreement.

"With that in mind, I've come to offer you this." He brought his arm from around his back, and in his hand was a tall pink candle sitting in a delicate wreath of pink roses. Wes held it out to her in the palms of both hands, as if it were an offering from a knight to his lady love as she looked down upon him from a marble balcony instead of a weathered old porch.

"Tell her what it means," Suzie prompted.

Tears rolled onto Louise's cheeks. *I hope I know what it means,* she said to herself. And finding the promise shining in Wes's clear eyes, she knew she did.

He climbed halfway up the stairs, the candle outstretched. "It means romance, Louise. And love that lasts forever. And I offer it to you as my personal plea that you will stay, here, with me…" he glanced around at his attentive audience "…with *us,* in Bayberry Cove, as my wife."

The woman who'd only thought of candles as a means to celebrate a birthday or combat a power outage suddenly became a true convert to their magic. She swiped at her tears and blinked hard, not wanting anything to blur her vision of Wes's fiercely determined expression. And because she'd always been a woman who dealt in absolutes, she said, "Are you fully and completely aware of what you've just said?"

He dropped the candle to his side and gave her a look so intense, so filled with longing, that she felt it curl her toes. "Don't leave, Louise."

Her eyes remained locked with his for a wonderful, magical moment of time. She was about to deliver her answer when Mason hollered from the parking lot, "Put the boy out of his misery, Louise. Say yes. Let him give you that cottage you want so much!"

Laughter sputtered from her lips. Real, honest, heartfelt laughter. And the citizens of Bayberry Cove seemed to utter a collective sigh of relief.

"And study for the North Carolina bar exam," Haywood shouted up to her. "This town needs a good lawyer." He put his arm around Kate. "Looks like I'm going to be in Ireland for a while going over the cases of a couple of miscreant offspring of my future wife's." He winked at Louise. "Don't know how long that will take me, and I can't leave these folks high and dry with no competent legal advisor."

"So what's your answer, girl?" Bobbi Lee said. "I've known Wes Fletcher my whole life. He's a bit stuffy, and he'll stand on his principles in the middle of the town square until grass grows up around his knees." She grinned at the object of her gentle chiding. "But he's a good man and he'll make you happy. And he told me he'll do the cooking or bring you to the Kettle every night."

Louise pulled her gaze from Wes and looked at Vicki, who had such a repentant grimace on her face that Louise knew her best friend had been a party to this little ambush. And then Vicki admitted it when she said, "Hey, anybody can be a little sneaky if it's for a good cause."

Louise laughed and focused on Wes again. She knew she would be here on the Fourth of July and beyond to witness the start of the candle store, the preservation of Currituck Sound and the continuing traditions of Bayberry Cove. And she would build her own future alongside this man in a little cottage that would once again be a gift of love.

"Bring that candle on up here, sailor," she said. "I feel like lighting a fire."

He gestured to his friends with his free

hand. "You can all go home now. Thanks for your help, but I've got a little private celebrating to do with my fiancée."

And while the folks of Bayberry Cove dispersed to their jobs and their homes, Wes climbed the rest of the way, turned Louise toward the door and took her inside, where he proceeded to do just that.

\* \* \* \* \*